"Tell me wh
Christmas,

The man dressed in a Santa suit pulled her out of the party and into the cold night air, under the dark velvet sky and the full pearl moon. He disguised his voice so she'd never tell who he really was.

Sighing, Nikki flung back her head. Lovely dark eyes that were as bright as the night sky searched the stars. Her shoulders were bare but the snowy night only brought a healthy pink to her skin. She bit her lower lip. "I want…"

He almost chuckled, since she still hadn't guessed it was him. "Yes?"

"I want Jon Sleet to fall in love with me."

He watched as her glossy eyes turned toward him—and widened in shock.

Jon pulled the hat and fake beard from his face. "Nikki," he said smoothly, coming closer and letting his lips hover above hers, "I think your dream's come true."

Dear Reader,

We're delighted to bring you a brand-new edition of the CHRISTMAS IS FOR KIDS romances you love. This year, four of your very favorite American Romance authors have gotten together to put these special stories under *your* tree.

And Jule McBride has *two* presents for you. In *Smoochin' Santa* she brings to life the character of little Christmas "Christy" Holt, the most precocious child you've ever met. At the advanced age of seven, Christy isn't sure if she believes in Santa anymore, but she's taking no chances and she's asked him for a family. Be sure you follow this mischievous little miss next month in American Romance #757, *Santa Slept Over,* the second book in THE LITTLE MATCHMAKER duet!

From Christy and all of us here at Harlequin, we wish you the peace, love and joy of this holiday season. May it last all year long!

Debra Matteucci
Senior Editor & Editorial Coordinator
Harlequin Books
300 East 42nd Street
New York, NY 10017

Smoochin' Santa

JULE McBRIDE

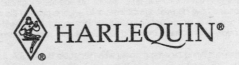

HARLEQUIN®

TORONTO • NEW YORK • LONDON
AMSTERDAM • PARIS • SYDNEY • HAMBURG
STOCKHOLM • ATHENS • TOKYO • MILAN • MADRID
PRAGUE • WARSAW • BUDAPEST • AUCKLAND

ISBN 0-373-16753-9

SMOOCHIN' SANTA

Copyright © 1998 by Julianne Randolph Moore.

Chapter One

"Whoa there! I said stop, little lady!"

"Guess again, mister." Seven-year-old Christy Holt wasn't about to let a nosy airline attendant come between her and the new daddy she'd picked out, so she kept hoofing it down the concourse as fast as her patent-leather shoes allowed. Trailing a wheeled carry-on behind her, she positioned her black velvet backpack in front of her so no one would notice the contents were alive and kicking. The being inside, who went by the name of Noodles, hadn't been baggage-tagged through proper channels, much less quarantined.

"Quit wiggling, Noodles," Christy commanded as the attendant's irate shout rose over a piped-in Muzak version of "Santa Claus Is Comin' To Town."

"Please...uh, little lady," called the man. "You're not allowed to be alone in the airport. Airline rules say you must be accompanied by an adult during the holidays!"

"Little lady?" Christy muttered under her breath. "Right, big man." She might be a second-grader, but her auditory canals worked just fine, and she could recognize male-chauvinist lingo when she heard it.

Judging by the footsteps pounding behind her, he was gaining on her, too, which meant she'd better get a move on and lose herself in the surging crowd of holiday travelers. "Giddy up, Noodles," she whispered with relish, even though the man was going to be hard to lose in this two-gate North Carolina airport. Still, Christy was glad she'd landed here, since she was about to meet her idol, Jonathan Sleet, and he was going to be a great dad.

"I said hold it right there, little lady!"

Training her gaze past the metal detector, Christy cased the joint, but seeing all the Christmas decorations between her and the exits made her heart suddenly hurt, since this would be the first year she wouldn't be awakening her mom and dad on Christmas morning. Not that it mattered. They were merely *biological* parents, and she was about to become the proud daughter of a cute, famous children's-book author. Since her parents had recently divorced, Christy reasoned the next logical step was to divorce them both and adopt a family of her own choosing, preferably one that included Jonathan Sleet.

Christy sighed. *A new family.* It was definitely what she wanted for Christmas, unless her plan to get her old family back worked. Her eyes drifted wistfully from a tall pine tree strung with white lights, to a decorated gift-shop window where Mr. and Mrs. Claus reclined in rocking chairs before a fireplace, surrounded by industrious elves. Outside, the snowstorm that had grounded Christy's plane was still raging, and thick, wet snowflakes were covering the red suit of the questionable-looking Santa Claus who was ringing a bell by a Salvation Army booth.

Christy did a double take. The only taxi waiting at

the curb was painted hot pink, and wired to the grill was a rope-pine wreath decorated with pink poinsettia blossoms. Pink was an awfully obvious color for a getaway car, but Christy guessed it would have to do. Feeling renewed determination, she kept her eyes fixed on the strangely painted taxi.

"Little lady, didn't you hear me?"

"Deep sigh," Christy muttered aloud before exhaling a lengthy breath of annoyance. She'd almost forgotten about the guy who was tailing her. Who did he think he was? The Hardy Boys of U.S. Airways? And why couldn't grown-ups quit meddling into little kids' private business?

Mustering a charming smile, Christy whirled around. The man was over the hill—maybe even as ancient as thirty—and anyone who looked so concerned for others should probably get himself some pets. He wore a navy suit, the lapel of which was skewered with a red pin indicating he was with the airline. Hoping Noodles didn't start wiggling again, Christy inclined her head politely, keeping her gaze all innocence. "Why, sir, could you possibly have been speaking to *moi?*" She'd been learning French at her New York private school, and now Christy thought the use of *moi* was a very nice touch.

The man, who was winded and gasping for breath, bent over at the waist. "You look here, little lady," he wheezed, sounding furious. "Are you traveling with your mother or father or what?"

Christy had half a mind to tell him she was traveling with "or what." Tossing the blond curls that framed her face, she was careful not to dislodge the emerald-colored wool pillbox hat that matched her conservative coat and mischievously dancing green eyes. Simultaneously pouting with feigned impatience and deepening her dimples, she gazed past the man. "Oh! There she is! My mom! See her?" Christy waved toward the phone booths and banks of screens announcing arrivals and departures. "Mama! Oh, Mama!" She blew some air kisses.

The man craned his neck around. "I don't see anyone."

Of course he didn't. Nevertheless, Christy looked terribly embarrassed for him and pointed. "She's right *there,* sir."

"Oh…yes. Yes, of course. I see her now."

Poor man. Not a single maternal type was waving back. "My parents greatly appreciate your concern," Christy assured before whirling around again. As she continued toward the exit—this time without the bloodhound—she caught a glimpse of her green, velvet-trimmed coat reflected in the gift-shop window and felt a rush of pleasure. No little girl could have looked more adorable, or less like a runaway.

Of course, Christy's mom would rather dress her in black leather, sunglasses and junior Doc Martens boots, but when it came to looking sweet and innocent, Christy knew she needed all the help she could get. Just this past week, she'd been grounded, sent to the corner for time-out, and had her phone privileges revoked. Everybody seemed convinced she was a junior-league Lizzie Borden.

Well, maybe Christy *was* born bad, but all that was behind her now. The instant her plane was grounded, the brilliant idea to run away had popped into her head, fully formed. As plans went, it was even better than climbing down the fire escape and playing in the park when Christy's last nanny, Rhea Morel, used to send her to her room for punishment. Christy frowned, thinking backwards from Rhea. Before that was Brietta, Lucy, then Joan and Brenda... Hmm. Christy guessed she *had* become a discipline problem after the divorce.

But now her life was about to change.

At least it would if she could jump this final hurdle—the metal detector. Eyeing it, she braced herself. Already, in the pandemonium of an emergency landing, Christy had given another girl the name tag that identified Christy as a parentless underage traveler. The girl agreed to flash the badge, so attendants wouldn't realize Christy had disappeared. Then Christy had air-phoned her dad to say she wouldn't be visiting him in L.A. until after Christmas. He was confused about the change of plans, not to mention the roaring sounds he said he heard in the background, but since he'd rather do anything than speak to Christy's mom on the phone, he'd promised to pick up Christy at the airport a week from now.

Which meant no one was expecting her, and she was free to see if Jonathan Sleet would be her surrogate daddy. Christy shivered all over with wicked excitement. "We're almost outside, so behave yourself, Noodles," Christy warned through clenched teeth as she fixed a game smile on a security guard at the metal detector whose name tag said Willy. "Hey," she called. "I'm not at all sure how X-ray machines work! Why, you must be awfully smart to run such a complicated machine, sir!"

"Well, miss, it's not so complica—"

"And I thought detectors were for when we come into the airport, not for when we leave." She grinned. "Oh, silly me!"

Willy winked as he lifted her carry-on onto the conveyer. "It's Christmas," he explained, "so we doubled security. We wouldn't want anybody smuggling out presents, now would we, miss?"

"Gosh, no, Willy!" Christy gingerly placed her backpack onto the conveyer. "I'd sure hate for anybody's presents to get stolen! Now, you'd better watch, Willy, 'cause my suitcases are coming through!"

Just as she suspected, Willy didn't even glance at the X-ray monitor. "How'd you know my name, missy?"

"Because I'm in second grade—" When she saw the contents of her carry-on in the half-turned X-ray screen, her mind raced. Would Willy notice Noodles in the backpack? "That means we learned to read last year," she babbled on. "Plus, I have an uncle Willy."

Whoops. Now Willy looked doubtful. "An uncle Willy, huh?"

Christy nodded. "Why, sure. Now, Willy, will anything bad happen to me if I walk through this detector? I mean, the machine won't magnetize me, will it? We learned all about magnets last year in first-grade science class and they sure sounded dangerous!"

Willy smiled indulgently. "Go on, miss. I'll watch and make sure you don't get zapped."

"Thanks!" Christy leaped through the metal detector, then edged around the conveyer so the X-ray screen was in view again. "Made it through! Thanks to you, Willy!"

He laughed. "Well, a little lady such as yourself wouldn't be the type to carry contraband, miss."

"*Moi?* Contraband?" Christy forced an innocent

giggle just as Noodles appeared on the X-ray screen. Flexing uncomfortably inside the backpack, only Noodles's backbone was visible and Christy prayed to God that the little bit of radiation wouldn't hurt him. Her lower lip suddenly quivered.

"Contraband," Willy was explaining now. "That's what we call illegal items people smuggle in."

"Smugglers?" Christy mustered a deep gasp, trying to sound impressed by Willy's acumen, but it was hard when her favorite pet was still on the screen, curled in a tiny, bony ball and looking like a photographic negative.

Her smile faltering, Christy scurried toward the end of the conveyer. As soon as the velvet backpack came through, she gently lifted it. "Deep sigh," she whispered under her breath, her heart pounding. They'd made it. Willy lifted off her carry-on.

"All set, miss?"

She lightly patted her backpack. "Thanks to you, Willy, I managed to smuggle out my contraband!"

He chuckled. "Merry Christmas, kid."

"Merry Christmas to you, too!"

Christy raced for the phones, relieved to see the pink taxi still at the curb. Inside a phone booth, she unzipped her pack to find that Noodles looked none too happy about his X-ray experience. "Big fat kisses," murmured Christy guiltily, sending a string of loud smacking smooches inside the bag. "Just hang in there."

Lifting Jonathan Sleet's latest book from beneath Noodles—it was one of two books in her pack—Christy double-checked the spelling of the author's name, then riffled through a phone directory. "Here," she murmured, running a white-gloved index finger down the page. "The Sleets. They're at number one Mistletoe Mountain." Staring hard at the address, she memorized it, then she shut the phone book. "I sure hope they like us, Noodles."

After all, not everybody did. Christy's second-grade teacher, who was supposed to be nice and supportive, said Christy was a delinquent. And when Christy first brought Noodles home, back when her parents were still married and both lived in New York, her dad had cussed and called the Central Park zoo. Even the zoo had refused to take Noodles. But Jonathan Sleet wouldn't feel that way, because he was everything wonderful—rich, famous, creative and cute—and he lived in a town where everything was perfect and magical. It was even rumored that the real Santa Claus kept a second home in Holiday Hamlet.

Not that Christy really believed in Santa anymore.

Still, if there *was* a real Santa, he supposedly visited Holiday Hamlet every Christmas Eve in a reindeer-driven sleigh, and this year Christy would be there to greet him. If this Santa was real, he'd have to grant her wish—and make Jonathan Sleet her daddy, or else get her parents back together again.

She glanced outside, toward the Santa at the Salvation Army booth. He wore a white wig and beard, but his eyeglasses didn't look right, and he was heavy in all the wrong places. "I wouldn't have fallen for him in preschool," Christy muttered.

But even if Santa didn't exist, this was an adventure. According to Christy's mom, Jonathan Sleet's books were so successful that his hometown had been officially renamed Holiday Hamlet and revamped to look like the magical Christmas town he described in his books. And her mom should know; she was Jonathan Sleet's editor. If Mr. Sleet really shared a mansion named the Christmas Castle with his wife and daughter, that meant Christy might also get something else she used to want for Christmas—a sister. Years ago, she'd begged her parents for one, but none had ever come.

Christy suddenly frowned. If Mr. Sleet was so successful, why had he suddenly quit writing two years ago?

Well, she'd find that out, too.

Impulsively, she turned over one of the children's books; on the back of the slender hardcover was Jonathan Sleet's picture. He was so cute that Christy wished time would stand still. If Mr. Sleet stayed the same age while she grew up, then Christy could marry him.

Of course, his biography said he already had a wife. "Too bad," Christy whispered, taking in his sparkly smile and wavy dark hair pushed back from his face. At least he had green eyes, which meant she could pass for his daughter. And if he wasn't agreeable to adopting her, Christy had a few tricks up her sleeve to convince him.

"Okay, Noodles," she murmured. "Deep breath. It's now or never." Surely Jonathan Sleet would want another little girl. Closing the book, Christy double-checked the zippers on her backpack, making sure Noodles was safely confined. Just last week, he'd escaped during a fancy mother-daughter Christmas luncheon sponsored by Christy's mom's office. Christy's mom's boss, the publisher, had screamed and dropped to the floor in a dead faint, and then Christy's mom had almost gotten fired.

"So you stay put, Noodles," Christy warned fiercely.

Then, feeling resolute, she picked up her bags and headed for the unconvincing Santa, the strange pink taxicab and the dark and stormy night.

GEEZ. The kid was truly something to behold.

Nikki Ryder hunched further over the steering wheel. With the cuff of her brown leather bomber jacket, she rubbed a circle in the condensation on the windshield to get a better look.

Between rapidly falling snowflakes and the rhythmic pass of the wipers, Nikki could see that the little girl was maybe four feet tall, tops. She was seven or eight—but going on a pretty regal thirty-five. Her calf-length emerald coat was trimmed in black velvet, which matched the velvet band on a green pillbox hat that made her look like a child movie star, circa 1950. Chin-length springy blond spiral ringlets fell from beneath the hat, just touching a neatly tied red-and-green scarf, and the white lace leggings that encased the kid's coltish legs ended at pointy-toed black patent-leather shoes. Right now, she was pressing a white-gloved index finger to her cheek as if deep in thought.

She looked like a pint-size first lady of the United States. Or at least a miniature senator's wife. "A *Republican* senator's wife," Nikki corrected.

Pretty weird. But she was definitely a welcome distraction from Nikki's darker thoughts. Not to mention the murderous impulses that all involved Buck Andrews. For nearly twelve hours, Nikki had been driving around, telling herself she was better off without

Buck. And yet she was so worried about the baby. Her eyes suddenly stung, then they widened.

"Tell me this little girl's not heading for my cab." Glancing in the rearview mirror, Nikki saw a car pull in behind her and decided it must be the girl's parents. *Face it,* Nikki thought, suddenly shaking her head. She could live to be a hundred and still never possess the little girl's poise. Nikki's father and brothers had done their best to raise a motherless girl, but Nikki had still wound up knowing more about plumbing and appliance repair than makeup.

"Yep. Men definitely want something else," she muttered. Probably bouncy blond something elses who liked the kind of thong panties Buck would have put in her stocking this Christmas.

Nikki glanced at the rearview mirror where the stocking from Buck's mantel now hung. Then her eyes skated along the dashboard, where she'd set up the small carved-wood figures of the nativity scene. Earlier today, it had also been on Buck's mantel.

She sighed again, fighting the tears with wry humor. "And to think all I wanted for Christmas was a new set of snow tires." What she'd gotten, of course, was a surprise pregnancy. And now Nikki wished she didn't know firsthand how much a child needed both parents. Not that her dad hadn't done his best.

Readjusting the baseball cap that, in tandem with an elastic band, held back her shoulder-length brown hair, Nikki glanced from the little girl's outfit, down to her own—a baggy pullover and bomber jacket, with baby-blue long johns that peeked out from holes in the knees of her lovingly faded blue jeans.

Suddenly, Nikki's mouth quirked. "Hope you're a boy," she said as if the baby could hear. Nikki wouldn't have a clue what to do with a girl. Not that she really had any preference—she'd love the baby no matter what—but the pint-size matron outside could definitely give her some pointers in femininity. At the thought, sharp, knifing pain suddenly arrowed through Nikki with such intensity that it brought a soft cry to the back of her throat. She knew it was a lie, but she kept thinking Buck would have loved her more if only she'd been more feminine. She shut her eyes against the emotions. *You're a survivor. Forget about him. You're going to make it on your own.*

When Nikki's eyes fluttered open, the girl was coming toward the cab and glancing around furtively as if someone was pursuing her. She paused beside the back door, then swung it open. When the dome light snapped on, Nikki nearly choked.

Too much! This girl was even wearing makeup! Nikki took in the lip gloss and smear of green eye shadow. Lord, what kind of parents would let a grade-schooler go out like that? Nikki hadn't been allowed to wear makeup until her senior year in high school, and even then guys had written her off as a hopeless tomboy.

Wheeling down the dial on the radio, Nikki slid back the Plexiglas partition that separated the seats and said, "Uh...can I help you?" The girl was so nattily dressed that Nikki almost accidently added "Ma'am."

"Number One Mistletoe Mountain. And step on it." With that, the little girl hoisted her carry-on and backpack onto the back seat, hopped inside and slammed the door.

And step on it? Where did the kid think she was— in a B movie? Using the passenger-side neck rest for leverage, Nikki twisted around. The girl was now gingerly positioning her backpack over the heating vent on the back dashboard, and the car behind them was pulling out. Guess that wasn't her parents. "You say you're going all the way to Mistletoe Mountain? You mean up by Holiday Hamlet?"

The girl nodded. Lifting a handful of dollar bills, she waved them over the seat. "I have plenty of money."

She sure did. Even in the dark, Nikki spotted a fifty-dollar bill. What kind of parents let a kid run around with that much cash? "Look," Nikki managed, "you really shouldn't wave money around like that. It isn't safe." She didn't want to frighten the child, but someone her age would make an easy target for a mugger. In fact, a mugger would do better to rob the little girl than Nikki. Nikki was almost broke.

The girl sighed impatiently. "Could you please just do your job and start the meter?"

Nothing like being bossed around by someone a third your age. "Well…Mistletoe Mountain's a long drive." Easily an hour. "Where's your mom and dad? Wasn't somebody supposed to come pick you up?" Nikki didn't even think airlines allowed children this young to fly alone.

"My parents couldn't come. That's why they gave me money for a cab. Now, could you please take me home?"

Nikki studied her in the rearview mirror. The expensive, impractical outfit and defensive tone said it all. Probably, her parents had money but didn't pay her enough attention. Nikki's hand dropped from the steering wheel to her belly, which was still so flat that it was hard to believe another life was really there.

She might not be able to offer the financial advantages this girl probably enjoyed, but Nikki did have a lot of love to give.

"Please," the girl said, looking close to tears now. "It's almost Christmas and I've gotta see my daddy."

Ah. So, maybe her parents were divorced and she'd flown here to spend Christmas with her father. Nikki's mouth set grimly, her heart suddenly aching for the girl. Men could be so damnably unfeeling. At the very least, this little girl's father should have come to greet her at the airport. What was wrong with people? "Don't worry," Nikki found herself assuring, "we'll get you home to your daddy, hon."

The girl swiped at her cheeks, looking relieved.

Geez. The man didn't even deserve a kid, Nikki silently ruminated as she flipped the meter switch and pulled away from the curb. *And I just might tell him so.* How could he neglect his own child? Was every man in North Carolina as self-absorbed as Buck? She exhaled a long-suffering sigh as she left the airport complex and got onto the interstate. This youngster had been sent out here—after dark and in the freezing cold—to catch a cab in a snowstorm. With the wind chill, the temperature had to be minus ten. Unbelievable!

Shaking her head, Nikki did her best to concentrate on the snow-slick roads, but the more Buck and the girl's inattentive father merged in her thoughts, the angrier she got. Glaring at the pavement, she realized the weather was worsening. Engine heat and warm tires had churned up gray slush, obscuring the road's center line, and the air had turned foggier, becoming so moist that even the car's heater couldn't stop the chill. Leaning, she turned up the defroster in hopes the windows would clear.

"Wait," she murmured after a few minutes, her pulse quickening when she thought she'd missed a turnoff. *No, that's only the Little Creek Township exit.* She wished she knew where she was going, but she was new to this area, having only moved to True Pines to live with Buck six months ago, and she'd never been to Holiday Hamlet. Most of her fares went the other way, back toward True Pines.

After another fifteen minutes, she glanced in the rearview mirror. "Radio okay?"

The little girl shrugged.

"Should I turn it up?"

"Please."

Well, maybe the child was more polite than she'd initially seemed. As Nikki turned the dial, "Rudolph the Red-Nosed Reindeer" flooded the car. Outside, the wind drove the snow down harder, further cutting Nikki's visibility. Frowning, she glanced at the gas gauge, which was getting low, then back into a wet night sky that was so dark and foreboding that it could have been Halloween, not Christmas.

Nikki told herself she wasn't worried. She could drive in any kind of weather. Last year's tires were still pretty good, and she had chains, but if the snow kept coming, she'd never make it back to town. Not that she'd return to Buck's. But where was she going? Her eyes scanned the roadside, looking for cheap motels. All she saw were the dark silhouettes of snow-covered trees.

She'd driven a few more miles when the little girl suddenly said, "How old are you?"

Nikki glanced at her in the rearview. "Uh... twenty-three. You?"

"Seven." Raising a white-gloved hand, the little girl pointed at the licensing information on the dashboard. "And your name's Nikki Ryder. I know 'cause I can read." She giggled.

Nikki raised an eyebrow. "You think my name's funny?"

"Yeah. You can't be a Ryder if you're a driver!"

Cute. Nikki smiled. "What's your name?"

"Christmas, 'cause I was born on Christmas. But I don't believe in Santa anymore, so I'm making everybody call me Christy for short."

"Have a last name?"

"Uh...Sleet."

And she thinks my name's funny? Nikki tried not to react visibly, but what kind of man would name his daughter Christmas Sleet? Didn't the kid get teased at school? Nikki might not have planned her pregnancy, and she was admittedly scared spitless about the future, but at least her child would have a normal name. Anita Lynn after her mother, if it was a girl, or Bruce, after her dad, if it was a boy. Anything but Buck.

Her whole face suddenly felt tight with unshed tears. Sternly, Nikki reminded herself that she wasn't the only person with troubles this Christmas. Maybe the poor kid needed to talk. Very gently, she prodded, "So, neither of your parents could pick you up, huh?"

Christy lifted her chin haughtily. "My dad's too busy, 'cause he's a world-famous author." She shimmied out of her seat belt.

"Please keep your seat belt on," said Nikki.

"Only after you look at my dad." The little girl's gloved hand thrust over the Plexiglas partition, holding a paperback book with a white cover. "Whoops." She snatched back the book and found another, this one a slender, glossy hardcover. "See? My dad's name's Jonathan Sleet, and his picture's on the back."

Nikki glanced over. She felt so raw from what had passed between her and Buck this morning that her heart's sudden stuttering took her completely by surprise.

"Cute, huh?" said Christy.

Cute wasn't the word. It was only a head shot, but the set of the man's broad shoulders suggested a powerful body that would move with grace. He was wearing a V-neck sweater beneath a tweed jacket that made him look professorial, and his face seemed well-lived-in. While his cheekbones were maybe too broad and his lips too thin, the thick chestnut hair and green eyes would capture anybody's attention. Where the daughter's eyes sparkled like wet emeralds, the father's were darker, mossier, and more penetrating. If the roads hadn't been so bad, maybe Nikki wouldn't have looked away so soon. As it was, she averted her gaze and leaned closer to the windshield.

"He writes children's books," Christy chattered on. "He probably had a creative brainstorm tonight or something, so he couldn't come get me." She exhaled loftily. "Nikki," she explained importantly, "when you live with a creative genius, you simply have to learn to make allowances."

Oh, you do? Nikki bit back a furious sigh. So the guy had actually explained his inattention to his daughter by saying he was a "creative genius." Obviously, he thought his career was more important than good parenting. Judging from the man's picture, countless women in addition to his daughter probably *had* made allowances for him. And benefited from his creativity. Nikki glanced at the book again and swallowed hard. The barely concealed feral glint in those mossy eyes definitely said the man could be very…creative.

She shifted uncomfortably. "C'mon, hon, get back in that seat belt."

Christy squirmed dutifully into her harness. "I can't believe you never even heard of my daddy."

As if I'm culturally backward. "I'll be sure to look him up," Nikki managed to say politely. And then she'd tell him what she thought of his brand of parenting. What an irony. You'd definitely think a man who wrote children's books would be more attentive to his own child. Silently, Nikki vowed that not one dime of her hard-earned money would ever go to buy Jonathan Sleet's books. She was definitely boycotting a man who couldn't even pick up his child at the airport. Didn't he know how dangerous it was to let a seven-year-old catch a cab by herself? Nikki shook her head again. An interesting face didn't count for much if the man couldn't even take care of his daughter. Someone really should talk to him.…

Suddenly something intruded on her mental tirade. "Come to think of it, I do remember something about a children's-book author living nearby."

"Well, he does. And our town's just wonderful!" Christy leaned forward, plunging into a glowing account of her father's career. Until two years ago, he'd regularly published a series of books called Everyday's a Christmas. The stories concerned the adventures of a little girl, one very much like Christy, who lived in a magical Christmas castle on Mistletoe Mountain, overlooking Holiday Hamlet.

Of course, Nikki seriously doubted that on Christmas Eve all the trees on the mountains twinkled because they'd been decorated by angels. Nor did she believe that the streets were paved with diamonds, or that silver swans glided across the ice on the ponds, as Christy claimed, but the descriptions the girl offered were certainly charming.

Supposedly, the stately old houses all had turrets, wraparound porches, and gingerbread trim that looked good enough to eat. And, regardless of which road a little girl was traveling, she was always exactly in the center of the universe. Inside the town square, which was really a circle, was a statue of Santa Claus so bright that you had to squint to look at it, and around the circle were shops: Mrs. Gloria Honey, who owned the general store, dispensed free sweets, as did the cobbler, Mr. Hobbler, who carried a red-and-white cane made of real candy.

By the time Christy finished with the wild descriptions, Nikki had almost forgotten that the author of these charming fictions treated his daughter so badly. She found herself murmuring, "That sounds really great, Christy." What Nikki wouldn't give right now, to have a magical place to run to, where everything sparkled and came out right in the end.

That place sure as hell hadn't been Buck Andrews's duplex in True Pines, North Carolina.

Gripping the wheel tighter, Nikki fought another sudden urge to cry. She wished she'd listened to her father and brothers when they'd warned her about Buck, instead of spurning their advice and running off. Not a day had gone by in the past six months that Nikki hadn't wanted to call home. Her father's heart had broken during their last fight. Nikki knew that now. Still, she couldn't bring herself to drive back home to Kentucky with her tail between her legs. At least not yet.

She thought of all her belongings, which were in the trunk. And of the stunned expression on Buck's face this morning when she'd wrenched the Christmas wreath right off the front door, wired it to the grill of the cab, then squealed out, her tires spinning slush and ruining his jeans.

The satisfaction was only fleeting. Having a child was a lifelong responsibility that she'd have to bear alone. She just wished she'd find a place to spend the night. A church was visible beside the interstate now, but not a Holiday Inn or Best Western was in sight. As Nikki's eyes strayed over the life-size nativity scene on the church's lawn, she felt a sympathy with Mary—another woman who'd been pregnant, traveling and looking for a place to stay the night.

"At least she had a husband," Nikki murmured wistfully.

"Huh?" said Christy.

"Nothing," Nikki returned, deciding that staying in a motel during Christmas was going to be depressing. And expensive. Glumly, she stared at the thumping wipers that pushed snow from one side of the windshield to the other. At least she owned her own, which meant she could set her hours and drive all night if she wanted. Later, maybe she'd simply park in a warm garage somewhere and try to get some shut-eye. She heard a yawn. "Sleepy back there?"

"I'm awake," Christy assured her.

Barely, Nikki thought. Jonathan Sleet could have at least put his daughter on a morning flight if he wasn't bothering to pick her up.

"Don't worry." Nikki pointed to an exit sign. "We're almost there."

But as she took the dark exit ramp off the interstate, Nikki felt a sudden prickle of unaccountable foreboding. Had she taken a wrong turn? Had the day, which had begun so badly, just turned worse? The snowy night had gotten even darker, her gas gauge was low and there were still no stations in sight. She thought this was supposed to be a touristy Christmas town, but all the shops along the main street were already closed for the night. Driving around the town circle, Nikki noted the Santa Claus statue and murmured the names from street signs. "Elf's Avenue. Reindeer Run. Santa Street."

This was definitely the place. And the sleepy houses, with their snowy lawns, really were mostly Victorians. But where were the lights? The decorations? Not a single ornament twinkled from the white-tinged branches of the trees lining the road. Holiday Hamlet looked dead as a doornail. It was closed up tight as a drum and as empty as a dry county on a payday-Friday night.

Maybe it was just because of the storm. Feeling edgy, Nikki turned down the radio so she could concentrate, then followed an arrowed sign that said Mistletoe Mountain. As the road narrowed, becoming less navigable, she nibbled her lower lip, staring at the halos around her headlights. In their eerie glow, she could see the hard-driving snow, and she realized the storm wouldn't be stopping tonight. Trees—mostly oaks and sycamores—arched over the road, their leaves creating crusty snow-heavy canopies that deepened the shadows. Suddenly, her heart skipped a beat, and she glanced between the rearview mirror and Christy's backpack on the back dashboard.

Geez, Nikki could have sworn the backpack moved. But it couldn't have. Blinking, she realized her imagination was starting to get the best of her. She'd been driving too long and concentrating doubly hard because of the weather. Flexing her hands on the steering wheel, she rolled her head, trying to work the ache from her shoulders.

Christy's voice suddenly quavered from the back seat. "Are you sure this is Holiday Hamlet?"

Nikki squinted. "The sign said so. I thought you lived here."

"I...uh...I used to."

Nikki's heart squeezed again. Christy must have moved away with her mother after a divorce or something. No wonder she was so anxious to see her daddy.

As she took a turn, Nikki came face-to-face with another sign that pointed straight uphill. It said Christmas Castle Straight Ahead. So, the town really had been fashioned after the fictional town in Jonathan Sleet's books. Nikki guessed that sometimes life imitated art, rather than the other way around. "The Christmas Castle," she murmured, deciding it had a nice ring. Too bad the steep incline was a solid sheet of ice. Nervously, Nikki licked her lips.

"Can we make it, Nikki?"

Hearing the anxiety in Christy's voice, Nikki set her jaw with determination. Someone, at least, was going to have a family reunited at Christmas, even if Jonathan Sleet didn't deserve such a cute, loving kid.

Thinking of the rift with her own father, Nikki felt another pang of heartache. Tonight, she'd give her eyeteeth to be back home, warm and safe in Kentucky. Too bad she could almost hear her dad say "I told you so." She found herself saying, "Don't worry, Christy. I promise I'll get you home to your daddy."

Backing up, Nikki took the hill at a run, the engine of the taxi whining into high gear, the tires spinning slush. Midway up, her wheels now gliding on solid ice, Nikki wondered if she should have made the foolhardy promise because suddenly the snow tapered off, and a dark stone mansion became visible on the mountaintop. Nikki gasped. "That's your daddy's house? That's the Christmas Castle?"

Christy sounded strangely uncertain as they continued gliding closer. "Uh...yeah."

Somehow, Nikki had imagined a cheerfully lit Victorian with wreaths and electric candles in every window, a decorated spruce in the yard and life-size figures on the lawn depicting Santa and his reindeer-driven sleigh. The place ahead was more like an ice castle. Huge and Gothic, it was a forbidding sprawl of steep roofs blanketed with snow and towers and turrets that dangled with icicles. It was completely dark, save for one thin, ghostly flicker of light emanating from the uppermost reaches of the highest, oval-windowed turret.

There was no stopping the sudden, unexpected fluttering of Nikki's heart. Or the unsettling sensation that Jonathan Sleet was up there waiting especially for her...

Chapter Two

Up close, Jonathan Sleet's creepy old stone mansion was as disturbing as the man's dark green eyes and even more forbidding. Snow tumbled from the perilously pitched roofs, and winter-bare trees cast spooky shadows over the extensive, sloping, snow-blanketed grounds. Wooded forests formed the property's perimeter and, in the darkness, trees seemed to be marching toward the house like soldiers about to overtake an enemy fort. Christy's teeth chattered as Nikki let the heavy lion's-head knocker fall on the door again.

"Thanks for c-coming to the door with me, Nikki."

As if Nikki had a choice. Who would leave a child at a place like this during a blizzard, then simply drive away? Anxiously, Nikki blinked in the inky darkness, wishing the man had at least bothered to turn on an outside light for his little girl. As brittle leaves blew across the stone floor of the wraparound porch, they rustled over the toes of Nikki's boots, making her think of tumbleweeds in ghost towns. She shivered as an air tunnel of howling wind whipped past. "And you're absolutely positive nobody gave you a key, hon?''

Christy bobbed on her toes to keep warm, her blond, bouncing curls barely visible in the dark. ''N-no.'' Her teeth chattered. ''But maybe…uh, daddy left the door unlocked for *moi*.''

''*Moi?*''

''It m-means me in French.''

''I know, but…never mind.'' Nikki glanced around, thinking that leaving the door unlocked would be safe enough. Nobody would break into this place unless they were looking for vampires or Quasimodo. She pushed at the heavy door, her ungloved hands feeling like ice, and she sucked in a quick breath when the door swung inward. Christy's small hand slipped into hers and held tight, as if the girl was afraid to enter her own house.

Nikki wasn't feeling so confident herself. The cold imposing place was making her extremely conscious of her duty to protect the new life growing inside her. A life, she thought with sudden, almost physical pain, that would be coming into this world without a father. Glancing at Christy, she suddenly wondered if having a bad father was better than having none at all.

Fighting the urge to turn tail and run, she pulled Christy's carry-on over the threshold and propped it inside the door. Even its light weight was disturbing since the small suitcase couldn't possibly hold enough clothes for a visit. Christy needed much heavier attire in this weather, wool sweaters and thermal underwear. And why hadn't her mother dressed her in a parka? The child couldn't play outside in a velvet-trimmed coat.

"Whaddaya say?" Nikki managed perkily. "Want to leave your backpack here until we find your dad?"

Christy's tone was hushed. "Uh…no. I'd b-better hang on to my pack."

"Just how long are you visiting, anyway?"

"Uh…a week." Christy's tremulous whisper was heartbreakingly tentative, making her sound strangely lost. "Until after Chri-Christmas."

A week, Nikki fumed, gripping Christy's hand again and inching inside. What was the poor kid supposed to do? Sit around in these fancy grown-up clothes for a week, keeping her white-gloved hands clasped in her lap? Nikki winced as the wind pushed the door shut behind them with a bang. Judging from this incredibly cool reception, Nikki feared Christy's dad hadn't even bothered to get her any Christmas presents. *What a schmuck.*

Edging through the pitch-black foyer into what seemed like a hallway, Nikki squeezed Christy's hand reassuringly. "Hello? Hello there?" Nikki slid her free hand along the wall, searching in vain for a light switch as she advanced. "Anybody home? Mr. Sleet? Jonathan Sleet? Are you here?" Despite the dark, Nikki could tell that the place was big because her words bounced back, echoing hollowly.

Christy's voice sounded thin in the dark, and her patent leather shoes were making soft, faint clicks on the hardwood floor. "Uh…Daddy?"

When no one answered, Christy's trembling fingers squeezed more tightly around Nikki's. "It's no warmer in here than it was outside," Nikki murmured nervously as they continued creeping along. The drafty place felt utterly deserted. Glancing upward,

Nikki doubted she had the nerve to go in search of the illuminated turret.

Nikki, it's been a long day. Take it easy. There's nothing to fear here. She'd grown up with brothers who weren't above slipping slimy creatures into her lunch box, so old houses shouldn't unnerve her. *Nor should men with big-boned bodies, intellectual clothes and penetrating green eyes.* At the deeper thought, Nikki felt a prickle that started at her nape and slid down her spine. She suddenly raised her voice angrily. "Dammit, if you're there, Jonathan Sleet, you'd better answer me."

"Quick breath." Christy inhaled sharply. "You cussed."

"Sorry," Nikki managed, thinking that was nothing compared to the language she intended to use when she found Christy's father. Nikki raised her voice impatiently. "Are you there or not?"

Still nothing.

Her hand hit a door jamb. Skittering her fingers around the smooth, cold molding, she suppressed a shudder. Relief flooded her when she found—and depressed—a dimmer-style light switch. Finally. Overhead track lamps came on, shining crisscrossed beams of light into the room. Only now, when she found herself standing in an ordinary, everyday kitchen, did Nikki realize how hard her heart was pounding. See, she chided herself, there wasn't a bogeyman in sight.

But something seemed...hinky. Strange. Blinking against the room's brightness, Nikki watched her underage fare place her backpack gently on the gray marble dining table in the center of the room. After that, she removed her hat and gloves, folding them neatly and slipping them into velvet-edged coat pockets. Nikki didn't know much child psychology, but she sure hoped these clothes were to the girl's taste—and that she wasn't dressing like a miniature adult because she was so desperately trying to parent herself.

Geez...there definitely wasn't a whole lot of parental warmth in here. The kitchen felt sterile to Nikki, decorated in gray, black and red, with gleaming gray tile flooring and institutional-looking stainless-steel appliances. The oversize oven range and refrigerator suggested that Christy's father entertained for large groups. Just looking around made Nikki hungry for her father's cozy red-and-white-checkered kitchen back home in Kentucky. Nikki could almost see her mother's old framed needlepoints and the white, ruffly curtains. She could hear the rough masculine voices, too, all the boisterous ribbing, knee-slapping and laughs.

When her eyes settled on the counter, she saw crumbs and hoped they meant Christy's father was here. But maybe the place was deserted. It was still so cold that she could see her breath. Ice had crystallized on the inner panes of the windows. "Maybe you'd better put your gloves back on, hon."

"It *is* kind of cold," Christy conceded.

"Freezing," Nikki returned as the fancy track lights flickered. Great. That explained the open box of candles on the counter, and why the town looked so dark. Everyone was experiencing power outages due to the snowstorm. Nikki stared up as the overhead lights strobed, dimmed, then returned to normal. Should she get the flashlight from the cab?

"If I can find some food—" Christy gingerly opened the refrigerator door and peered inside

"—would you stay a minute and eat with me, Nikki?"

"Don't worry, I'm not leaving until I turn you over to a responsible adult."

Christy sounded relieved. "Good."

"Besides, I'm hungry myself." All she'd had today was a banana and a pint carton of milk, but now her stomach was rumbling, reminding her she was feeding two. Earlier, she'd been too angry to eat.

As Christy rummaged, Nikki's eyes flitted to the window. Wind banged the shutters against the house and pushed branches against the windowpanes. Sweeping gusts were still driving the snow straight down. If Christy's dad didn't materialize soon, Nikki was going to get stuck here. Coming up, the mountain had been a solid sheet of ice. Soon, going down would be impossible.

Her eyes pierced the darkness, penetrating her own image reflected in the glass. She searched the shadows beyond. Geez...this was sure turning out to be a weird Christmas. Suddenly, her eyes detected a movement. Someone was behind her! She gasped, whirling around.

But he was gone.

If it *was* a he. She shook her head, wondering if it had been her imagination. But she was certain she'd seen someone in the window. Had he been behind her? Or outside?

"What's wrong, Nikki?" Christy asked nervously.

"Nothing," Nikki managed, not about to frighten the child. But what had she gotten herself into? Maybe she should have made Christy call her dad before driving all this way in the snow. She glanced at the child, who was carrying a loaf of bread and a jar of peanut butter to the table. "Since it's sandwich stuff, I can make it myself," Christy announced proudly.

"Good for you," Nikki murmured, turning toward the window again. Without warning, the lights flickered. There he was! Nothing more than a shadow. She spun around once more, but the room suddenly went dark. In the silence, the wind whistled, and Nikki's blood ran cold. Dammit, it was probably just Christy's father. Maybe she startled him as much as he did her.

"Nikki?" Christy whispered, her voice sounding a few feet away and to the right.

"I'm here." Why wasn't the man identifying himself? "Uh...Mr. Sleet?" Nikki ventured, blinking in the darkness.

"The jury's still out."

She heard a lot in that one sentence, more than she wanted to—how his soft, twanging North Carolina drawl seemed to be touched by a mysterious, bone-deep darkness that came from his soul, and how the sad, sexy voice made her feel something for him, an answering sadness or unexpected pity that appeared and passed too quickly to be examined. Judging from how the words projected, the man was even bigger than his photo suggested. A lumberjack type. Not that Nikki was going to react to a little overbearing masculinity. Just this morning, Buck had taught her everything she'd ever need to know about men. An image of her father suddenly flashed in her mind, as if to remind her there were still a few good men left in the world.

"Come on," she finally said. "Enlighten me. Who's there?"

"Who's asking and why?"

Once again, she noticed more than she wanted to—that despite his down-home twang, the voice was cultured, hinting at more than average book-learning. Even worse, Nikki realized she was tempted by the challenge she heard in it, and she suddenly regretted her greatest character flaw, which was that she always rose to the bait. Swallowing hard, she schooled herself not to forget Buck and countless other things that had caused her heartache. But she still hadn't managed a response when the light snapped back on, and she found herself staring at Jonathan Sleet.

In that first instant, she knew he liked the way she looked. Male appreciation glimmered—and promptly vanished—from eyes that were more the color of sage than moss. He was both rougher and better-looking than his picture. Taller than she'd imagined, with wider, stronger shoulders and an older face. The eyes that weren't exactly inviting were now studying her with feigned detachment.

She met those eyes. "Well, I'm sure you're happy to see us."

Lips that should have been too thin to be sexy compressed in what wasn't much of a smile. He leaned in the kitchen doorway. "Not really. You have a name?"

The man didn't even bother to look around and make sure his daughter had arrived safe and sound. Casually, Nikki touched the brim of her baseball cap, gently tipping it. "I'm Nikki Ryder."

That wasn't what he was after, and out of sheer perversity, she wasn't going to offer more. Her eyes flickered over him, studying him as calmly as he was studying her, and she realized he'd come down a notch in the world since his last photo session. Oh, his body didn't show it. It was so jewel-hard it could have been carved from the marble of his dining table, but stiff, devil-may-care whiskers had replaced a smooth jaw, and hair that had been dark brown now had a few silver strands tangled in with the chestnut. He wasn't wearing a stitch of tweed anymore, either, just snug jeans and a heavy fisherman's sweater that had faded to green-gray. The oilskin coat tossed carelessly over a dining chair was damp, suggesting he'd been out in the storm not long ago.

"Well, Nikki Ryder, what the hell are you doing here?" The Carolinian lilt of his voice was incongruent with the gruffness of his words.

Somewhere to her right, Nikki sensed Christy was shrinking against the refrigerator. "I'll just assume you're Jonathan Sleet," Nikki returned. "Now maybe you'd like to restate your question. This time without the profanity."

His eyes darkened with what might have been temper, and Nikki suddenly registered their perceptive awareness. Writers were rumored to be more intuitive than the average Joe, and now Nikki decided it was probably true. Nothing had ever made her feel quite so naked as Jonathan Sleet's stare at this particular moment. If someone told her he was seeing her past, present and future, she'd believe it.

He blinked his wide-set eyes as if realizing he'd stared longer than was polite. "I said, what are you doing in my house?"

He really had some nerve, seeing as Nikki had brought his daughter home in a snowstorm. While she knew it wasn't at all appropriate to challenge him in front of Christy, she couldn't stop herself from saying, "Anybody ever tell you you're a real charmer?"

"Not lately."

"Geez. Wonder why they haven't mentioned it?"

He shrugged. "Who knows?" His eyes trailed over the backpack and hat on the table. "I see you're making yourself at home."

"It's a little cold in here to be homey."

"And I like it this way. Now, how'd you get up here? That mountain road's frozen solid. You couldn't have driven."

"Well, I did."

He glanced toward the window and the snow, then looked at her as if she were crazy. "You *drove*?"

"I'm a professional. I came in my cab." She raised a staying hand. "And please, keep the remarks about woman drivers to yourself." Nikki jerked a thumb toward his daughter. "I'd think it's pretty obvious why I'm here."

Jonathan Sleet turned slowly, staring at Christy as if he'd never even seen her before, and Nikki's jaw dropped in outraged astonishment. Wasn't the man even going to say hello? Surely, he'd give the poor little girl a hug or a kiss. Christy was obviously worn out from traveling, and she'd been so anxious to get here. Nikki suddenly realized Christy had probably put on the fancy, obviously uncomfortable clothes just to impress her daddy. Her heart tugged at the thought.

"Why you're here might be clear to you." The man's eyes had lasered into Nikki again. "But maybe you'd like to share the information."

Nikki wasn't about to give him the satisfaction of forcing her to state the obvious, but she wished she could ignore how his eyes slid from her baseball cap to her bomber jacket and jeans. It was definitely the wrong time to cry, but tears suddenly threatened. Even worse, he seemed to notice, and he frowned in a way that made him look a lot more hospitable.

"Are you all right?"

Damn him for being so perceptive. "Is that concern in your voice?"

His thin lips compressed. "Guess you're fine," he muttered, dragging a hand through his hair and pushing it back from his high forehead.

But she wasn't fine. She loved this old fool baseball cap, and the jeans were her favorites. So, why couldn't she feel more comfortable with herself? Why did Jonathan Sleet's eyes make her suddenly wish she looked like more of a woman? She blinked back the tears. "Don't bother to say thank you," she managed. "But in the middle of a storm that you were apparently too busy to go out in because you're such a creative genius, I—"

"A creative *what?*" He gaped at her.

"Genius."

"Who said that?"

"Your daughter." Nikki pointed a thumb toward Christy. "The one I just brought home for Christmas."

Jonathan Sleet turned, his smoldering, suspicious eyes looking very serious and dangerous as they settled on Christy. "My *daughter?*"

Poor kid. As Christy hopped nervously from one patent-leather shoe to the other, her hair danced and she clasped her hands in front of her. Her sparkling green eyes shifted uncertainly, and the shy smile she shot her father made Nikki ache for her. Obviously, these two hadn't seen each other for a very long time.

Tremulously, Christy said, "Hi there, Daddy. It's *moi.*"

"DADDY?" he whispered hoarsely. Was this some kind of sick joke? He no longer had a daughter or a wife. It was why he'd been holed up, why he hated the holidays. In fact, it was why Jon Sleet hated pretty much everything known to man.

He stared at the child. Lord, she even looked a little like Jenny might have looked now. She was a cute thing. Blond and green-eyed, so dressed up she could be heading for church. Just looking at her made his heart squeeze with pain.

"Hi Daddy," she ventured again.

Vaguely, he wondered if he was having hallucinations. "Who are you?" he croaked. He definitely wasn't her daddy. And no child saying so could realize how many wounds she was cutting open. What kind of game were these two playing? One look into the kid's duplicitous, mischievous eyes would tell any fool she was fibbing.

She blushed with guilt, but her voice only got bolder. "I'm Christy Sleet," she announced, edging from the refrigerator to the dining table. "And you know it, Daddy."

He knew no such thing. He forced himself to turn to the woman. Had she really said she was a cab-driver? Looking at her, his chest got tight again. And he felt something else—a strange, heady excitement and a gentling of his spirit. It had been a long time since a woman was in this kitchen, two years. And Nikki Ryder was a woman—no matter how hard she tried to hide it with those boyish clothes. His eyes drifted from her baseball cap to her jeans, then lingered where her cute, powder-blue long johns peeked through the artful holes in the knees. Even when she wasn't speaking, he could still hear the put-on ruggedness of a voice that was probably sweeter and softer than she wanted it to be. Language was his business, so the Kentucky accent was unmistakable, and he found himself wondering how she'd gotten so far from home. Suddenly, he reminded himself she was an intruder. "You two stay put."

"Don't worry." The little girl sounded both eager to please him, and as if she were acting out a part in a TV crime drama. "We won't move a muscle."

He almost smiled. Might have, if he hadn't forgotten how, two years ago. Or if he was in a mood to welcome strangers. Turning on his heel, he headed down the hallway, not flicking any switches until he reached the outer floodlights. Stepping coatless into the fierce cold, he squinted against the driving snow, strode down the stone steps, then suspiciously circled the sedan in the driveway.

It did have a taxi light on top and a meter inside. But otherwise it was the strangest car he'd ever seen. Hot pink and decorated for Christmas, even down to a nativity scene on the dashboard. He studied the figurines, then frowned when he realized some were missing. What had happened to Joseph? The stocking looped over the rearview mirror was embroidered with the name Nikki, so he guessed she hadn't been lying about her name. She was unusually trusting, too, judging from the fact that she'd left the keys in the ignition. Taking them, Jon circled the car and opened the trunk. A mess was inside—tangled clothes, enough over-the-counter remedies that she could have dumped a medicine chest in here, two tennis racquets and a basketball...

Deciding he'd seen enough, he shut the trunk. He told himself he didn't even really care who the woman was or why she was claiming the kid was his daughter. He just wanted them gone.

Turning, he headed for the house. When he reached the kitchen, he leaned in the doorway, crossed his arms and simply waited for an explanation. When none came, he said, "Okay, so you're really a cab-driver named Nikki, but that's not my daughter."

Nikki's eyes widened. "Oh, come on!" She glanced helplessly around, as if she didn't want to argue in front of the child. Lowering her voice, she said, "What seven-year-old would ask to be brought here for Christmas if she wasn't a relative of yours?"

Good point. He was vaguely aware the kid was watching this sparring match with a fascinated expression. "I'm telling you, that's not my daughter."

Nikki made a soft, exasperated sound. "Uh...I'm not sure what to say."

He took a harder look at her, since she really seemed convinced that the child hovering near the dining table was his. Nikki Ryder, he decided, had a sexy face. No two ways about it. Her long, slender neck was nice, too. Large brown eyes were offset by thick eyebrows that she hadn't tweezed to nothing, the way some women did. She had a long, straight nose. A full lower lip, and healthy-looking, very square teeth. She didn't wear makeup, but then she didn't need to. Thick soft hair peeked from under the jaunty baseball cap she obviously thought made her look so tough.

"Through staring?"

He decided he even liked her attitude. She didn't scare nearly as easily as most. "Not really."

"Then it's too bad I've got to run."

Most women would have by now. "Somehow, I was hoping you'd say that." As he spoke, the child inched forward, tiptoed around the dining table and tried to slip past him. He grabbed her arm. "Where do you think you're going?"

She wiggled out of his grip. "To get my suitcase, so I can unpack."

Unpack? He was so stunned he let her go. As the girl darted down the hallway, he stared at Nikki. "Mind telling me how you plan to get down the hill in this mess?"

"Hey, thanks for the hospitality," she shot back, "but don't worry. I'll slide down on my backside if I have to. I'm sure not staying here."

"At least stay long enough to tell me why you think that's my daughter."

"Sorry—" She was already taking long strides toward him. "As you can imagine, it's been fun meeting you. A real barrel of laughs. But now I've just got to go."

When she reached the doorway, he unceremoniously grabbed her arm. This woman wasn't going anywhere unless she was taking that child. Her chin snapped up as if pulled by a live wire, and her eyes narrowed. "You don't want to grab me," she warned.

Unfortunately, his gaze had settled on lips that made him remember how much he used to crave long, deep tongue kisses that made a woman's toes curl. "I already did."

Her eyes flashed. "I grew up with three brothers, and I'm not above getting physical."

He almost wished she'd hit him; maybe that would bring him to his senses. Instead, a bemused smile glimmered on his lips. "You want to get physical?"

She shook off his grasp. "Look, I don't want any trouble here. I'm truly sorry for whatever domestic dispute you're having with your wife. Or ex-wife. But I don't want to be involved. I think you should try to make it up with your daughter. She's cold, she's hungry, and she's tired. She's had a long day of travel. Now please—" She glanced through the door. "I've really got to go now."

He could merely stare. "You can't. I'm serious. That's not my child."

Something in his eyes must have gotten through to Nikki because she finally looked doubtful. "I picked her up at the airport. She gave me this address."

What was happening here? This woman believed he was the girl's father, but why would a child he'd never seen before hire a cabdriver to bring her here? "Are you lying to me?"

She stared back. "No. Of course not."

She looked honest. And strangely vulnerable beneath that tough facade. He suddenly wished he hadn't pulled her so close. Next to him, she was more petite than he'd realized, a tiny spitfire of a woman, and in the drafty, crisp clean air, her scent was doubly sharp. It had him imagining how her hair would look, loose around her shoulders or draped across his chest.

"Please listen," she said.

It was hard not to when her voice was like something warm pouring right down his throat. The sudden thud of his heart reminded him that he'd been holed up too long, licking his wounds. He glanced around uneasily. He really had to move away from this woman. Find the kid and send them both packing. But her eyes held him.

"Jonathan," she began again. "My guess is that you have some nasty feelings for your ex-wife."

"And you think that's why I'm denying the girl's mine?"

Nikki nodded. "I'm sure of it, Jonathan."

"Jon. People call me Jon." At least they had the last time he'd bothered to talk to any of them. And it had been a while.

"Uh...Jon." She cleared her throat, her soft brown eyes making something inside him squeeze tight. "You must love your daughter."

At the mention of his child, pain sliced through him again. "She's not—" He might have finished, but the first woman he'd laid eyes on in two years placed a sweet, imploring hand on his chest. He felt her fingers on his sweater, how her eyes warmed his face. It was no use. He was perceptive about people, and knew that once this woman got a notion lodged in her mind, nothing could shake it loose. He better track down Christy and get the truth out of her. God only knew what havoc she was wreaking in the far corners of his house.

"Please," Nikki said again. "You can't let whatever happened between you and your wife get in the way of your relationship with your little girl."

What happened with my wife? In the space of a heartbeat, the old anger that always ghosted through him came to the surface. "You're making some false assumptions," he managed. "It doesn't matter. But I want you to leave this house. And take that child."

"Take her where?"

"Wherever you found her."

Something agelessly female came into Nikki's eyes then. "I'm not leaving until I'm sure your daughter's all right here."

He grunted softly. "Please don't decide to start playing the diplomat."

Nikki crossed her arms. "You didn't bother to come get your daughter at the airport. You didn't so much as give her a hug when we came in. There was no food prepared, no Christmas decorations up, even though she's spending the holidays with you."

He nodded. "Wouldn't those suspicious things tell you something?"

"What?"

"That she's not my daughter." When the lights flickered, he hoped there wasn't another power outage since he didn't want to have this conversation at all, much less in the dark.

Nikki blew out a short, peeved sigh. "I swear," she warned, "if I have to stay here until Christmas, you're going to make your little girl feel welcome."

"Nothing like female solidarity," he said dryly. Well, since Nikki wasn't going to leave a little girl alone with him, all he had to do was get rid of Nikki. Christy would be right on her heels. What kid would want to be left with a strange man?

"Look, you'd better take her now. She needs to go right back to her mother's." Or wherever she came from. "What kind of Christmas is she going to have here?" He glanced around. "You're so right. I haven't even prepared..."

The smile Nikki sent him somehow curled his blood. She said, "There are still some shopping days left before Christmas, Jon."

He was getting desperate. "This is no place for a kid. Now get her and get out."

When Nikki didn't budge, panic slid through his veins. The lights flickered and, as his eyes drifted over her lips again, he realized he had only one choice.

Nikki's eyes suddenly widened as if she'd read his mind.

Just as the lights went out, she uttered a jittery, stupefied laugh. And then his lips caught hers in the dark. As much loneliness as he'd felt, as much need, Jon expected the soft pressure to make him come undone. He wasn't disappointed. The fleeting kiss left countless impressions—the pliable yielding of the womanly body she tried to hide, the softness of her lower lip, a mouth that tasted faintly of banana. And then he felt a sweet throbbing ache between his legs that made him wonder what had come over him. He'd never acted this way before. But then, what did he have to live for, these days? Instead of releasing her, he wound up pulling her closer.

Nikki's first punch smacked his shoulder and brought him to his senses. Her kneecap followed, connecting with his thigh. She was still staggering back when the lights flickered on. "Sleet," she growled, furiously lifting off her baseball cap by the brim and slapping it against her thigh. "What is *wrong* with you?"

Good question. All he knew was that he was aching. Her mouth had been all heat and salt, and now he felt strangely helpless as his gaze settled on her glistening lips again. "I'm not a nice guy," he forced himself to say. "That was the point."

She slapped her palm to her head as if dumbfounded. "That's why you kissed me? To prove you're a jerk?"

"You're swift, Nikki."

"Please," she shot back, slapping her cap back on. "I had your number the second I laid eyes on you."

"We haven't known each other all *that* long."

"Long enough."

When she spun around and fled, he was still tasting her. And nothing could have stopped Jon Sleet from following.

Chapter Three

"C'mon," Nikki pleaded, feeling panic-stricken as she turned the key in the ignition. "Why won't you start?" Reaching beside her in the seat, she found her gloves and put them on.

At least Jon had quit following her. She stared anxiously at the house through a circular spot she'd rubbed in the windshield. She guessed he'd gotten the message when she slammed the front door in his face. She didn't take kindly to assault. And when it came to accepting children into his life, the man wasn't any better than Buck. "Poor Christy."

Inhaling sharply, Nikki felt the bitter cold air searing in her lungs. Every inch of the rest of her still burned from Jon Sleet's mouth. No matter how hard she tried to push the recollection from her mind, she could still feel his tongue miming what the rest of him so very obviously wanted to do to her. What an animal. It felt like he'd captured her hips between his hard-muscled thighs, making absolutely sure she felt...

Don't go there, Nikki. Heat flooded her cheeks. "And I had no choice but to kiss him back," she whispered defensively. The man came on like he'd been locked up in that house for years. He wanted love, too, that was the worst thing. No man could kiss a stranger like that if he wasn't desperately lonely. He'd probably even fooled himself into thinking he was trying to push her away, but Nikki knew better. "A confused man and a bad divorce." It wasn't a winning combination, but looking briefly through a window into Jonathan Sleet's world had aroused Nikki's empathy for the lonely man and his daughter.

"Oh please, just get me out of here," she muttered, trying not to think of Jon's cute, misguided daughter in her grown-up little outfit, looking so anxious to please her daddy. Nikki turned the key over in the ignition again. "Nothing," she murmured, fighting panic. Was she out of gas? Was the battery dead?

Another more disturbing thought came: Had someone tampered with the car? Glancing around, she half expected to see some old hunchbacked family retainer making off with her heater hoses. Had Jon Sleet disabled her car when he'd left the house? Was he trying to trap her here for some reason? And what about Christy? When she said she was going to get her suitcase, Nikki could have sworn she'd heard the front door open. Had Christy come out here?

"Stop it," she muttered. A seven-year-old, no matter how wily, couldn't disable a two-ton Chevy. Willing her heart to stop racing, Nikki squirmed uncomfortably on the freezing vinyl car seat and considered her options. Even if the cab started, she'd never get off the mountain in this snow, not without a tow truck.

Inside the house, lights had been snapping on. Now Jon ran past a window. Shuddering, Nikki watched him move. His bulky sweater hid plenty of hard, flexible muscle—she'd found that out—so his powerful grace didn't come as a surprise. Nevertheless, she couldn't believe he was really chasing his seven-year-old around the house. Guilt assailed her. She couldn't leave that poor little girl here alone. Maybe she should be a Good Samaritan and stay until morning....

"I'd rather face a firing squad than Jon Sleet."

Her mouth set grimly. But she should at least go back in, get his ex-wife's number from Christy and call. Something here was really fishy. Drawing a steadying breath, she grabbed a flashlight from the glove compartment, got out of the car and slammed the door. Even as her breath fogged the frigid air, heat flooded her again. The man's kiss shouldn't have affected her. His lips were too hard, his tongue too invasive. And yet that kiss had such need in it, such hunger...

Geez...you'd really better get out of here. Reaching inside the car again, Nikki popped the hood. She was resourceful, she reminded herself as she circled the car. She could get off this hill—and away from Jon Sleet. She tried to tell herself Christy would be fine; after all, she was his daughter. Besides, Nikki didn't believe in meddling. What had happened between a husband and wife wasn't her business. Live and Let Live, that was her motto.

Lifting the hood, she shined the flashlight over the engine. Jiggled some wires. But nothing was missing. Nothing was out of place. She wrinkled her nose against a waft of peanut butter. Funny she should smell it out here, since Christy had made her sandwich inside....

She thought she heard a shriek.

Her head snapped up, and she stared at the house

just as Christy flew past an upstairs window, running as fast as her legs could carry her. Her miserable excuse for a father followed. Blinking against the driving snow, Nikki tried to ignore the cold air burning her lungs. Face it, she was stuck. Even if she wasn't, she couldn't leave Christy. Once the child's mother realized her ex had been holed up in a dark house like a hermit, and that he hadn't even decorated for Christmas, she'd want Christy home. Nikki would drive Christy back to the airport and put her on the next plane. Except the planes were probably all grounded by now, she realized. Well, she'd cross that bridge when she came to it.

First she had to deal with Jon Sleet. That decided, Nikki gripped the flashlight like a billy club and strode resolutely toward the house.

HE WAS GETTING too old for this.

Breathlessly, Jon hauled Christy back into the kitchen by the scruff of the neck, carrying her suitcase in his other hand. Even though he wasn't hurting her, she yowled as if he were a monster. "Let me go!"

Releasing her, Jon stared at Nikki, feeling as if he'd seen a ghost. After the way she'd slammed the door in his face, he hadn't expected to find her leaning against a wall with the phone receiver wedged beneath her chin. Even worse, the quickening of his pulse told him how much he'd secretly wanted her to come back. "Thought you'd left."

"Believe me, I'm not that easy to get rid of."

He arched an eyebrow. "Come back for more?"

Nikki merely rolled her eyes.

But she'd liked the kiss. He knew by the surprised way she stared at him the split second afterward, before anger overtook her features. Now she was self-consciously fiddling with the bill of her baseball cap, and nervously tapping the phone's dial-tone button as if praying an operator would answer soon. She'd put on lightweight leather driving gloves, the kind with snipped-off finger holes that usually had Velcro at the wrists. Hers snapped. He said, "Who are you calling? Nine-one-one?"

She recradled the receiver, her tone faintly accusatory, as if he'd cut the wires to keep her here. "No one. Your phone's dead."

They both knew it was the kiss that bothered her, not the phone, and as his eyes drifted over her, he could barely believe he'd possessed her mouth so completely only moments before. He'd never kissed a stranger—in fact he'd kissed few women other than his wife—but now that he knew how good it felt, he was tempted to do it again. "The phone was working an hour ago."

She stiffened. "Well, it's not working now."

"Don't take it out on me. I don't work for Ma Bell."

"Did you disable my car?"

That came out of the blue. Was she serious? He glanced around the kitchen. Redecorating it had been one of the last things his wife had done, but he'd meticulously removed all the frills—the bright yellow blinds, red-ruffled curtains and window-box herb gardens. It seemed strange to have a woman in here now. *And such a sexy woman,* he thought looking at Nikki again. She was a diamond in the rough. Not even the tight rubber band and boyish cap that held back her hair could hide its silken texture, no more than her lack of lipstick could obscure the sensual curves of her mouth. Jon suddenly decided that the degree he was attracted to her was exactly the degree to which he wanted her gone. His lips twisted with irony. "So far, I've made no secret that my goal was to get rid of you. Why would I disable your car?"

"Who knows? You seem like a strange guy. Maybe you wanted me to stay and take care of your daughter until you can send her back to her mother's. Maybe you feel you're incapable of caring for her alone."

The words rankled. Not that Nikki Ryder knew anything about his capabilities or how he felt he'd failed his family. "Who are you trying to call?"

She sighed. "Christy's mother, if I can get the number from you. Or maybe the local sheriff."

"What? To find out if I'm a fit parent?"

She shrugged uncomfortably. "I just thought…"

Great. Steve Warwick would love that call. Back before Jon had decided to systematically wreck his life, he and Steve had been best buddies. Now Jon would rather clear up this mess without talking to Steve, or anyone else in town for that matter.

His eyes narrowed. Maybe Nikki had some hidden agenda that had brought her here. "I looked in your car," he said with a casualness he didn't feel, trying to ignore the rapt, fascinated expression on Christy's face as she watched the exchange. "If you were really working, why are you driving around with a year's worth of clothes in your trunk?"

When Nikki's eyes widened, he noticed that her eyes were more than brown; they were a rich, deep caramel with flecks of honey-gold and sunlight. "You looked in my trunk?"

"You left the keys in the ignition."

She stared at him. "Why my clothes are in my trunk is none of your business."

Fine. He turned his gaze to Christy. "Sit." He pointed at a kitchen chair, and she sat dutifully. Crouching in front of her, he dropped his eyes over her outfit and decided she looked like a pint-size poster girl for a Junior League fund-raiser. He said, "You've really confused this cabdriver, so you'd better tell me who you are."

The little girl smiled sweetly, her bright eyes saying she was starting to enjoy the havoc she was wreaking. "I'm your daughter. Don't you remember me, Daddy?"

Staring into the kid's heart-stopping, devilish green eyes, he decided she was awfully cute—at least if you ignored the makeup she was too young to wear and the fact that her tiny oval fingernails were painted bright red. He concentrated on the flaxen curls and pert ski-jump nose. "You'd better quit fibbing."

Her eyes widened. "Or else you'll give me that awful truth serum again, right, Daddy?"

"Truth serum?" Nikki questioned, stepping anxiously forward.

As if he really drugged small children. He shot Nikki a droll glance, knowing full well how this situation appeared to her. God only knew what she thought of him. His own emotions were still at war— he was angry about the intrusion and confused about what the child was up to; yet he somehow felt as if he'd been rescued. Hell, the only thing in his date book for tonight was drowning himself in self-pity.

Taking in Christy's makeup, he heaved a sudden sigh and muttered, "Who would let a kid walk around like this?"

Nikki was eyeing him. "Her parents?" she suggested mildly.

So Nikki Ryder really thought he'd encourage little girls to paint their faces. Wonderful. He sighed. "Elizabeth Taylor didn't wear that much face paint in *Cleopatra.*"

A dreamy look came over the kid's eyes. "*Cleopatra...*" She clasped her hands theatrically to her chest. "I love that motion picture."

Jon could only shake his head. Where on earth had this strange child come from? Somewhere out there her parents were probably worried sick. Eyeing the phone, he dreaded the call he needed to make to Steve, but authorities had to be notified the child was missing.

Getting up, he headed for the sink, returned with a damp washcloth and grabbed the kid's chin. The resigned way she pursed her lips, shut her eyes and tilted back her head made his heart suddenly wrench. A thousand times he'd washed his own daughter's face like this. For a second, he squeezed his eyes shut against the memories, then he opened them again. Christy was still patiently waiting to have her face washed. Nikki might be wary of him, but Christy sure wasn't.

And why would she be? he thought, grimacing. The fool kid had him exactly where she wanted him. His gentle touch belied the scowl on his face as he dabbed her baby-soft skin. Blusher, pink lipstick and green eye shadow bled onto the white cloth. "There." Crossing the room, Jon tossed the cloth into the sink.

"You should leave it on," Nikki suddenly said.

He squinted at her. "You think I should leave the makeup on her?"

"No." Nikki laughed. "The sink. My dad's a plumber. If you don't let the water drip in this kind of weather, your pipes will freeze."

She had a nice laugh. It was deeper and more throaty than he'd expected, given her petite size. And she mentioned her father with affection. Maybe that explained the overgrown-tomboy look. Was she the only child of a man who'd wanted sons? Jon didn't want to be curious, but he was.

Christy said, "You'd better do what Nikki says, Daddy."

He shot the child a long sideways glance, then he turned on the faucet, letting it dribble. Crouching in front of Christy again, he said, "Okay. Fun's over. Start talking."

"Moi?"

He stared at Christy a long moment. *"Oui.* Who do you think?"

Pinching her thumb and index finger together, she made the motion of zipping her mouth shut.

Fine. He gave her his most bloodthirsty eyebrow-waggle and sliced an index finger across his throat, indicating what would happen if she didn't start talking. If she wanted, maybe they could solve this whole dilemma in pantomime. Or in pidgin French.

Christy giggled.

He'd known she would. Maybe he'd even wanted her to. After all, he couldn't stand the fact that Nikki thought he was a bad father. Or just plain old crazy. How on earth had she convinced herself he'd come unhinged because of a divorce? Chewing the inside of his cheek distractedly, he wondered what to do next. Torture was out of the question.

Nikki ventured closer, a hand on her hip. She obviously felt uncomfortable in a stranger's house, but she wasn't going to leave until she felt sure Christy was safe. He wondered if he should get out old photo albums with pictures of Mary and Jenny, but even that wouldn't necessarily prove Christy wasn't his. Besides, those pictures were personal. What had happened to Jon's wife and daughter wasn't any of Nikki Ryder's business.

Christy's pursed lips twitched in amusement over his predicament. He knew from experience that there was no greater glory in youth than besting a grown-up. "I guess you'll want to lock me in my room now, Daddy," she crooned, "and punish me the way you usually do."

"I do not—"

Gasping, Nikki stepped behind Christy's chair. Placing a protective hand on the girl's shoulder, she leaned close, her eyes brimming with concern. When she spoke, Jon decided her voice was far too gentle to waste on such a devious child. "Hon, has your daddy ever...ever hurt you?"

His lips parted in mute protest. Hurt her? Right about now, he could kill this kid. What a little manipulator. Why couldn't Nikki see this kid was using her? Wrapping them both around her little finger? Everything she said roped Jon in deeper, making it seem as if she really was his daughter.

Christy gazed soulfully at Nikki. "You mean, does Daddy beat me and things?"

Jon groaned. "Beat you? And things? What *things?*" As if he was some monster. "I've never even seen this child before today."

Nikki ignored him. "Yes...has he, hon?"

The kid glanced nervously around. "Not really."

"Just sort of, huh?" Jon could merely stare. To be so thoroughly had by a grade-schooler was humbling. He forced a smile. "Thanks for all your honesty, darling."

She smiled back. "You taught me never to fib, Daddy."

Daddy. The word suddenly knifed into him, cutting open the wound left by a little girl he needed to forget but never could. If Christy knew how much heartbreak she was causing, she wouldn't call him "Daddy." Jon would gladly die right now if he could only hear Jenny call him that once more. And yet, staring at Christy, his gaze softened.

At least until she made a show of shivering. "Since I'm finally here, Daddy, could you turn up the heat? It's really cold. Mommy might get mad if I die of pneumonia."

His tone was dry. "I'll take that under advisement."

Nikki was now fiddling with the zipper on her bomber jacket, sliding it up and down a two-inch trajectory. "You know, it *is* a little cold in here...uh, Jon. And we wouldn't want her to get sick."

The woman's misdirected concern was starting to try his patience. "Do you have any idea how much it costs to heat a place like this?"

"With or without you in it?" she shot back.

Touché. "So, you think I'm a cold guy, huh?"

"Yes. And your child's welfare should come before your pocketbook, Mr. Sleet."

Maybe. Except this wasn't his child. And he'd been unemployed for two years.

"A child's welfare must come first, Daddy," Christy echoed.

"Thank you," he muttered. He glanced at Nikki again. "Anything else?

Her voice turned prim. "I think you know what else."

He did. The way her gaze drifted over him made him suddenly conscious of his disheveled hair, and of his faded jeans and bulky sweater. He could use a shave. Eyeing her baseball cap and ponytail, he found himself wondering how she'd gotten her strange mix of toughness and sensitivity. He also wondered how her thick hair would feel in his hands. Brown was too easy a word to describe the color. It was rich and earthy, shot through with strands of deep red and honey. Well, when it came to Nikki Ryder, Jon decided he wasn't in the mood to make any promises regarding his behavior, so he simply turned to Christy again. "You know you can't stay here. People must be looking for you. I need to know who you are and where you're from."

"Nikki," the little girl wailed.

"Jon," Nikki said quickly. "I don't know why you're doing this to her. It's cruel. Apparently her mother thought she should spend the holidays with you."

He realized interrogating the child in front of Nikki was no use. Maybe she'd talk if he got her alone. He gave it one last try, fighting dirty. "You know Santa forgets naughty little girls…"

"Oh look," said Nikki. "I think you've made her cry." She leaned and smoothed Christy's hair, while the child blinked back imaginary tears. "You poor thing," Nikki murmured.

Funny, he thought, glancing between Nikki and Christy. One was dressed like a grease monkey, but probably had the heart of a saint. The other was dressed like a million bucks and belonged in the lower tiers of Dante's *Inferno*. Without warning, Jon gave up and reached into Christy's coat pockets.

Nikki gasped. "What are you doing?"

"Don't worry, I'm not assaulting her." He was definitely starting to wish Nikki believed he wasn't this girl's father. He glanced over the contents of her pockets: white gloves, a white handkerchief, a tiny gold pen, a small heart-shaped gold locket on a chain. He opened the locket, but the pictures had been removed. Had Christy removed pictures of her parents because he'd recognize them? Did he know her from somewhere?

No, he'd never seen her.

Leaning forward, he peeled back her velvet coat collar and read the designer label. The outfit hadn't come cheap. Her locket was twenty-four karat gold with a diamond chip, too, and she was also wearing a sapphire ring. Did he have any wealthy acquaintances who had children?

He couldn't think of any, but then he'd pushed away a lot of people in the past two years. Images of the charmed life he and his wife had led after the success of his books flitted through his mind. Knitting his eyebrows, he crossed the room and lifted Christy's carry-on onto the tabletop, next to the backpack.

"What are you doing now?" Christy asked warily.

"What's it look like?" Unzipping the bag, he frowned and began lifting out items of clothing. They were also well-made and expensive, but they were for warm weather. Sundresses and two bathing suits. Shorts and tank tops. In a side pocket, he found more cash than he'd ever carry.

Nikki made a sound of disapproval and edged so close that her scent was like a bobbing hook cast out to him. "I knew that suitcase felt too light." She turned to Christy. "Why didn't your mother pack warm things for you, hon?"

"Uh...my mom was too busy to help, so I tried to do my best." Christy frowned. "What? Did I do a bad job, Nikki?"

"Oh, no," Nikki assured. "You did just fine, hon."

Without even looking, Jon knew Christy was batting her pitiful eyelashes. And now Nikki thought Christy's mother—his supposed ex-wife—was as bad a parent as he was. He kept riffling.

"You're messing up my stuff, Daddy," Christy ventured.

Damn right he was. He ignored her. Maybe there was something in that little velvet backpack. Lifting it by the shoulder strap, he drew it to his chest, against his thick wool sweater.

Christy leaped from the chair. "Don't open my pack, Jon!"

Lifting it high above her reach, he stared down. "So it's not 'Daddy' anymore, huh?"

She glared up, craning her neck and looking genuinely upset. "If you tell me your real name," he bargained, sinking to bribery, "then I won't look in your pack."

Her emerald eyes glittered with fury, and her tiny hands tightened on the chair. "Give me my pack, Daddy."

Given her misbehavior, Jon hardly felt guilty about lording his superior size and strength over her. With the pack still held in the air, he pulled down a zipper, stared inside—then dropped the pack as if he'd been burned.

"Noodles!" Christy shrieked in terror.

Right before the backpack hit the floor, Jon swiped at it, managing to grasp it. Lifting it to the table again, he realized his heart was pounding dangerously hard. After a second, he stared at Christy in censure.

She smiled weakly back, a small trembling hand now pressed to her heart. The devilment in her eyes had been replaced by adoration that touched him more than it should have. "Thank you, Jon," she said, her breath fluttering. "You saved him."

Unfortunately, Nikki didn't seem to notice that Christy was no longer calling him "Daddy." She was warily eyeing the bag. "Saved who?"

"Noodles," Christy said with a relieved sigh.

As Jon turned toward Nikki to explain, she suddenly lunged and gripped his biceps. Glancing at the backpack, Jon saw why. Noodles was wiggling through the unzipped opening.

He wasn't a big snake, as snakes went. A two-foot baby boa who was beige and brown with black markings. Jon was half-inclined to draw out the moment, seeing as Nikki was clinging to him for protection, and he was now Christy's hero. Nevertheless, he leaped. Grabbing the area that passed for a neck on a snake, he coaxed the creature back inside and zipped the bag.

After a long moment, Nikki said, "I have only one question."

Jon glanced at her. "Hmm?"

"Is that thing poisonous?"

He shook his head. "No." He couldn't help but

shoot her a glimmer of a smile. "It's the kind that squeezes things to death."

Nikki smiled back tightly. "Great."

Christy hovered over the backpack, looking hurt. "Nobody ever likes him, but he's nice. He really is, Nikki."

Nikki definitely wasn't as tough and intimidating as she'd wanted him to think. Her voice was still faint. "I'm sure he is, hon." She blew out a slow breath. "Christy, you're so, so…" She finally settled on "So well-put-together. Why would you want a *snake?*"

Catching Jon's eye, Christy giggled. "'Cause I'm real good with cold-blooded creatures." Everything in her twinkling green gaze said she was talking about him.

"Good thing, Christy," he returned, staring out the window where the snow was raining down. "Because it's beginning to look like you're stuck with me, kid." His heart suddenly missed a beat. "So are you, I'm afraid," he added. "I don't think either of you can leave tonight."

As Nikki's wary eyes darted from his to the near whiteout beyond the window, Jon tried not to remember what the soft touch of her mouth had done to him, or to remember how he'd felt—just for that one second, when she'd clung to him for protection.

Jon hadn't felt so good in years.

IT HAD TO BE past midnight. Christy clutched a candle she'd stolen from the kitchen counter and wished its weak, flickering light would illuminate the upstairs hallway. She'd put on a white sweater Nikki had brought from the cab; beneath, she was wearing only a sleeveless nightie her mom had packed for the trip to her dad's in California, which meant she was freezing.

Shivering and advancing slowly on tiptoe, she wished she could turn on the lights. But Jon might wake up. Or Nikki. She blushed guiltily. Okay, maybe she'd laid it on a little thick about Jon being a bad dad. And what if the peanut butter she'd put in Nikki's gas tank hurt the car? She winced. A good little girl wouldn't have cut those phone cords, either. But then Christy couldn't let Nikki call the sheriff.

Besides, once she'd seen this creepy place, Christy wasn't about to stay here alone. Something had gone very wrong. First, her idol had whiskers and a gruff voice, not at all like the Jon Sleet who was supposed to be funny and cute. Second, the Christmas castle he'd written about was supposed to be well-lighted and smell of pine trees, cider and roast turkey. Frowning, Christy very much doubted that Santa Claus really had a house here. Oh, he probably did need a vacation home, since ordering around all those busy elves would be a highly stressful career. She guessed Santa's needing a getaway was like how her parents used to want a beach house in the Hamptons.

But there was nothing Christmassy here. All the decorations were packed away in a storage room that Christy had found earlier; there were boxes of lights, ornaments wrapped in tissue paper and wreaths made of pinecones and nuts. Why would Jon take down such cool decorations?

"He must have freaked out," she whispered aloud to ward off her fear of the dark. It happened to grown-up men. Especially if they were around thirty or forty.

When she talked to her girlfriends on the phone, Christy's mom said the midlife crisis was the worst.

Christy reached the end of the hallway, and after a moment's deliberation, turned right, hoping she wasn't lost. She peered over her shoulder. How would she find her way back? What if she ran into Jon?

At least Noodles was safe in the bedroom where Nikki was sleeping. He'd be warm, too, since Jon had built them a fire. Christy blushed guiltily again. Nikki was so nice. When she saw they were out of peanut butter, she'd put away the sandwich fixings and made Christy and Jon roast beef and real mashed potatoes for dinner. Then she'd insisted she and Christy share a room, which was fine with Christy. Still, Christy wasn't sure whom Nikki wanted to protect—Christy or herself—and she felt a little disappointed. If *she* was the adult and Jon had kissed *her,* she wouldn't get mad. At least not if he shaved and got a haircut.

Christy stopped and peered inside a room, wishing she could see better. Quietly shutting the door, she flicked on a light. It was a master bedroom, and there were women's clothes in the closet and drawers. No men's clothes. Hmm. After carefully examining everything, she turned out the light, headed back into the hallway and stopped at the next door.

Her heart was pounding now. It was so silent and creepy in here. Goosebumps rose on her arms—and they weren't from the cold. Edging inside the next room, she shut the door, then hit the light switch.

Her lips parted in wonder as she took in the white antiqued bedroom suite, with its canopy bed piled high with dusty pale pink pillows. She'd recognize this room anywhere. It belonged to Jenny, the heroine in Jon's books who had so many wonderful adventures. Fear niggled at her. She guessed Jenny wasn't just a character, but Jon's real daughter—and yet this didn't look any more lived-in than the other rooms. Swallowing hard, she thought of the little girl in Jon's stories, who felt like a best friend to Christy. But where was Jenny? Had Jon really gotten divorced, as Nikki thought?

She drew in a sudden breath. Since Jon's wife and daughter were gone, maybe Nikki could marry Jon! Jon already had a crush on her. Christy thought she had seen him kiss her. It was just too bad she was responsible for Nikki's bad impression of Jon. But Christy could change all that....

Suddenly, her eyes widened. Holding her breath so she wouldn't make a sound, she flipped off the light. Was someone coming?

Carefully opening the door, she crept into the hallway, clenching her teeth to stop their chattering. Wrapping her fingers tightly around the candle, she glanced one way, then another. Everything was pitch-black. *Just keep moving.* Eventually she'd find Nikki again. Meantime, she'd better not think about old houses. Or ghosts. Trouble was, Scrooge kept coming to mind, since Jon was just like him. *Oh, no. What if the Ghosts of Christmas Past, Present and Future reach out and grab me?*

She heard something! It was right behind her. She yelped and ran. Losing her grip on the candle, she felt it tumble to the floor. But she kept running. The ghosts of Christmas were right behind her! They were going to punish her because she was such a bad girl!

The ghosts snatched the back of her nightie. Sucking in a deep breath, she released her most piercing scream. It was one she frequently practiced, since she wanted to be an actress when she grew up. Flailing her arms and legs, she thrust out one foot and landed a solid kick that elicited a curse in the dark.

She frowned. The ghosts of Christmas didn't cuss. "Jon?"

"What are you trying to do? Burn down the house?"

"Oh, Jon," she said breathlessly. It really was Jon. "I thought you were a ghost!"

"Really," he drawled dryly. "How dramatic."

At the far end of the hallway, a light snapped on and Nikki appeared, wearing a cotton nightgown she'd gotten from the trunk of her car. When Jon saw her, Christy heard him draw in a sharp breath. And no wonder. Nikki's body was silhouetted in the doorway with the light behind her, and you could practically see her underwear. Christy wished there was some way to warn her.

Looking highly suspicious, Nikki snapped on the flashlight she'd put under her pillow, shooting its beam down the long hallway. "What's going on down there?"

"Christy's snooping around," Jon explained. "And she dropped a lit candle on the floor."

He was right, of course. She'd been bad again. Spying and pawing through his wife and daughter's things. He'd be furious if he guessed where all she'd been. "I was cold!" she whined defensively. "And Noodles can't sleep in a backpack all night. He'll get cramps."

"Please," Jon muttered. "Snakes don't get cramps."

"Noodles can. He isn't a regular snake. He needs an aquarium. And I need more blankets!"

"I left three blankets in that room, Christy. And I built you and Nikki a fire."

Ignoring him, Christy wiggled from his grasp and ran down the hallway. Lunging, she wrapped her arms around Nikki's waist before Jon could figure out where she'd really been.

"You okay, hon?"

"I just wanted to kiss Daddy good-night," Christy ventured contritely.

Nikki surveyed Jon for a few more suspicious moments, then she shut the bedroom door.

Christy sighed. At least her parents weren't looking for her yet. Deep sigh. She'd known when she raided her piggy bank and decided to bring her considerable life savings on this holiday trip that something remarkable would happen. She didn't even feel very guilty about the extra cash she'd stolen from her mother's wallet. In fact, she'd merely *liberated* it. Really, if you thought about it, the money was just a loan.

And all for a good cause. Because maybe Jon and Nikki really would fall in love. As Nikki tucked her in for the second time that night, Christy started making plans....

LONG AFTER she'd said good-night to Christy, Nikki lay awake. Her body ached from driving, and the day had been so full of emotions that she was sure she'd go out like a light. But now she couldn't sleep.

Through slitted eyes, she gazed over the footboard, toward the two mustard leather wing chairs in front of the fireplace. The fire had burned low, and for long moments, Nikki nestled her head on the pillow, listening to the soft crackling of the embers and the even breathing of the sleeping child beside her.

As Nikki's eyes drifted shut again, a silent tear slid down her cheek. How had she wound up here? And how could she be feeling attraction for a man when she'd just left another one this morning? Shouldn't she be back in Buck's bed in True Pines, trying to make the relationship work because of the baby? And yet she knew that was an impossibility.

She could still see Buck standing in front of the bedroom window this morning. Over his shoulder, she'd seen a bright red cardinal fly through the sluggish gray sunrise as Buck said, "Ever since we moved in together, you've been trying to make me get married."

"Make you?" She'd gasped. "I thought you *wanted—*"

"What? A bunch of brats?"

She couldn't remember who yelled first. But he'd said she didn't know how to act like a woman or please a man. And then he'd said that, given the way she dressed, maybe she even wanted to *be* a man. Now she wondered if that was before or after he'd called her a bitch. She squeezed her eyes tight against the tears. Oh, she knew they'd only been cruel words meant to hurt her, but maybe that was the point—the words did hurt. More than anything she'd ever felt. She bit back a sob she knew would wake Christy.

And then she wondered what she was doing with her life. She'd always been such a good girl, cooking and cleaning for her father and brothers, since that's what girls were supposed to do. Boys hadn't paid her much mind in school, and when they did, her dad usually got a protective glint in his eyes as if he intended to run them off with his shotgun.

Then her brother, Matt, brought a fellow trucker home for the weekend. Buck was nice, she'd thought. He'd kept visiting, and it was obvious he was coming back for her, not Matt, since he always brought flowers and took her out, giving her a thousand reasons to put on a dress. The attention had made her feel so feminine, so soft, and so even if lovemaking wasn't everything she'd imagined, she'd decided to move to True Pines.

After that there were fewer flowers, and less talk of love and marriage. She'd found herself doing what she did at home, mostly cooking and ironing shirts. She'd tried to tell herself it was just an adjustment period.

At least until the man suggested she have an abortion. Now Nikki wished she knew what advice her mother would have offered, had she lived.

She'd tell you to do whatever makes you happy, Nikki.

Swallowing hard, she opened her eyes. Trouble was, for reasons Nikki couldn't even begin to understand, Jon Sleet's kiss had made her start thinking that *he* could make her happy.

But he couldn't. Maybe nothing could right now. Bringing a hand from under the covers, Nikki lifted it and gently touched Christy's cheek. Somehow, that helped her sleep.

JON DIDN'T KNOW what had possessed him to come in here. Sprawling in an old, red-leather armchair he used to love, where he used to do his best thinking, he glanced around.

His study was a man's room, with dark paneling, subdued area rugs on the hardwood floors, and gilt-framed paintings that hung by the door—one of this house, another of the church in town where he and Mary had gotten married. It was a writer's room, too, with floor-to-ceiling bookshelves and an oak table he preferred to a desk. Near a window was his computer and an old manual typewriter, his first.

For years, he'd wanted to write the Great American Novel. But in the end, it was the stories he'd made up for Jenny—to ease her fears, teach her about life and to make her laugh—that had given him fame. And more money than the considerable sum he'd inherited.

Not that money mattered much. His eyes fell on a whiskey bottle resting on the arm of the chair. Twisting off the cap, he lifted the bottle, then paused, trying to tell himself that he didn't care if Nikki Ryder wouldn't like his drinking. But because he did, he recapped the bottle. And then he swallowed hard. Just remembering how womanly she'd looked an hour ago, framed in that doorway with the light shining through her white gown made heat pool in his groin. He'd inadvertently glimpsed the full shape of her, from her softly sloping breasts to the curve of her waist and the flare of her hips. He wanted her, there was no denying that.

He released something between a groan and a sigh, and he glanced around again. Until tonight, there'd been so few distractions around here. The west-wing turret where he spent much of his time was quiet, though here there were memories—and plenty of them. The study was dusty, too.

No doubt he looked as unkempt as the room. Without wanting to, he saw himself through Nikki's eyes: A good-looking, but rough and unshaven man, living like a hermit in a cold stone house. Suddenly, he wondered if she was awake, and if she'd been listening to him prowl around in the night. When exactly had he started staying awake until dawn and sleeping until noon? Oh, he wasn't entirely reprobate. He occupied himself with the books he loved to read. But then, Christmas always brought the old ghosts racing back.

Amazing, he thought now, what two short seconds could do to a man's life. There was a second before— when you felt serene and filled with the spirit of Christmas. When you were wondering which present your little girl was going to like best.

And then there was a second after—when your best buddy, Sheriff Steve Warwick, knocked on the door and informed you that your wife and child were never coming home.

A second, Jon thought now, was a lifetime.

His long fingers curled around the bottle, and he stared into the warm amber liquid. Just as abruptly, he released it and got up. With a final glance around, he strode from the room, pausing only once in the hallway, where he turned up the thermostat. Not that he'd go out of his way for his houseguests, he told himself. It hurt too much to have a woman and child here at Christmas. But it wouldn't kill him to bring in some more wood from the shed and keep their fire going while they slept.

When he reached Jenny's bedroom, he turned on the light—and promptly shut his eyes. For a second, he just couldn't bear to look. When he opened them, he saw Christy's small handprints in the dust of the white-antiqued French dresser. Somehow, they reminded him of the plaster-of-paris handprint pies Jenny used to make for him every year. Five of them were in a drawer of his study. Five years…

Even now he could remember the ice storm they'd had that night, the last night he'd seen her. Ice weighed down gutters and forced the slender branches of saplings to bow, and cables swooping between phone poles snapped in two, leaving live wires trailing fire through the snow. The storm hit True Pines worse than here, but Jon would never forget watching it while his breath fogged windows where the ice had crystallized in intricate snowflake patterns. That ice had looked both beautiful and so dangerous. Why hadn't he begged Mary to stay at her mother's in True Pines that night? Why hadn't he been able to convince her the roads were too dangerous?

But it was Christmas Eve, and Jenny desperately wanted to come home for the annual Christmas party at the inn. She was determined to see both her daddy and Santa.…

Before the feelings overwhelmed Jon, he headed for his daughter's closet. There was an aquarium in there, and the least he could do was find it for Christy. As he jostled shoe boxes and old board games, he recalled how Christy had looked at him when he'd caught her falling backpack…how a blond child, so like his Jenny, had clasped trembling hands to her chest and breathlessly said, "Jon, you saved him!"

Jon, you saved him!

As if he was a better man than the wretch he'd become. For a second, he'd felt like a hero again, at least in a young girl's eyes. He thought of Nikki gripping his arm, too. Lord, he'd wanted to hold her and kiss her again.

But as he pulled the aquarium from the closet, he was still feeling the heartbreak of the past, and he decided he'd better avoid Nikki Ryder. She was too intriguing, too attractive. Every time he took in her baseball cap and torn jeans, he wanted to put his stamp on her, to make her a woman. *His* woman. So, while the storm lasted, he'd make himself scarce, giving her free rein of his house.

And when the snow stopped, he wanted her gone.

Chapter Four

"Nikki?"

"Hmm, Christy?"

"See my old bedroom? Isn't it cute?"

"Adorable. The furniture's very grown-up. But why didn't your daddy put us here last night, since it's your room?"

"Uh…guess he didn't want to clean it. See? You can write your name in the dust. Besides, I think it hurts Daddy."

"What hurts him, hon?"

"My room. And the one he shared with my mom, because it reminds him she's gone."

"Well, he's still got his little girl. Want to talk about what happened?"

"Uh…they divorced. And see, I live with my mom now, which is why most of the clothes I left here are too little. I'm sure glad we found the ones with the tags still on them that were too big when we bought them. Ever since the Big D—that's the divorce—Daddy's been alone. He's lots more normal when there's a woman around. If he only had a wife…"

"CHRISTY, I don't feel comfortable looking through your mother's things."

"But we're still snowed in, and the phones don't work. Have you seen the dresses Mom left? See? Daddy loves fancy dresses."

"I can see that. Especially backless ones."

"You'd look great in backless dresses, Nikki. Ever think about wearing your hair fluffed out?"

"Uh, fluffed out?"

"You know, all bushy."

"You mean like Pamela Anderson?"

"Yes!"

"Geez, Christy, it never once occurred to me to wear my hair like Pamela Anderson's."

"C'mon, please. You could even put on makeup. I've got some lipsticks in my bag."

"I'll just bet you do, Christy."

"And with some eye shadow and blusher, you could make my dad really horny."

"What!"

"You could make him horny. Bess Kelly—she's in my class—she says horny's when a man gets all sexy and wants to get married."

"Well, I don't care what Bess Kelly said. Don't use that word again. And no offense, Christy, but I'm not here to please your father."

"But he's so sad. He used to shave and get haircuts and everything. Now look at him."

"No."

"Please. I mean, you don't have to marry him, but—"

"I am *not* marrying anybody."

"At least wear a fancy dress for my dad."

"I said no."

"You don't really mean no. I can tell."

"When a woman says no, she means no, Christy."

"WHICH ORNAMENTS do you like best, Nikki—the paper reindeers or the handmade wooden gingerbread men? And what about these glass snowflakes? They're prisms to hang in the window. Aren't they cool?"

"Hmm. I guess your dad quit decorating for Christmas after the Big D."

"So, couldn't *we* decorate the house, Nikki? If we don't, Santa won't even know he's supposed to stop here!"

"You said you don't believe in Santa. Besides, your daddy might get mad...."

"Forget Daddy! He's a Scrooge."

"You have a point, hon. But I have a better idea."

"THIS IS your better idea?"

"Quit complaining and hand me that can of Pledge. Think of yourself as a busy elf, doing something nice for Daddy."

"Yuck! This whole can's rusty."

"Well, he hasn't polished furniture for a while."

"When the house is clean, can we make cookies with those cookie cutters we found that're shaped like angels and Santas? I bet Daddy's hungry for some cookies."

"I love how you always look after your dad's best interest."

"Well, *I'd* like some cookies, too, Nikki."

"I figured. Now, could you please hand me that wet rag in the bucket?"

IT TOOK the better part of two days, but Nikki and Christy had fun, singing Christmas carols while they cleaned Jon's house. Meantime, the storm kept coming, bringing dark skies, power outages and fierce winds that pushed the snow in blinding sheets. Now Christy shielded her eyes, trotting toward the barn in oversize snow boots, her legs sinking thigh-high in the drifts.

"I'm running ahead, Nikki, okay?"

"Sure."

If Nikki hadn't felt confident, spending a few days with Christy convinced her she was ready to be a mother. She loved the little girl. But where was Jon? Turning into a hard wind, Nikki glanced anxiously toward the house, her eyes searching the shadowy windows.

He was up there somewhere.

So far, he hadn't materialized again. Geez…was it because of the kiss she kept recalling at the most unlikely moments? Even Nikki's dreams were touched by rough stubble and a strong male scent. Unlikely intoxicants, to be sure. And yet she kept thinking about casual affairs where people took what they wanted with no emotions…

Not that she'd ever experienced such a thing. But where was Jon? Was he regretting how forcibly he'd kissed her? Had he lain awake that first night, recalling how his strong hands pulled her to him, and how he'd cradled her hips with his thighs?

Nikki shuddered. He could at least show up long enough to dispense with this awkwardness. He'd say hello. She'd say hello. Then he could go right back to what he'd been doing—avoiding her.

The first morning, she'd opened her eyes, seen the snow, and known she wasn't going anywhere. Christy slept beside her, a fire crackled in the fireplace, and that disgusting snake had been moved to an aquarium, outfitted with a pebbled floor, water bowl and climbing stick. Nearby were kid-size snow boots and more winter clothes that might fit Christy. That Jon had sneaked into the room and seen her sleeping had made Nikki's insides feel jittery; that he'd fixed an aquarium for his daughter's pet was unexpectedly sweet. "Tell me if you need anything," his note said. All day, she'd expected him to appear.

When he didn't, it strengthened her resolve to try and help repair the distanced relationship between him and his daughter. Not that she minded playing baby-sitter. But why wouldn't he visit with Christy?

He was still on the premises. Nikki knew that much because they were snowbound. Besides, last night she'd left out a casserole that had vanished as surely as cookies left for Santa. Sometimes Nikki heard footsteps. Or glimpsed Jon's shadow when he headed to the barn. She was beginning to think she was sharing quarters with a handsome ghost. Maybe the Spirit of Christmas Turned Sour. Or a taciturn elf. Except, of course, Jon Sleet kissed like a man. Feeling eyes on her back, she fought the urge to turn toward the house again. Was he watching her?

As Nikki followed Christy inside the well-maintained barn, the musty, earthy scents of hay and horses made her nostrils flare. Christy waved, continuing toward the other end as Nikki edged near the closest stalls. She didn't know anything about horses, but these looked like good animals. She leaned over, stroking a flank that quivered.

"Hey there, Mr. Ed," she whispered, reading the nameplate above his stall. "You, too, King." As she petted the sleek coat, she realized it was coarser by the underbelly, silken behind the ears. "How you doin'? Looks like Jon keeps the barn cleaner than his house.''

Jon. Just speaking his name made her body tighten. As much as she tried to deny it, Nikki could still feel his hard, solid chest against hers, and smell his masculine scent while her mouth longed for another claiming kiss. Like these horses, he was a strong, proud, male animal. But there was more to him—she was sure of it after snooping around his house—a gentleness he needed to reclaim. She started, realizing her eyes had drifted to the stallion's underbelly, to the bold evidence of its maleness. Abruptly glancing away, she found herself staring into glossy, black eyes that held such power....

She swallowed, feeling oddly shaken. How could only one encounter with Jon make her so aware? At night, the covers worried her skin, and when cold winter air touched her face, she craved human warmth. She could go find him....

She tried to tell herself she was only motivated by her desire to see him and Christy get closer. Besides, she could never respect a man who ignored his own daughter. No doubt Jon *thought* he had reasons, since Christy probably reminded him of a wife he'd doted on.

The unused master bedroom proved he had loved her. There was a big bedstead. And fine jewelry that was still in the boxes. Delicate cut-glass decanters of perfume were aligned on the dresser and smelled of heaven. She'd worn dresses fit for a queen. Sleek, sexy backless numbers with jeweled straps, and cloudy chiffon confections. When he traveled, Jon had sent her humorous postcards, some of which Nikki had guiltily glanced over.

Once upon a time, Jon Sleet had been a romantic.

Even now, his home remained beautiful. The neglected rooms held original art and ornate antiques. Judging from the Christmas decorations, the place must have once been magical during the holidays. So, why had Jon's wife left without taking her jewelry or clothes, leaving Jon in such pain that he'd never even reentered the bedroom they'd shared? Geez...it must have been a helluva fight.

"Nikki!" Christy suddenly waved wildly from the other end of the barn. Nikki chuckled as the little girl tripped over a hay bale in her excitement, nearly falling into a water trough. "Hurry, you gotta see this!"

"I'm coming. Hold your horses."

Christy giggled. "I can," she shouted. "Wanna know why I can hold my horses, Nikki?"

"Why?"

"'Cause we're in a *barn*."

The kid was too much, Nikki thought, shaking her head as she approached. Her dad didn't know what he was missing. "What's up?"

"Look!"

Nikki's eyes widened as she peered into the stalls. "Reindeer?" She'd never seen a live one. They were larger than she'd have guessed, and friendlier—one was letting Christy rub its nose. Above each stall was a nameplate, and Nikki's heart skipped a beat as she read, "Dancer, Prancer, Vixen..." For a jarring minute, she felt as if she were Christy's age again; she could almost see the reindeer hitched to Santa's gold sleigh. "Your daddy keeps reindeer?" she managed.

Christy glanced up with puzzled sincerity. Lowering her voice reverently, she said, "Maybe he's been taking care of them for Santa."

Nikki's heart pulled. "I thought you said you didn't believe in Santa. That's why everybody's supposed to call you Christy now, not Christmas."

"Well, I *want* to believe in Santa."

Staring into the little girl's suddenly hopeful eyes, Nikki sighed. "So do I, hon." Glancing around, she wished so many Christmas wishes would come true. She wished her baby was coming into the world with a father to love, that Christy had the stable family life she deserved, and that Jon Sleet's romantic side hadn't been destroyed. Call it woman's intuition, but after snooping around the house she somehow suspected Jon was one of the most worthwhile people she'd ever run across. Or he had been. "C'mon," she said. "I've changed my mind. We've got work to do."

Christy groaned. "I'm tired of being an elf."

"You won't mind this time."

Christy looked doubtful. "I won't?"

"Nope." Nikki grinned. "Because we're going to decorate your daddy's house."

JON COULD ONLY stare.

Each ornament hurt. Each bulb. Each scent. Staring into the living room, he felt so murderous that he barely registered the Christmas carols playing on the radio. The snowflake-shaped prisms he'd bought during a book-signing trip to Germany years ago hung in the windows, transforming the day's gray light into hazy rainbows that touched the tiny ceramic angels lining the window sills.

Already, he'd seen the kitchen, where reindeer decanters perched on the counter. And the guest bathroom, where pine-tree-printed toilet paper was on the roll. He'd almost forgotten the nut-cluster wreaths that now hung outside, against the ground-floor windows, and how this house could smell of lemon oil, home-baked cookies and hot apple cider.

His angry gaze trailed over the living room again—from the china nativity scene on the mantel, to the needlepoint stockings, then over Mary's collections of handsome, mustached nutcracker soldiers and squat Santa Clauses. A candlelit carousel, Jenny's favorite decoration, depicted the Christmas story—Mary and Joseph traveling, the three wise men bearing gifts and Jesus in the manger.

Christy was kneeling on the floor, wearing one of Jenny's sweaters and not a bit of makeup. Somehow, Nikki had managed to transform her from a shrunken adult into a bona fide child. Oblivious of Jon's presence, the little girl lifted delicate ornaments from a box and gently unwrapped them from tissue paper. "Nikki," she said, pouting. "What can we do with the ornaments if we don't have a Christmas tree?"

"We'll think of something."

"But we need a tree."

For a moment, all Jon could feel was the past—the soft patter of a child's footsteps, the peal of laughter. And then he couldn't help the anger that slid through his veins. It wasn't their fault they were snowed in, and Nikki Ryder probably didn't even want to be here. If the truth be told, he even respected how she was making the most of things. How many people in her circumstances would have spent all this time entertaining a stranger's child? Watching her from the windows as she and Christy played in the snow yesterday, he'd realized Nikki was truly a good-hearted woman, and he'd felt genuinely touched.

But the two had been going through Mary and Jenny's things. Even though Jon had left Jenny's sweater out for Christy to wear, it now hurt to see her wear it. His gaze swept over the smallest, homiest room in the house, with its fireplace and dark wood mantel, comfortably worn sofa and braided rug. Everything reminded him of how perfect Christmases in this house used to be.

For the past couple of days, Jon had made himself scarce, letting Nikki and Christy amuse themselves. When it came to the little girl's lies about being his daughter, he had never even forced the issue. What was the use? They were snowbound, without phones, and nothing could be done yet. But now he wanted every ornament taken down.

Nikki was up on a ladder, humming happily and wiring a wreath to the mirror above the mantel—as if what she was doing wasn't tearing him apart with memories. His gaze skimmed down the back of a white sweatshirt to her skintight jeans and cute roundish behind, until his eyes settled on where her Frye boots hugged a wobbly rung. He sighed. With his luck, she'd fall and sue him. Her hair was still stuffed under the fool baseball cap, leaving her slender neck bare, and despite his foul temper, his eyes lingered, caressing soft creamy flesh that promised more delicacy than her outfit.

Christy persisted. "If Daddy wasn't so mean, maybe we could have a tree."

This was getting too bizarre. Jon should have guessed Christy would only keep lying about being his daughter, though. He might have lost his desire to write, but when it came to spinning stories, this kid was a natural. "Christy—" Somehow, he'd kept his voice even. "Why don't you scoot? Nikki and I need to talk."

Looking startled, Christy glanced up. A second later, she'd reacted to his tone by vanishing.

Jon advanced.

When Nikki turned on the wobbly ladder, looking equally surprised by his sudden appearance, he saw that the front of her sweatshirt depicted Santa's reindeer-driven sleigh. Her heavy boots teetered as she took a careful step downward, venturing a tentative smile. "He lives."

"Such as my life is," he muttered, feeling hardly in the mood for banter. Sidling close to the ladder, he stared up. "What did you expect? Guided tours? An itinerary? My best roast duck?"

She arched an eyebrow, shoving a hand into her back pocket as she edged another step downward. "If you've come out of hiding to be a surly old Scrooge," she returned, her light tone undercutting the words, "Christy and I would rather be alone. We're entertaining ourselves just fine."

He dragged a hand through his hair, pushing it off his forehead as he glanced around. "I can see."

"Well, you can't expect us to sit around feeling bored." Another sudden step down made the ladder sway. One arm started pinwheeling back, almost comically, while the other jerked out of her jeans pocket and sought a handhold. Finding none, she plunged— and her full weight hit Jon square in the chest. Grabbing what he could—her left buttock and right arm— he staggered back. But just as he regained his footing, his boot heel slipped on an ornament. His feet tangled with Nikki's and he wound up on his back with her on top of him.

"Did you survive?" he managed gruffly. His chest felt tight, and his heart was pounding too hard. He told himself her weight had knocked the wind out of him, but knew he was really reacting to the soft, warm proximity of her.

Her breathless voice was husky, damnably husky—and way too close. He smelled something sweet, either her breath or hair. "Oh, Sleet," she muttered. "Did you really think you could hurt me?"

Never. The soft body on top of him felt warmer than the long hot bath he'd just taken; her skin was more smooth than the soap. Her baseball cap had tumbled off, and the thick, luxurious red-brown hair he'd fantasized about now swirled around her shoulders. It stroked his clean-shaven jaw, making him glad he'd taken a razor to it. Not that she was the reason he'd shaved. Or bathed. Or put on clean jeans, a pressed white shirt and cologne. *Yeah, right.*

She wiggled on top of him.

For a second their eyes met, and the world seemed to stop. Jon was aware of how close their mouths were, of the uneven sound of her breath. He knew she was smelling the scent of his cologne, and that the clean fabric of his starched shirt was smooth beneath her palms. She pushed at his chest, and one of her legs fell between his, bringing her hipbone against his groin. God, she felt good.

She exhaled an annoyed sigh. "Are *you* okay?"

He forced a growl. "Fine." Rising abruptly, he pulled her up with him.

She gasped as he released her. Staggering back a pace, she nearly fell over the toppled ladder. With a short, dutiful sigh, he caught her elbow and righted her once more.

"Uh, thanks," she said, tugging the hem of her sweatshirt down over her hips. "I think."

The rich-textured hair that had felt like velvet against his cheek now framed her flushed cheeks. Down and disheveled, it made her look so stunning that it took his breath. For an instant, he forgot why he'd come in here and felt almost compelled to say something about the obvious attraction passing between them. Did she feel it as strongly as he did?

Unfortunately, she was glaring at him. She slapped the baseball cap against her thigh and wiggled it back on her head as he righted the ladder. She said, "I can see you're just as magnanimous as when we first met."

"I pride myself on manners."

She sighed again. Glancing around at the tissue paper and sheets of old newspapers in the floor, she slid her hands nervously down the sides of well-worn jeans. "Uh, look, you wanted to talk to me?"

Suddenly, his eyes narrowed. Why hadn't he thought of it before? "Oh, come on. Stern, Wylie and Morrow sent you, right?"

She frowned at him. "Huh? I never heard of those guys."

She did look blank. So much for the flash of brilliance. But his old publishing house, SWM as it was sometimes called, occasionally sent people—usually assistants, barely out of college—to coax him to write children's books again. His Everyday's a Christmas series had earned a king's ransom for SWM, and they'd been none too happy when he'd gone over the edge.

But would SWM stoop to sending a child and a woman posing as a cabdriver? Maybe. Jon's family was gone. And for businessmen, the almighty buck always lived on. *Now, there's the Christmas spirit for you.*

Nikki was eyeing him carefully. "Who are those people?"

"My old publishers. Never mind. Just do me a favor and take down these decorations."

Her lips parted in protest. "Please, Jon. I...I know how you must feel."

The soft way she said his name almost made him relent, but her presumption rankled. "How could you begin to know what I feel?"

"Because I've been in your house for two days." She paused, weighing her words. "I know you loved your wife very much. And my guess is you're ignoring Christy because she reminds you of her." She gestured vaguely at the room. "I was afraid this might remind you of how the house used to look at Christmas...."

"It does." And it was breaking his heart. Anger surfaced again, conveniently submerging that heartbreak. "How did you know where to put the decorations, anyway?" She'd arranged the room almost as Mary would have.

She looked surprised. "Your daughter knew."

Impossible. He frowned. Had Christy been here before? Had she been a friend of Jenny's? *Forget about it. Whoever she is, she'll be gone before Christmas.* "You'll take those decorations down," he said simply.

"Don't get dictatorial with me."

"Dictatorial? It's my house." Feeling thoroughly taken aback, he sincerely wished he could forget the flavor of her mouth. For the past two days, her presence here had haunted him. She left her scent in rooms, crumbs on the counter, and those sporty-looking gloves in unlikely places. His gaze flicked over her. "I've made sure you two were comfortable. I realize you're snowed in and there's nothing you can do about it. But you're overstepping your bounds now."

She put a hand on her cute, curving hip. "But what if the snow doesn't let up? What if Christy doesn't get back to her mom's before Christmas?"

He'd go crazy, that's what. "The snow will let up. By tomorrow, you'll be off the mountain." And he'd forget all about her.

"But Christy and I are going stir-crazy," she protested, leaning an elbow through a rung of the ladder. "And you…well, Jon, you can't deprive your daughter of Christmas."

His daughter. Not that again. He sighed. "Who do you think you are?" he asked softly.

Answering temper flashed in her eyes, turning them a brickish color, like clay in the roads after a rain. "Geez! I'm the unfortunate soul who wound up bringing your daughter home, that's who. Now, I suspect you're drowning yourself in self-pity because your wife left or something, which is fine with me, but I can't just sit here and watch you ruin your daughter's Christmas!"

"Please—" This time, he was fighting like hell for neutrality. "Just take down the decorations." But it was pointless to argue. Her brown eyes were flashing with anger and righteous determination. Given how riled she got about the welfare of a stranger's child, he decided she'd be hell on wheels if the well-being of her own were ever in question.

"Sleet," she fumed.

Under other circumstances, he might have been amused by her continued use of his last name. "What, *Ryder?*" he found himself shooting back.

"I'm beginning to think you're spineless, that's what! I mean, you've never even cleaned out the master bedroom and your daughter's room."

His heart pounded. "You were in the bedrooms?"

She made a point of taking a slow, deep breath. "I'm doing the best I can with Christy," she continued in a measured tone. "We've cleaned, made cookies, and I've sat through at least a hundred hands of Old Maid." She lifted a staying hand. "Not that I mind. Your daughter's a delightful girl. In fact, I've learned more about makeup application than I ever thought I'd know. But you can't expect a seven-year-old to stare at *Oprah* all day between power outages. Your daughter wanted to decorate—"

He thought he'd explode. "She's not my daughter!"

The words hardly had the desired effect. Nikki clapped her hands to her face, and took another deep breath, rubbing the heels of her palms against her eyes. When she looked at him again, her gaze had softened and she reached out, her slender fingers settling on the front of his white shirt. Glancing down, he noticed her nails—Christy must have gotten to her because they were now painted pink. "C'mon," she said, her low-voiced Kentucky drawl rolling over him. "Why haven't you spent time with us, Jon?"

He had his reasons. The main one being right in front of him.

"Why don't you stay and help us decorate?" Her

tone had gotten even sweeter and more gentle. "Please? I want to do anything I can to help you and Christy. A little girl needs her daddy."

She was relentless. Why wouldn't she quit trying to pry him out of his shell? Somehow, one of his own imploring hands wound up settling on her waist. "You should mind your own business, Nikki."

She edged back from his hand, taking a stance— one uniquely hers, that he was getting to know intimately. One hand was on her waist, her shoulder forward. The other was behind her, clamped on her hip just above her buttock. Her parted lips were slightly twisted with disappointment, as if she'd known him for years and suddenly had reason to quit believing in him. He told himself not to react, but he felt strangely guilty. "Please," she said again. "Why not get reacquainted with Christy? Just help us finish decorating, hang a few ornaments…"

He stared at her mutely. He started to try and tell her that Mary and Jenny were gone—*dead*—but he feared sharing his heartbreak with this woman would bring them even closer. Dangerously close, judging by the sparks they generated. "If you don't take these things down, Nikki, I will."

"You'd really ruin her Christmas?"

Whatever attraction was between them had nothing to do with shared interest or common ground, and neither of them wanted to feel it. But here it was, still palpable between them in spite of their argument. "Please, if you don't take the things down, I will." When she said nothing, he turned on his heel, telling himself he was leaving her where he wanted her, so livid she was shaking.

He heard her stamp her foot. "I can't believe you'd deprive a child of Christmas, Jon Sleet!"

"Believe it," he shot back.

And yet hours later, when the first gray light of dawn was still indistinguishable from the falling snow, Jon found himself staring out a window. He couldn't fathom why the child was lying. And he somehow hated letting Nikki Ryder get the best of him. But he rose anyway, throwing on his oilskin coat. And then he headed up Mistletoe Mountain with an axe, to cut them a Christmas tree.

As she entered the living room the next morning, Nikki felt her spirits lift. She'd been sure Jon wouldn't take down the decorations, but you never knew. She definitely hadn't expected to find a bushy pine strung with lights nestled in a tree stand, or to be sitting here, hours later, watching him help Christy hang the ornaments.

"Careful, there," he was saying as Christy rose on tiptoe, carefully holding out a delicate glass bulb. Taking it from her, he easily reached the higher branches.

He'd come in a while ago. Warily at first, like a hungry animal circling a warm fire. Saying a gruff hello, he'd edged around the braided area rug, then seated himself in an armchair, next to the couch where Nikki was sitting.

Silently, they'd watched Christy decorate the bottom branches. When she could no longer reach, Jon had risen wordlessly to help. Now Nikki wanted to thank him for the tree, but she was afraid he might get uncomfortable. She wasn't about to risk scaring him off when he was finally getting along so well with his daughter.

Watching him and lightly tapping her foot to the Christmas music on the radio, Nikki decided he sure cleaned up good. Yesterday, when she'd fallen off the ladder, she'd been shocked by the transformation. Today, she simply enjoyed. He'd shaved again, and he was wearing the same cologne. His hair was a little long, but it was neatly combed, pushed away from his high, broad forehead. Her eyes settled where the dark, heavy, silver-shot waves brushed the collar of his sweater as he leaned back, hanging a velvet ball. Then she took in the perfect fit of his jeans. She decided, not for the first time, that he was an extremely handsome man.

He turned too suddenly, catching her gaze, and raised an inquiring eyebrow. Caught staring. Great. She cleared her throat. ''I was just about to ask if you wanted some hot cider.''

For an instant, his eyes turned wary. *Please don't ruin it,* she silently begged, sure he was about to become argumentative and push her away. *Not when you're having such a good time with Christy.*

She felt self-conscious as his eyes drifted over the sweater she was wearing. It was one of her best, a deep-chocolate-brown pullover that complemented her eyes and hair. Even though she didn't want to admit it, she knew she'd worn it for him. Lifting a hand to the brim of her baseball cap, she started to remove it, then changed her mind.

''Sure,'' he said, ''That'd be great.''

''Christy?''

''Nope, Nikki. I've still got some O.J.''

Moments later, when Nikki returned from the kitchen, Jon was kneeling on the floor, untangling hanging wires and listening to Christy's cheerful chatter. Pausing in the doorway with two warm mugs, Nikki's heart swelled. She'd known Christy could wrap her dad around her little finger, if only Jon would give her a chance. Seeing the father and daughter reestablish family ties would be more than enough of a gift for Christmas, she thought. Smiling encouragement, she entered the room and placed Jon's mug on a coffee table. "Watch out. It's hot."

He glanced up, awareness in his gaze. "Thanks."

For a second too long, she stared into his green eyes, noticing the hints of gold and gray. She was suddenly sure he was thinking about how he'd kissed her, and how their bodies had felt yesterday, hopelessly twined on the same spot on the living-room floor where he was now sitting. "No problem," she managed.

He smiled, and she had a quick impression of straight white teeth, and of the indentions—not dimples, not laugh lines—that curved beside his lips.

She smiled back. "And I'd begun to think your frown was permanent."

"Is that right?"

Color crept into her cheeks. "Not that I spend all day analyzing the quality of your expressions, Sleet."

His low chuckle was barely audible. "Well, there's not a whole lot to do in this weather."

Still gazing into his eyes, she suddenly thought of a few new ways to spend the time. She imagined he was thinking the same. Turning away, she seated herself again and sipped her cider. "So, you're a writer?'' It was a bad opening line, but she guessed it would do.

Reaching out with a long arm, he hung a silver star on a high branch, while Christy pointed, then he glanced at Nikki and shrugged. ''I don't write much anymore.''

Nikki sipped her own cider. ''Why not?''

A second before he looked away, his eyes narrowed, looking strangely distant and sad, making Nikki sorry she'd asked.

''It's a good thing Nikki got you a hot drink, Daddy,'' Christy suddenly piped in, thankfully short-circuiting the moment. ''It's still awful cold in here. I bet I could even get swine fever or the flu.''

Jon chuckled softly. ''Swine fever, huh?''

Christy thrust her neck out like a turtle. ''You'd better feel me, Daddy.''

''Feel you?''

Christy nodded. ''Uh-huh. But don't use the back of your hand to check for fever. Lips are a better thermometer. If you don't kiss my head, you could make a misdiagnostic.''

Now Nikki chuckled. ''A misdiagnostic?'' Most of the time, Christy spoke like an adult, but she was still misusing some words. She also acted much more mature when Jon wasn't around.

He frowned. ''If you're cold and want me to build a fire, why don't you just say so directly, Christy? You'd have a better chance of getting what you want if you just ask.''

Christy ignored him, curling a coy fist under her chin. ''Guess you'd rather build a fire than kiss me the way you kissed Nikki.''

Geez...thanks, kid. Nikki stared quickly down, studying her boots. When she glanced back up, Jon was looking at Christy again. He kissed two of his fingers, then pressed them to her head. "There. Your temperature's normal."

"That kiss wasn't so hot," Christy complained. "Maybe you need some mistletoe."

"Let me know if you find some. Meantime, I'll build you that fire."

He was slow, methodical. Bunching old sheets of newspaper from the boxes, he lined the fire grate, then laid on twigs from a wood box. Squatting with his weight resting on a heel, he leaned forward, his broad upper body filling the fireplace. For long moments, he silently stared at the burning kindling, waiting, and Nikki became conscious of the howling wind...of being alone with this man in a storm. Glancing through a window at the bare tree branches stirring in the wind, she was glad she wasn't alone. Glad for a man's protection, too, since she wouldn't know the first thing about building fires. As the warm flames grew, yellow-rose light seeped into the room, seemingly permeating the tree, the nativity scene and the stockings with its glow.

Her eyes caught Jon's. "It looks good."

He raised an eyebrow, shrugging a powerful shoulder. "The fire?"

She realized she'd meant the whole room. Him. Everything. "Yes," she said simply, glancing around. As her eyes returned to his, she could feel the tension between them finally lift. Some silent truce had been called and, for a moment, everything else around

them—the tree, the fire and Christy—became insub-
stantial background.

"I, uh, found my old bicycle in the basement,"
Christy suddenly said, pulling Jon's gaze away.
"Could I ride it in the barn?"

Jon's features tightened and a heartbeat passed.
Nikki frowned, sure he was going to push Christy
away again, but he finally offered a strained smile. "I
don't see why not," he said, rising and taking another
ornament from Christy.

"I thought of a rhyme, too. Want to hear it?"

Jon shot Christy a bemused glance. "Sure."

"It's Mr. Icicle rides a bicycle. But I need you to
help me make up some more. C'mon, you're a good
writer."

There was a long silence.

"You are," Nikki found herself venturing even as
the wariness returned to Jon's eyes. "I saw all your
books. When Christy and I cleaned the study, I...I
took one back to the room. I've been reading it to
Christy, and I hope you don't mind."

His voice was gruff, seemingly touched with feeling she couldn't quite understand. Had his personal
troubles made him lose his love of his work? Finally,
he said, "I don't mind."

"You shouldn't," she said. The story was won-
derfully imaginative, and calculated to build excitement about the spirit of Christmas. More than anything, it had made Nikki want to know Jon Sleet. The
real Jon Sleet. Not the grim visage he was currently
showing the world. Reaching high, he hung a tiny
golden angel.

After a few minutes, he said, "Mr. Icicle rides a

bicycle. But not a tricycle, 'cause he's fickle about his vehicles.''

Nikki couldn't stop herself. She suddenly chuckled, feeling as delighted as Christy at the silly rhyme. Staring at Jon, she saw his eyes sparkle with a humor she imagined once came easily to him. She finished, ''Gimme a nickel, and I'd tickle Mr. Icicle.''

''But his long pointy finger might prickle,'' Jon warned, his mouth curving into a droll smile. ''And put a woman in a pickle. Because when a man melts, he trickles.''

Nikki laughed and blushed, not missing the bawdiness.

''Wow!'' Christy gushed. ''You're such a great writer!''

''Right up there with Shakespeare,'' Jon said dryly.

Sobering, he turned his gaze from Nikki and hung a glass snowflake. Once more, Nikki trailed her eyes wistfully over his broad back, and an unexpected lump formed in her throat. Her hand moved to her still-flat belly, curving over and smoothing her sweater. She felt something warm curl inside her. More than simple awareness of the baby, it was a rush of emotion—wistful, joyful and excited. Glancing around, she took in the glow of firelight that bathed the room, and a quiet peace seemed to descend as she took in the small carved figures of the nativity. When her gaze settled on the manger, she thought again of the Virgin Mary, a pregnant woman who'd traveled so far.

Where would Nikki live with her baby? Should she stay in True Pines? Or move back to Kentucky, near her father and brothers? What kind of life did she want?

Suddenly, being snowbound here seemed to be a gift in itself. Maybe this was a moment out of time, where she could figure out where she was headed. Still looking over the glowing living room, and at the remarkably handsome man lifting ornaments onto the tree for his little girl, Nikki thought, *This. What Jon Sleet once gave his family is what I want for us.*

Chapter Five

The fountain that had been Jenny's prized delight was on flat ground, halfway up a hill beside the house. Inside its knee-high stone enclosure were filtered lights that had once sent red and green water jets over seven bronzed elves; they danced merrily around Santa as he leaned to hear a little girl's Christmas wishes. Now all the tarnished figures were hidden under crusty snow, and leaves and twigs filled the fountain's empty pool. Jon was sitting on the weathered stone ledge, his oilskin coat keeping the damp cold from his jeans, his back turned to the statuary, his hand firmly clasped around Christy's upper arm.

"Let me go!"

As if I'm inflicting mortal damage. Which I'm not. Glancing toward the house, Jon hoped Nikki gave him a few more minutes alone with Christy, so he could find out who she was. "Your parents must be beside themselves," he said, offering the stern, fatherly stare that used to make Jenny promptly admit her wrongs. Not so Christy. She yowled.

"I am *not* hurting you, Christy."

"Are, too! And you're going to get in trouble.

When Nikki brings your hot chocolate outside, I'll tell her you're harassment me!"

"Oh yeah, that's me. Scrooge to your wounded Tiny Tim." Jon's breath fogged the bitter cold air. "And Christy, it's *harassing* me, not *harassment* me."

"See," she shot back in an injured voice, her cold, red nose twitching with righteous anger. "You expect me to know everything even though I'm only in second grade. Well, I *don't* know everything." Suddenly she giggled, venturing an irresistibly coy smile. "At least not yet."

He forced himself not to smile back. "Please."

"No."

Maybe he should try flattery. "See, you're so darn smart you've reduced me to begging. Now where do your folks live?"

"Maybe I'll tell after I sled ride some more."

Threats weren't going to work. This child had an iron will. The harder Jon pushed, the less she talked. He gentled his voice, relaxing his hand and caressing her sleeve. "I know someone out there is really worrying about you right now, sweetheart."

She thrust out a petulant bottom lip that was bright red, from both the cold and the smear of lipstick she'd insisted on wearing. Even with the makeup, she was cute as ever, dressed in a red snowsuit Jon's mother had bought Jenny a couple of years back. The outfit was too big, his mother had said, but it was on sale and just too good to pass up. Jenny would grow into it. Jon's eyes drifted over her snug red knit hat, then dropped to the mittened hand that gripped the rope tied to Jenny's saucer-style sled.

"Long bored sigh," Christy said. "Why don't you let me sled ride, Jon? You're hurting me!"

"I'm gently rubbing your sleeve."

"But it hurts!"

"Good thing the phones are still down," he returned dryly. "Or else you'd probably call youth protective services."

That got a giggle out of her. "Good idea."

"How'd you get to be such a handful, kid?" At a loss about how to proceed, Jon released her and lifted his gloves from the fountain ledge; he'd removed them to untangle the sled rope, and now he slapped them against his thigh, dislodging the snow before he replaced them on the ledge.

Christy groaned. "C'mon, don't ask me more questions."

But how could he not, when strangers were sleeplessly pacing floors, wringing their hands and wondering where their little girl was? "Christy, this might feel like an adventure to you, but you're hurting your mommy and daddy."

"Guilt trips don't work on me," she said loftily.

What would? He wished he could hit on something. "Don't you even trust me enough to tell me your parents' names?"

She shook her head. "No."

Great. He'd reached the end of his rope. He'd been trying to inspire trust, showing her and Nikki the grounds, decorating the house, sharing meals and supervising while Christy rode Jenny's bike in the barn. For hours now, he'd watched her trudge up the hill with the sled, then coast to the bottom. Now his searching eyes settled where snowflakes glistened on her rosy cheeks. He watched her raise the mittened hand with which she was clutching the sled rope and scratch her nose. Then his eyes followed the arcing swing of the mitten back to her side.

"How'm I gonna pull my new sled, Daddy?"

"Guess you'd better look under the tree again, Jenny."

"So Santa brought me a sled, but you got me a rope to tie to it, huh?" A trusting hand closed over his. "That's why I love you, Daddy."

"Why's that?"

"'Cause you give me stuff 'fore I ever need it, like the rope for the sled. Is that 'cause you can see the future?"

"Nope, Jen. Daddy can't see the future."

If Daddy could have, he would have kept you safe.

Glancing away from the sled rope, Jon turned toward the kitchen window where bright light shined, looking so cozy in the gray air that Jon felt warmer. Nikki was at the stove, stirring cocoa, her lips moving as she sang carols along with the radio. She was wearing jeans and a sunny yellow sweatshirt, and she'd put on another baseball cap, this one with an electric-blue bill. Her hair was down, looking touchable even at this distance. With a faint smile, Jon wondered if the slow changes in her appearance had anything to do with him...the nail polish she was wearing, how she'd taken down her ponytail.

Seeing how at home she looked in his kitchen, he realized how much he liked having a woman here...liked having *her*. The daily sounds of another presence—her footsteps, the running shower—were strangely comforting. And yesterday, he'd had fun with her and Christy. He'd been deeply moved, too, by how concerned she was for the little girl. Well, maybe he could see into the future, after all. At least enough to know that Nikki Ryder would belong to a lucky man someday.

She didn't yet. She'd kissed like a woman who was still looking. But she'd get snapped up soon enough. How many women would brave a storm, just to get a stranger's child home for Christmas? How many would have made a man's house more comfortable, when she realized she was snowbound? Or tried to help repair a relationship between a father and daughter, when she thought it was in trouble?

A tiny voice suddenly sounded. "Don't be mad at me. Okay, Jon?"

Glancing down at Christy, he said, "I'm not mad. Just worried."

Sidling close, Christy hopped on the fountain ledge and scooted next to him. A second later, her hand wiggled into his pocket, the wet snow on her mitten melting against his palm and tingling. He'd forgotten this…the quiet strength in a little girl's hand, and the chubby pressure of small fingers. Wordlessly, he curled his fingers around hers.

She squeezed back, making his heart pull.

Her voice was a solemn whisper. "Can I ask *you* a question?"

"Sure."

"Why are you sad?"

He hadn't expected that. He shrugged, watching the flurries blend into the day's remaining light. Glancing back toward Nikki in the twilight gray of the afternoon, he saw a ringed halo around the porch light, and it suddenly reminded him of angels. He looked at Christy again. She was a good kid, and he figured she wouldn't have pretended to be his child if she guessed his had died. But who was she? Had she run away? Or gotten lost, then pretended to be his daughter on a misguided whim? It made no sense. But then, what adult could follow a child's logic? *You used to, back when you wrote kids' stories.*

"I guess I'm sad because I'd hate to think of my…" He glanced at the hills where Jenny had once played. "Of my little girl disappearing and never calling me."

"Well, I can't call anybody because your phones don't work."

He nodded. If phones worked, he'd have alerted the authorities already, and they'd be that much closer to finding her parents. Glancing around once more, he wondered if the roads would be cleared by tomorrow. Seeing Nikki in the window again, he was suddenly glad she thought Christy was his daughter. Judging from her obvious good-heartedness, she'd be worried sick if she knew Christy wasn't. Until Jon spoke with the sheriff and the airlines, nothing could be done, so at least she didn't have to share his worry. "If the phones did work, Christy, who would you call?"

She glanced away, swallowing guiltily.

He pressed the advantage. "I bet your parents have called the police. Maybe even the FBI if you were traveling over state lines…"

She pursed her lips.

Someone had to be looking for her. She was expensively dressed, well-groomed, and when he lifted the ends of her hair, the blunt ends attested to a recent salon cut. Hardly a child who wouldn't be missed. Between power outages, Jon kept watching TV, expecting to see announcements about a child meeting her description. He wished they'd report something about when the phone lines would be restored.

Suddenly squirming off the fountain's edge, Christy hopped to the ground, her boots sinking in the deep snow. When she turned, her green eyes glittered in the waning light, and her voice was fierce. "I don't want you to worry and get even more sad, Jon. Nobody else is worried. Nobody's looking for me."

"Christy, I'm sure they are."

"They aren't!"

From the doorway, Nikki suddenly yelled, "Sure you don't want your cocoa now, Christy?"

Christy raised her voice. "I want it later."

Before Jon could catch her, she whirled around and headed up the hill, her boots sinking and kicking up snow-spray, her body half-turned to haul the sled behind her. *Nobody's looking for me.* The words played in Jon's head, making his heart feel oddly heavy, because he believed her. Christy was lying about many things, but not that. A sudden chill passed through him, and he pulled a red wool hat from his coat pocket. Tugging it over his ears, he fished around for his cherry-wood pipe and lit it.

Nobody *was* looking for her, he thought, the warm tobacco helping him mull it over. Why not?

"IT LOOKED LIKE you and Christy were having a serious talk."

Jon blinked. When he slowly raised his gaze, Nikki saw that the snowy twilight had turned his serious, faraway eyes a deep gray-jade. It was a color so dreamy that something inside her melted. He removed the pipe dangling from the corner of his mouth long enough to allow his lips to flicker, then stretch into a full smile. "Sorry—" Replacing the pipe, he grabbed his gloves and brushed snow off the stone ledge beside him. "I was in La La Land. Have a seat."

"Thanks." She offered him one of the steaming mugs she was carrying, then laid down an old newspaper to protect her jeans and seated herself. "Here. This'll help warm you up." Her eyes settled on his hat. "Anybody ever tell you you look like Santa?"

"Santa?" Jon glanced down at his washboard-flat belly as he pulled on his gloves.

She shook her head. "I meant because of the red cap and pipe."

"Oh." He nodded, puffing once on his pipe. As he blew smoke across the mug, chocolate and cherry-smoke scents wafted to Nikki, smelling warm and invitingly masculine on the crisp, cold air.

"I didn't know you smoked."

"Not often. Only a pipe. And usually outside." He squinted and sniffed, then sent her a slant-eyed sideways glance. "Chanel Number Five?"

She blushed. "Christy's. She spritzed me."

He smiled. "Smells good. I love that stuff."

Secretly, Nikki realized she'd hoped he would. It was why she hadn't washed off the scent. "Well...I never smelled tobacco in the house." She'd noticed other things, though. How little he slept and that he loved books. They were everywhere, shoved through stairway bannisters, stacked in bathrooms, crowded on tables. He was a voracious reader.

A long companionable silence had fallen, broken only by Christy's gleeful squeals as she plunged downhill on the sled. After a moment, Nikki squinted. "Should we help her pull the sled back up?"

"I tried. She wants to do it herself." Jon sipped the cocoa gratefully. "Thanks. This hits the spot. I was starting to freeze out here."

"Sorry. No marshmallows."

He shot her another smile. "I think I'll live. I have a standing order for grocery delivery, and never even considered putting marshmallows on it."

Smiling back, she sipped her own cocoa to ward off the chill. The snow had tapered off, and now the wind's howling was nothing more than a low, soft rustle of branches. Nikki's eyes strayed over the sloping snow-blanketed hills and landed where ancient-looking trees bordered the surrounding forests; the undersides of their twisted limbs were dark, the tops crusted with snow. It was strangely beautiful here, strangely peaceful, and everything held a hint of the sublime. *Even him,* she thought, surreptitiously taking in Jon's profile. She liked the hard strength of his face, the straight nose and solid-looking jaw and cheekbones.

"Watch me this time!" Christy yelled.

"We're watching," Jon shouted back.

Nikki waved as Christy pushed off. The saucer-sled spun in circles as it descended, and Christy faced them for a minute, her eyes wide, her small red mouth open in an excited O. With a wistful sigh, Nikki said, "I love kids. And your daughter's cute as all get-out."

Jon was silent a long moment. When he spoke, his voice carried an answering wistfulness. "Yeah...the kid's cute."

"And this place is a child's dream."

Or was. Nikki glanced behind her at the unused fountain that had probably once been delightful, then at Christy who'd reached the bottom of the hill. She pointed, laughing as Christy tumbled off the sled into the snow. Beside her, she felt Jon's rumble of a chuckle; it warmed her as much as his body, which pressed down her side. "I like it," Nikki said. And then wondered if she meant the property, which was wild and overgrown, or the feel of him beside her.

"Like what?"

She shrugged. "Everything. This place." Looking back toward the house, her eyes lingered on the spooky spires and turrets. "It was kind of scary at first, but it grows on you." Especially now, since Jon had put up some outside lights. The wreaths and electric candles she'd imagined should be here were now in the windows.

When he turned, their eyes locked briefly. He looked as if he wanted to say something, but didn't know how to start. She watched him puff on the pipe again, her eyes following the mixture of foggy breath and sweet-smelling smoke on the whitish air. The damp cold started seeping through the newspaper to her jeans, cooling the backs of her thighs.

He finally spoke, his voice a slow, almost gruff drawl. "I'm...I'm sorry about the night you came, Nikki."

She was still taking in the hard angles of his jaw, the smooth planes of his cheeks. "You're sorry?"

"I shouldn't have kissed you like that."

Ever since, while he'd shown her around the grounds and helped decorate the house, she'd thought of nothing else. Not that she had the nerve to say so. "Uh, not to worry." That seemed neutral enough.

"I just don't want you to think..."

She shook her head quickly, wishing they weren't

having this conversation. Despite the freezing air, she felt heat burn in her cheeks and hoped their redness passed for windburn. "Believe me, Sleet," she found herself saying, "I don't think anything." As if she had no thoughts at all! She sounded like an idiot now. And she didn't really want him apologizing, either. Dammit, more than once, she'd wanted him to kiss her again. "What I mean is, uh—" Taking off her cap, she toyed with the brim. "I don't think..." *Whatever you don't want me to think.*

The attempt at clarification only made things worse, and another silence fell, this one uncomfortable, she thought. She finally shoved the cap back on her head, and he abruptly picked up the conversation where they'd left off.

"I grew up here with my parents until they moved to Florida, for the weather," he said. "This place was built by my great-grandfather—three greats back. When he was young, he was an explorer in Alaska." He flashed her a quick smile. "At least until he struck gold."

His rich relatives seemed a far better topic than how he felt about kissing her. "Gold, huh?" She decided Jon Sleet's strong nose and regal cheekbones made him look as if he'd come from old money. "I guess that should make me nervous."

He squinted at her. "Why?"

"Well, this place is so full of heirlooms and history." Suddenly, she chuckled. "I grew up with my dad and three macho brothers. But then I guess they had their traditions, too."

"Such as?"

"Leaving the toilet seat up."

The deep sound of his laugh surprised her, it was

so like music, and the cold air suddenly tingled on her face; in a burst, she felt very alive—and all from nothing more than his voice. He said, "What else?"

"Racing stock cars on Saturday. Flapjacks on Sunday. Football on Monday." Unexpectedly, her heart wrenched, and she longed to hear the booming voices of her father and brothers again, and the scrape of their heavy boots on the kitchen's old linoleum. "Alaska?" she said, glancing at the Santa statue behind her. "Sure your grandfather didn't come from the North Pole?"

Jon's smile made his eyes light like candles. "Wondering if I have elf blood?"

She tilted her head, studying him. He looked more like a Scottish Highlander. Or an Irish sailor, with that dark hair and the green eyes that so often settled somewhere distant. He had smooth skin, too, that could have been weathered down, washed clean by years of salt spray and north winds. "Now that you mention it," she finally said.

"What?"

Frowning, she lifted a pant leg and stared at his thick gray socks. "Green legs. Geez, I should have known." Smiling, she met his gaze again. "No wonder you keep to yourself. Pointy ears can be a real embarrassment in public places."

He nodded. "I try to tell myself they're a conversation piece. Besides, there is one good thing about being an elf." He shot her a smile. "We can make a helluva gift."

The man wasn't talking about wielding a hammer and nails, and in Nikki's mind's eye, she saw him sprawled naked in bed on Christmas morning.

He said, "Why are all those clothes in your trunk?"

The question took her by surprise. Maybe he'd meant it to. "You don't beat around the bush."

"I don't mean to pry. I'm just curious. I told you I looked in your trunk the night you got here."

"A fight…" she said after a long moment. "I left the man I'd been living with for a few months." It was probably more information than she should have offered, but she was surprised at how steadily she'd said the words. She took another sip of cocoa—it was cooling fast in the freezing air—then she watched as a snowflake drifted over the mug's lip and melted. The same flakes were catching in Jon's dark eyelashes, tingeing the tips white.

"So, it's over between you?" She tried not to read too much into the solemnity of his voice.

"Yeah."

"For good?"

She swallowed hard, schooling herself not to misinterpret the more-than-casual interest in his eyes. "Yeah."

After a moment, his mouth quirked. "Let me guess. The wreath on your car was previously on the front door of the place you shared with…"

"Buck." Nikki nodded sheepishly.

"And the nativity on the dashboard was on your mantel, as was the stocking that's now hanging from the rearview mirror?"

Strangely, she, too, was beginning to see some humor in this. "You must be psychic."

"And you simply couldn't leave Buck without taking the mistletoe that now hangs from your dome light?"

"Nope. Too mad." Nikki had worked so hard, decorating the house for Christmas, getting ready to tell Buck about the wonderful gift they'd been given, their baby. "I was so mad, I guess I took everything that wasn't nailed down," she admitted with a sad chuckle. Without mentioning the baby, she felt strangely compelled to give Jon a thumbnail sketch of her relationship with Buck. She finished by blowing out a long sigh. "I thought I loved him. I never would have moved in with him if I hadn't. I guess I don't have much luck with relationships."

"Never?"

Finishing off the cocoa, she set aside her cup and shrugged. "No. I guess it all goes back to a Christmas dance my first year of high school. It was the first real date I ever had, and the guy's car broke down. Since I didn't want to be late, I tugged on some coveralls he had in the trunk and fixed it."

"Depleted the guy's testosterone reserves, huh?"

"Could I help it if he didn't know how to check his oil?" She suddenly chuckled softly, shaking her head. "Maybe my whole life might have been different if I'd waited for triple-A like a normal girl. It's what Kitty Powell would have done."

"Kitty Powell?"

"Blond, perky cheerleader. You know the type."

"Nikki," he returned softly. "You *are* a normal girl."

The warmth of his eyes made her feel breathless and self-conscious, but without letting it show, she tipped the bill of her baseball cap. "Thanks. But all my life, I hung around boys..." Sighing, she continued, talking about their farmhouse in Kentucky, telling him how, when she was only two, her mother had died from complications during an operation. She told him how there weren't many girls to play with, and how she'd always been a nuisance, tagging along after her big brothers. At least until Buck.

"So, you wanted to be on your own?"

"It was past time." She shot him a quick glance. "Unfortunately I didn't strike gold." Suddenly, she wished Jon's sympathetic green eyes didn't seem to see so much. And she wished she had someone to whom she could confide the rest of her story. It had been barely a month before she'd started to suspect Buck wanted nothing more than a glorified housekeeper, and she'd wound up deciding that lovemaking was something she could live without. Her throat tightened, and once again she wondered what advice her mother might offer now. "I guess I was trying to prove something to my family by leaving."

The easy tenderness in Jon's voice curled up inside her like a kitten. "You have every right to make mistakes, Nikki."

Except hers had big consequences. She was carrying Buck's child, and now she almost admitted it aloud. It struck her that not a soul in the world even knew about the life growing inside her. Not that it was appropriate to tell Jon Sleet.

He said, "I bet you learned a lot."

"I hope I did." *Enough to be the mother I never had.*

"You did." He sounded so sure. "You know more about what you want from a man."

Another wave of self-consciousness came over her, since what she wanted was the kind of passion she'd felt from Jon's kiss. Somehow, she managed to sound vague. "I suppose."

"Talk to your family the day you left?"

She shook her head. "No. And now I can't call." She wanted to, though. When her father and brothers had warned against her deepening relationship with Buck, she'd accused them of wanting to keep her tied down at home, just so she could cook and clean for them. But they loved her. All her life, they'd tried so hard. When the boys weren't accepting her as one of their own, showing her how to mend fences on the farm or tinker with stock cars, they were making amends for her lack of female supervision by going overboard, buying her things with too much pink and too many ruffles.

Jon finally said, "Sounds like you're a close family."

"We are. I love them." But she hadn't heard her father's voice since she left home. "Maybe because of that I—I like seeing you and Christy patch things up."

Some emotion she couldn't decipher crossed Jon's features, making her wish he'd open up with her, as she had with him. But he simply said, "You'll talk again."

The day's long, deepening shadows fell across his face where his cheeks were ruddy from the cold and darkening with evening stubble. Pipe smoke sugared and warmed the air, clouding around him, making her think of Santa Claus again.

"Well," she said, glancing away and feeling suddenly awkward, "I'd better get inside." She slapped her hands on her knees, as if ready to make her move, even though she felt she could stay here forever talking to him. "Christy's probably about worn herself out, and she'll be hungry."

He glanced at Christy—she was halfway up the hill, hauling the sled behind her—and he nodded.

"Well, uh, maybe the phones'll be back on tomorrow. Or the snowplow will make it up here. I—I really appreciate your letting me stay, Jon."

He was merely watching her, seemingly registering her mild embarrassment. Another sexy smile played on his mouth. "I guess I could have set you up in the barn."

She smiled, then felt a swift catch of breath as images of the Christ child's hay-filled manger entered her mind. Thoughts of her own child followed; she had so much to think about. "I'm glad there was room at the inn," she said lightly. "I do appreciate the bed. Thanks."

"You're welcome." He paused. "It's nice having people around."

For some reason, her chest felt tight at the admission. She slapped her knees yet another time, now conscious of the cold, and of the warm fires burning inside. Somehow, she forced herself to stand. "I'll start dinner. You're pretty well-stocked. Fried chicken sound good?"

He glanced up at her. "I'll cook, if you'd rather watch Christy."

"I like a man who offers. But I enjoy it."

"You're good at it, too."

"You liked that casserole, huh?"

His shoulders shook with suppressed laughter. "It would have been better if you and Christy hadn't eaten so much of it."

"Sorry, but we have to eat, too."

"This time make extra. I'm thinking ahead to midnight snacks."

"Glad to." She gazed down into eyes that held astonishing depth. Jon Sleet might have been born with a silver spoon between his lips, but life had apparently dished out plenty of things that were hard to swallow. Just as she leaned and lifted her empty mug from the fountain's edge, he surprised her by raising his gloved hand to her cheek. The gentle, unexpected touch made time stand still, and she felt suddenly conscious of everything: the softness of the glove's leather, the smells of leather and smoke, of how the snow flurries danced between them. When his thumb stroked her cold skin, the soft caress of buttery leather sent her heart pounding. She still couldn't move, only lowered her eyes.

He murmured, "Maybe I wasn't clear."

She managed to stand as he dropped his hand, even though her knees were weak. "About?"

His voice was unmistakably husky. "I was sorry about the *way* I kissed you. But I didn't mean to imply I didn't like the way it felt."

Did that mean he liked it? Probably. For a second, she was sure he was going to kiss her again, but he merely lifted his hand and brushed his thumb—once, twice—across her lips.

And then, very unsteadily, she walked back to the house.

"I'M READY for you to tuck me in, Daddy."

Waiting in the hallway, Jon sighed, realizing his talk with Christy today had done no good whatsoever. How could he make her trust him enough to tell him who she was? He frowned. If she didn't start talking, things would get worse once the sheriff was involved. Steve might be legally bound to turn her over to an agency. Clearly, Christy didn't understand the implications of what she was doing.

He lifted his voice. "Ready or not, here I come."

Christy squealed, "I said I was ready!"

Smiling, he entered the room. As he came up behind Nikki, his eyes drifted over the gentle slope of her shoulders. His hands followed, resting on them, lightly squeezing the tired muscles and making the fabric of the dress she'd changed into bunch beneath his hands. She'd said she'd changed because her jeans got wet outside, but he was sure she'd done it for him. The dress was casual, and of royal blue that matched the bill of her baseball cap. Long and baggy like an oversize T-shirt, the dress was more cute than alluring. Drawing in a deep breath of her perfume, he wished he'd kissed her outside. He could have so easily, wanted to so badly…

But she deserves so much more.

He could read between the lines; Buck hadn't done much for her, sexually or otherwise. And he could kill the guy for giving her anything less than royal treatment. Quickly, he reminded himself there wasn't really anything going on between them. She was here for one reason—she was snowbound. Shrugging off the thoughts, he gazed over Nikki's shoulder at Christy.

"Big fat kisses," Christy murmured, gazing lovingly into the aquarium. Lifting Noodles out, she kissed the grim line that passed for the snake's lips.

"Yuck," Jon muttered in Nikki's ear.

"Disgusting," Nikki whispered in agreement as Noodles's long, forked tongue wiggled over Christy's cheeks. "But like she said, she's good with cold-blooded creatures."

He chuckled. "You really thought I was cold-blooded?"

Nikki glanced over her shoulder. "Yes."

"Changing your mind?"

"Yes."

"Care to elaborate?"

"No."

He laughed softly. "You're a helluva conversationalist, Nikki."

She grinned and stepped away from him to fold down the covers. "C'mon," she said to Christy. "Hop in, hon."

Christy lunged for the bed, racing past the fire Jon had built while Nikki finished the dinner dishes. Christy was scrubbed clean, her cheeks still rosy from the outdoors, and she was dressed in a long-sleeved cotton nightshirt that was probably Nikki's. The sleeves were rolled so many times that they bunched at her wrists. Once again, he thought Nikki was nice to do so much for the little girl. And yet Nikki obviously enjoyed it. Someday, she'd make a good mother.

And you'd be a good father. The thought came from nowhere. He *had* been a good father, Jon thought now. But he'd never do it again. Over these past days, he'd felt his heart start to open up, and Nikki Ryder was making him crave a night where he wouldn't be alone. He'd started to feel a tenderness he'd forgotten, too, but he'd never risk his heart again. He'd never have a child.

He watched as Christy snuggled under the covers, pulled them right beneath her armpits, then thrust out her arms so they lay flat on the bedspread. She breathed in deeply and announced, "Deep sigh."

"Deep sigh," Nikki said in return.

He smiled. It *had* been a long, fulfilling day. And now the big old bed that could easily sleep a family swallowed the sleepy-looking child. Jon slept little, always had, and tonight he knew he'd stoke the fire while Nikki and Christy slept.

The first night, the two had shared this bed because he hadn't been expecting them. Now he was glad they hadn't asked for separate rooms. He liked to watch them sleep—Nikki, on her stomach with her fiery brown hair spread over the pillow; Christy on her back, curling against Nikki and hogging the bed's center, where she was now. Nikki leaned over the bed and gently tossed Christy's hair. "You okay, hon?"

Christy nodded.

"I put your water glass right next to you, and we'll leave the door open a crack."

Strange, he thought as he watched them, how easily habits were established. How, without even realizing it, you got to know all the little things about people that meant so much.

He turned off the light and edged around Nikki. As he pulled the covers under Christy's chin, his chest squeezed with emotion. She looked like an angel, with her cherubic cheeks gleaming in the soft light and her spiraling blond curls glinting with golden red from the fire. He started to lean back—Nikki had retreated to the door—but Christy's small hand stayed him.

"Tell me a story."

His breath caught. How many times had his own little girl said those words, begging for the stories he'd created just for her? He could almost see Jenny, squealing and running merrily to bed, excited because he was coming to tuck her in and spin yarns until she drifted to sleep. Now his gaze settled on Christy's eyes—clear, green eyes that reflected the simplicity of youth. The hair he brushed from her forehead felt like silk. "Not tonight. I—I'm fresh out of stories."

She toyed with the thin gold-chain bracelet on her wrist and whispered, "Some other night?"

"Maybe."

Her emerald eyes flitted to his. "Can't you think of stories anymore?"

From the mouths of babes. His voice was low. "I guess I can't."

He didn't expect her to sit up then. Didn't expect the small fierce arms that suddenly circled his neck, or the painfully tight constriction of his chest. God, he'd forgotten how fiercely the little ones hugged. His own hands lifted—maybe to stop her, maybe to steady himself—but they wound up pressing against her back, holding her close.

"It's okay, Jon," she whispered. "I don't need any story."

He barely heard her. He'd squeezed his eyes tight, drawing in the soft-washed scent of her hair, feeling its silk brush his cheek. For just a second, he was holding his own child again. He felt suddenly conscious of the small bones of Christy's back, of her fragility.

"I'm sorry you don't have stories anymore, Jon," she whispered.

Jenny would be sorry, too. When Christy turned her head and gently pressed her lips to his cheek, he was sure he'd just been kissed by an angel.

His voice was hoarse with emotion. "Good night."

"'Night," she returned easily.

He'd forgotten that about little girls, too. Their emotions were like rainbows. Fast to appear. Fast to fade. The spectrum of colors as broad as the sky. She'd just shaken his world, but already, she was snuggling into the covers again. He watched as her eyes drifted shut, and he knew she was only seconds from sleep.

Out in the hallway, he caught Nikki's hand, realizing that for the first time in a long time, he really didn't want to be alone. "Let's do something."

Nikki's smile lifted his spirits. "Suggestions?"

He glanced through a window at the snow-filled night. "A midnight swim?"

She shrugged. "I did find a deck of cards."

"I know. Christy already beat me at Old Maid." He smiled. "Unless you're suggesting we switch to strip poker."

"What, Sleet?" She sized him up with those incredible brown eyes. "Are you that desperate to lose your shorts?"

He shook his head. "You'd never win."

She stared at him for a long moment, nibbling her lip and looking as if she was telling herself not to rise to the bait. And then she said, "Five-card stud. Sevens are wild."

Chapter Six

"Oh, Sleet—" Nikki grinned with relish, tossing down a card and picking up another. "I warned you I had brothers. They taught me everything I know about strip poker. Getting cold yet?"

"Freezing," Jon assured her, even though the kitchen was warmer than it had been for years, filled with softly inviting light and scents of the chicken and warm rolls Nikki had made for supper.

"Geez, so sorry you're freezing," she said.

He smiled, watching as she surveyed her cards, then merrily resituated them. "First, you're not really sorry. And second, you've at least been kind enough to leave me my pants."

"So far." Nikki laughed, training her sparkling dark eyes on a belt slung over a chair. "Too bad there's nothing left to hold them up with."

Jon blew out a mock sigh of frustration. "As Winston Churchill said, 'There are some things up with which I will not put.'"

Nikki frowned. "Huh?"

"I'm a writer, remember?" he murmured. "And you put a preposition at the end of your sentence." He'd turned his chair around and was sitting backward, straddling the seat. Resting his elbows on the chair back now, he looked over his cards again. Great. He was two stitches from the buff and stuck with another lousy hand.

"Don't start getting personal about my grammar just because you're losing again, Sleet." Nikki's lips twitched as she watched him fold and re-fan his cards. "You know, it's not the hands, but what you do with them."

"I'm not touching that one." Or she might find out just what kind of touching his hands wanted to do.

"You're not touching— Oh," Nikki suddenly said, color rising in her cheeks. "I get it now."

"Don't worry. You might not get your own double entendres, but you're wicked at five-card stud. At least this modified game that your brothers made up."

"You think that's why I'm winning?"

Jon merely frowned, suddenly wondering if he should stoop to cheating, just to keep his pants. Raking a hand distractedly over his bare chest, he caught her gaze.

She looked thoroughly pleased with herself. "You *are* a sight for sore eyes," she said, resting her elbows on the gray tabletop and coyly fanning herself with her splayed cards.

He started to tell her she could use a lesson in winning graciously, but he settled for staring at the backs of her cards, wondering what was on the other side. Knowing Nikki, she had four of a kind. Of course, he did have the ten, jack and ace of diamonds. It was a start. When he glanced up again, the gaze she dropped over the thick brown hair liberally covering his chest made his whole body tighten. "You wouldn't look at me that way," he warned. "Not if I was over there."

"Idle threats," she said loftily.

But they weren't. When he'd touched her cheek outside, his body had flooded with want. He'd seen desire in her eyes, too, and hesitation, probably from her experience with Buck. Jon had longed to feel the soft give of her lips beneath his mouth again, and to erase the pain of whatever Buck had done, but with Christy around, he'd thought better of it. He just wished Nikki would divulge more about the fight, but she hadn't. "Keep pushing me," he teased as he took his turn, "and we'll see what's idle."

"Definitely not your mouth."

"I'm the victim here," he protested as she drew cards. "A poor, sensitive man who's been stripped of all his clothes during a freezing blizzard and put on display like an object."

"Display?"

"A very pretty woman keeps staring at my bare chest."

"Now there's a backhanded compliment, Sleet."

"If you want it right up front, Ryder—" He shot her a grin. "You *are* pretty."

She did her best to look annoyed as she took another turn. He chuckled softly, thinking that when the smoke cleared and things settled down between them, they had fun together. She said, "You're just getting cabin fever. In this blizzard anything would look good to you. Even the wildlife."

"Baby," he found himself teasing, his green eyes twinkling. "You *are* the wildlife."

Color exploded on her cheeks, though her voice remained mild. "If you don't start concentrating on your hand, that pretty girl who's been staring at your chest is going to be staring at a whole heck of a lot more."

"You had a real poker face," he shot back. "Right up until you started turning beet red."

"We'll see who's about to turn red."

She had a point. He was the one who was about to lose his pants. He stared down again, debating. Should he sacrifice the pair of twos? The chances of drawing the king and queen of diamonds were slim, but he decided to live dangerously and discarded. He picked up the two of clubs and frowned. He should have held on to the twos. The six of hearts wouldn't do him any good, either. *Goodbye pants.*

Nikki took her turn, then stared hard at her new hand. "Uh, do you mind if I ask you something?"

"What?"

"Are you wearing long johns?"

Guess she picked up something good. "No, ma'am. You're fresh out of luck. Just jeans."

She looked stricken. "But you do have underwear, right?"

"In my drawers, no pun intended? Or am I wearing them now?"

She rolled her eyes. "It's a simple question."

As dire as his predicament was getting, Jon couldn't help but laugh. "Guess you're about to find out the answer, Ryder."

She fiddled nervously with the bill of her baseball cap, looking unusually adorable. "Look, Sleet, maybe I should give you some kind of handicap. You know, like you get another wild card or something."

He tilted his head, as if considering, but really he was just looking at her. She did look pretty; the blue color of the dress was good for her, enhancing her hair that looked penny-brown in the low light. He finally shook his head. "It's bad enough I'm half-naked, but having a woman let me win would destroy whatever's left of my fragile male ego."

She sent him a long look that said his masculinity was quite intact. "That's the thing about big strong men—" She shook her head sorrowfully. "They never accept help from women."

"Hmm. I think that was a backhanded compliment."

"Just draw your cards, Jon."

He drew the queen of diamonds and had to fight not to grin. She was searching his face. He wagged a finger. "Don't bother looking at me like that. You won't find any clues in my eyes."

She leaned forward anyway, peering at him as if to detect what he'd drawn. Finally giving up, she took her turn. He liked how her full, sexy eyebrows knitted together in concentration, how she chewed on a thumbnail.

"If you don't speed it up, my clothes will *rot* off of me."

"I'm thinking," she said distractedly.

Unbidden came the notion he didn't want her to think at all. He wanted her to feel his body against her when he swept her away with another kiss. "Okay." She nodded as if satisfied with her hand. "You go."

He drew the king of diamonds. Piercing her with his eyes, he said, "I'm ready for show-and-tell."

"Let's see what you've got."

He raised an eyebrow. "Sure you're ready to see it all?"

"I meant I want to see your hand, not your..." She blushed again.

He fanned his cards on the table. "Royal flush."

He loved watching the expressions play on her face—the astonishment since she hadn't yet lost; the quick relief that he wasn't going to finish stripping for her, followed by horror as she realized she was wearing only a dress and no stockings.

"I know your bedroom slippers are under the table," he teased with a soft drawl. "So, don't you dare try to put them back on and pretend they were an article of clothing you were previously wearing."

She exhaled a long suffering sigh. "Four of a kind," she said, plopping down four sixes. "But you see, I don't need to take anything off because I *let* you win."

"Oh no." He shook his head. "Rules are rules. But since *I'm* a gracious winner, I'll help you. I've already decided which article of clothing you have to remove for me."

"I bet you have," she said, eyeing him warily as he rose and slowly began circling the table. "What do you *think* I should take off? *Think* being the operative word."

He paused, his breath catching. He suddenly wanted her so much. Her silly tomboyishness touched something deep at the masculine core of him, and he wanted to prove to her that she was more of a woman than she knew. He kept moving, his voice turning husky with words that were out before he completely thought them through. "Nikki," he promised, "you're going to take off something that will make me very, very hot."

Her fingers pressed the base of her throat as if to

calm an accelerating pulse. Stopping in front of her and staring down to where she remained seated, he noticed her eyelashes. They were thick, luxurious. Velvet brown eyes gazed up from beneath them, imploring him not to demand her dress. "Sleet," she said flatly, raising a staying hand. "Game's over. C'mon, I've only got on a bra and panties."

"A bra and panties," he murmured as he gazed down at cheeks that were darkly pink and soft, like roses, and at her bright, sensual eyes that glittered with awareness.

When her voice hitched with an excitement she was trying to hide, he realized she was half-titillated by the prospect of undressing. "Please," she huffed. "I think we've had enough suspense. What do you think I should remove?"

"This."

The second before he touched the bill of her baseball cap, she inhaled sharply. The fool cap was so much a part of her that she'd apparently forgotten she was wearing it. Lifting it, he reached and fluffed her fiery brown hair, then he edged closer, set aside the cap, and traced a finger down a lush hank, following it onto her neck.

She looked determined to pretend that nothing was happening between them. "So, taking off a baseball cap does it for you, huh, Sleet?"

She didn't sound the least bit tough; her voice was shaking. "Yeah, and you'll never know how much, Nikki."

Suddenly, he felt that the air had left the room. They'd both stopped breathing. Looking into her eyes, he realized his body was poised, tensed and towering over her. He felt both strangely moved by her uncertainty and surprised he was getting so aroused from nothing more than this. As the last of her tomboyish toughness drained from her face, she looked plain old nervous, and he was aching for her, his jeans feeling suddenly tight with what all he wanted to give. Hoping she read the good intentions in his eyes, he slid his fingers under her hair again and gently stroked a warm hollow beneath her earlobe. His voice lowered, turning almost gruff. "I want to kiss you again. And I want to be in bed with you tonight, Nikki."

Her voice sounded strangled. "I figured."

Strands of her silken hair brushed the back of his hand until his mind felt drugged, and when his fingertips touched the unsteady pulse at her throat, he longed to touch her much more intimately. Just as he closed the scant inch of space still left between them, she turned her head. Her cheek glanced off his belly—the hollow of her eye touching just above his pant's fly, her eyelashes fluttering near his navel.

He could have moaned, but he didn't. Reflexively, his hand tightened on her neck, staying her, so her head curled against his belly. Her chin wound up grazing the snap of his jeans, and when her arm circled his waist, the hug brought her breast to his groin. Soft as heaven, it curved to the masculine shape of him. He couldn't breathe. His hand stopped rubbing her hair. "Come here," he said, urging her up. Her slightly dampened palms pressed his chest as she rose, and then her hands slid over his shoulders and loosely around his neck, as if she was afraid to hug him too tight.

His fingers skimmed her jaw, tilting up her face so he could stare deep into her eyes. "Make love to me,

Nikki.'' He brought his lips closer. ''And let me make love to you, too.''

''Sleet—'' Her voice trembled slightly. ''Just because we're two adults who happened to get stuck in a snowstorm...''

He tilted his head, surveying her and wishing she understood what he felt right now. ''I'd want you in the sunshine, too.''

The sudden trembling of her lower lip and her tentative nod of assent made him wonder at her experience. He suspected Buck had been her first lover, but Jon knew it was better not to ask. Nikki needed to feel vulnerable, not exposed. ''You won't be sorry,'' he whispered in assurance, rubbing a thumb over her lips before pressing his own to hers. ''It's been a while for me, Nikki,'' he said, drawing away. ''I want to experience everything a woman has to give. Everything I know will bring her pleasure in return.'' He smiled into her eyes. ''Game?''

She managed a nod.

Leaning, he swept warm lips across hers again, and his fingers followed, bracketing her reddening lips, framing them as his mouth descended once more with his deepest, gentlest kiss. Exploring her teeth, he found ridges only a tongue could discover, and stroking the insides of her cheeks, he tasted what only a lover ever would. As her tongue filled his mouth, parts of him wanted to beg because she made his loins ache with such fire.

There was nothing in the world like what Nikki Ryder was doing to him. Nothing more healing or more electrifying. And yet Jon needed more...so much more. He leaned away, taking both her hands gently in his. "Come with me, Nikki," he said simply.

She sounded strangely lost. "After you, Sleet."

HE LEFT HER in the small, cold room where he slept. It was sparsely furnished, with a straight-back chair wedged between a window and a full-size quilt-covered bed, and an antique armoire that sat in a corner. The windup clock on the bedside table said it was ten. It felt later. Nikki sat on the bed to wait, but she was too nervous. When it came to sex, Buck had always made her feel she was lacking.

Getting up, she hugged her arms to her waist and moved toward the window. The venetian blinds were up, and she could see the sky now, since the storm clouds had lifted. Jon was still out there—in the clearing night and under the full moon—shining a flashlight into the cab's trunk where the condoms were supposed to be. What if she was wrong and there weren't any? She couldn't get pregnant, but she'd feel better with protection.

She sighed shakily. "I know there're condoms in there." There had to be. She'd taken everything from Buck's but the kitchen sink.

She watched Jon rummage. He hadn't even put on a sweater. He'd dashed out right into sub-zero temperatures, bare-chested and pausing only to pull on the boots he'd lost at poker. That's how anxious *he* was.

Her heart pounded as he shut the trunk and ran back toward the house. She reminded herself that what was about to happen was just sex. Probably, this was just something she needed to do, to prove she was desirable. She wouldn't entertain any feelings for

Jon because—at least judging from how he'd left his old bedroom—he was still in love with his ex-wife.

"Oh, geez," she murmured. "I think this is a mistake." Because she already more than liked Jon. Watching how he'd warmed to Christy, accepting her back into his life, had touched Nikki. And now she had to know if he was as passionate as his kisses promised. Raking a hand through her hair, she realized her baseball cap was gone, and she somehow wished she had it with her.

And yet when Jon came into the room, her doubts lifted. He was breathless and smiling. A burst of cold came with him and scents of fresh air. Because the moon-touched silhouette of his powerful body took away her breath, she was glad for the dark.

Turning, he locked the door. She swallowed hard; she hadn't even thought of Christy waking and finding them. Setting down the condoms, Jon leaned and caught her easily. *"Brrr,"* he rumbled, wrapping strong cold arms around her. "You're so warm."

And she was. Shamelessly warm from the first moment he'd touched her. Hot now, as his cold lips settled on hers, and as his hands molded over her hips, reminding her of where they'd left off. Offering her tongue, she felt the deliciously cold kiss heating, then burning through her as his strong, greedy hands lifted the hem of her dress. Pulling it up, his palms grazed the sides of her cotton panties, then settled on her waist. His gravelly words against her lips were lazy and breathless and touched her womanly core. "Sorry it took me so long to get back to you."

She leaned away, letting him string kisses along her neck. She could barely think. "What held you up, Sleet?"

"Oh, you know, Ryder. I was braving a blizzard." The deep, barely audible, lust-touched chuckle that sounded between his kisses spilled right into her blood. "But I just kept thinking of the carrot dangling in front of me."

Her voice was raspy in a way she'd never heard before. "Carrot?"

"Yeah, you."

"Glad you're back. I—" Her breath was cut off as he urged her to arch against where he was so hard. When she did, her insides got crazy and jittery.

His ragged voice caught on her splintered nerves. "Your trunk's a mess," he managed, brushing back her hair and kissing the base of her throat. "Looks like you wiped out the place."

Her voice was unsteady. "I did." As another wave of heat suffused her, so did a rush of anxiety. What if he thought she wasn't so hot in the sack? What if he saw her body and was no longer interested? As if to somehow prove her female power, she boldly slid her hands over his chest, grasping strands of chest hair. Touching him as she'd never touched Buck, she played with his nipples, rolling them between her thumb and fingers until he moaned, "Oh, Ryder, what you do to a man."

She kept going, maybe too fast, as his lips found hers again. Touching each new inch of him, she explored his flat belly and ribs while they kissed. And then she unzipped his pants. Her hand shook as she slid it inside, over his boxer shorts, and then it shook even more as she squeezed the length of him, feeling the hardness and heat. She glided her fingers along the shaft, but he pulled back, his voice a soft pant.

"Nikki," he said, brushing his lips across her cheek. "Slow down."

"But…" As much as she wanted him to know she could please him, she stopped the intimate caress.

Leaning back another fraction, he looked at her with eyes that were impossibly gentle in the dark. "What?" he managed.

Her cheeks burned and her breath caught. "I…I just wanted to make you feel good." Despite the languid heat coursing through her, she was panicking. This man was rich. Sophisticated. Talented. And probably still in love with his ex-wife.

"Good?" He loosed a half moan, half chuckle and caught her hand, sliding it back to where his jeans were open. "You've been feeling how good you make me feel." Lifting both their hands, he stroked her cheek. "But you're going to feel good, too."

Suddenly she felt very confused. "Oh, Sleet," she said shakily, her heart thudding. "What are you doing to me?"

"Making you a woman."

Damn him for being so perceptive. She swallowed again. But nothing could calm her strangely wired body; her skin felt too sensitive, her breathing too shallow, her heart was beating too hard. His hand came between her legs, and their labored breaths mingled at the brief touch. Somehow, she wound up on the bed with his knee sliding between her thighs, the soft, worn denim of his jeans gliding high on her thigh. She felt so nervous she had to try to talk. "Geez…uh, where were the condoms?"

"With the rest of the medicine cabinet. Somewhere between the aspirin and Comtrex." He eased her dress over her head, and as his starved gaze fell to her bra, his voice turned to gravel again. "They were buried under a shirt I'd love to see you in."

She was so nervous, she wanted to tell him she'd never been with anybody but Buck, but her mouth was dry as cotton, dryer still when he didn't lift his eyes from her bra. "Sweater?" she croaked.

Gently, both his hands molded over the simple white cotton cups. "No," he whispered. "A tank top that would barely cover your skin. This skin." He unhooked the front catch of the bra. "This pretty skin."

His hands, warm now from touching her, cupped over her bare breasts. She'd always thought her body was too boyish, since she was long-waisted, with low hips and only handfuls of breasts. But the fingers exploring her stiffened nipples made her forget she'd ever felt anything less than beautiful. So did the tender wonder in Jon's eyes. Especially when he reached behind him, tugged her baseball cap from his back jeans pocket, and sweetly snuggled it on her head, huskily saying, "Wouldn't want you to feel buck naked."

Somehow, she managed a laugh. "Please don't use the word buck."

He chuckled softly at the wordplay, then promised, "After you make love to me, you'll never think about him again."

"Talk about ego." But Nikki was pretty sure he was right. She reached for him again, but he merely whispered, "Don't go getting anxious again. It's my turn." And then he explored her thoroughly, until he was hiking his knee higher, forcing her thighs further apart. Slipping off her panties, he opened her intimately with a finger stroke, revealing the source of her pleasure. Feeling agitated, she tried to fight the moisture gathering there, but he continued to touch, another hand molding her breast while his mouth found her nipple, suckling.

"Oh, Sleet," she murmured huskily.

"Don't ask me to stop, Ryder," came a sweet, soft taunt. "You know how tough you are. You can take it." But she couldn't, she really couldn't. With every kiss, Jon Sleet was stripping away her false bravado, and the finger he gently pushed inside her made her cry out now with crushing vulnerability. Arching her hips, she felt him go deeper and she thrust out her breasts for his tongue. "Sleet," she rasped, hoping she didn't sound as overwhelmed as she felt. "You're pretty damn good at this." He was making her whole body burn.

Right before his mouth captured hers again, he said, "You don't even know how good yet." And then he kissed her hard, sending damp fire down to where she'd gotten so moist, and to where his practiced fingers were eliciting an empty gnawing in her womb. Dammit, Sleet, she fumed moments later. She felt hot all over now because of him. Agitated. Frustrated. If something didn't happen soon…

She suddenly whimpered.

His hopelessly kind voice came from somewhere out of the dark. "Put your arms around me, Nikki."

She flung them around his neck, so she was holding him tight when she climaxed. Still deep-kissing her mouth, he let his tongue send sweet dark sensations though her as she shattered.

After that, he was too lost to soothe her. Instead he gasped, his finger still deep inside her. "Oh, Nikki," he managed, his voice broken. Not a moment later, he rolled away, stood and crossed the room. Watching him, her eyes fell over his broad shoulders and the smoothness of his skin, then shifted down to the hard muscles of his backside and thighs—a sight that made her ache to have more of him. Emotion pulled at her as she became more conscious of their many differences—of how small he made her feel, of how much more soft and shapely. He was all hard, sleek muscle covered with hair. And when he turned, her eyes sought his aroused manhood, nestled in a tangled pelt. Right now, it was all the proof of her femininity she needed. Maybe it was all she'd ever need.

As easily as breathing, he put on a condom. As he came back across the room, she sat up to meet him. Her skin was burning with the fever of need and Jon was lying between her legs, his voice raw as he guided himself into her dampness.

He went slow, pushing in each inch of his heat until she cried out for another release. Again and again, her lost whimpers brought him to her—his mouth finding hers to kiss, his hips thrusting, filling her with shared pleasure. And when he plunged with a last deep kiss, he pulled her with him into a darkness that a woman could only share with one man—her lover. It was a place from which Nikki never wanted to return.

NIKKI HAD BEEN so worried about what they'd say or how they'd act afterward, but now she simply smiled and said, "Maybe we should have gotten dressed."

"I like you like this." He untied the belt of her robe, opened the sides, and gazed at her breasts in the light of the kitchen as his warm hands snuggled around her waist. Leaning back, he kissed each nipple, smiling when they stiffened against his tongue.

"Uh…" Feeling suddenly uncomfortable, she glanced around. Didn't he know how powerful their lovemaking had felt? That she needed to step back and process it? "I thought you were hungry."

He looked up, his moss green eyes dancing. Before now, they'd held such sadness that she hadn't guessed they could sparkle so much. "Are you kidding?" he said, retying her robe. "I'm starved."

He was wearing a robe as well, and the whispery dark silk slid against his body when he moved, outlining his powerful form as he opened the refrigerator. He lifted a plate of fried chicken to the counter, then poured two glasses of milk. He didn't bother to sit down, but leaned against the counter, holding out a chicken leg. She took a bite.

"Thanks, Sleet," she said softly.

Kissing a crumb from her lip, he handed her another drumstick. "Here. Have your own."

For long moments, they munched silently. When she tossed away a last bone, he lifted her hand and licked each finger clean. "Told you I'd want a midnight snack."

She smiled. "But who knew we'd be sharing it?"

He shrugged, echoing, "Who knew?"

Polishing off her milk, she let him dab her mustache with the corner of a paper towel. He was so easy. Obviously a man who'd spent time around a woman. *A wife he's probably still in love with.* Nikki pushed aside the unwanted thought and glanced toward the window. "Think the plows will make it up here tomorrow?"

"If they don't, we won't make it off the hill. Maybe not until the next day."

Make it off the hill. She knew the words shouldn't bother her. Jon and Christy were getting along, and she wasn't needed. What happened tonight was nothing more than a brief affair, something to while away some snowbound hours....

But she hadn't expected something so perfect, something that would touch so many parts of her...and now she was in way over her head. How was she going to deal with the emotions? How could she not fall for a man who'd loved her body as he had? She wished she had the nerve to ask him how he felt about her.

He said, "Maybe the phones work now."

"Might as well give them another try."

He kissed her lightly, then crossed the room and lifted the phone from its usual place on the counter. Coming back toward her, he picked up the receiver and listened. "Still dead." He recradled it, then glanced over his shoulder, suddenly frowning.

She raised an eyebrow. "What?"

He didn't answer.

Her eyes followed his along the floor. And then she squinted. The phone cord wasn't connected to the wall. It wasn't apparent until he'd taken the phone off the counter. Leaning, he picked up the end. "It's been cut."

When he glanced up at her, the suspicion in his eyes took her by complete surprise. Right before he strode from the room, he said, "Wait here."

She tapped her foot impatiently, wondering what was happening. Moments later, Jon returned with two more phones and plunked them down on the kitchen table. "Someone's cut all the cords."

Fury suddenly flooded her. "Geez, Sleet. I guess you're accusing me?"

He glanced around. "Who else is here?"

"Oh, you," she burst out, her Kentucky accent deepening with the emotions and twanging like a banjo. "You don't believe for a minute I'd do such a thing! You're just using this to push me away! God, it's like how you denied Christy was your daughter." She stamped her bare foot on the floor. "You know what, Sleet? You're a crazy man!"

Ignoring her outburst, he leaned forward, his eyes serious, his stance saying he wouldn't tolerate deviousness. "Who are you?" he demanded. "And why did you and that little girl come here?"

Chapter Seven

Jon grunted softly, prodding King's underbelly with his boot heels and squinting against the white sunlight that glanced off the snow-covered horse trail leading to town. He was still kicking himself for accusing Nikki of cutting the phone cords last night. After cussing him out, proving her brothers had taught her some choice words in addition to how to play poker, she'd gone to her and Christy's bedroom, slamming the door.

She'd been right, too. He had been pushing her away. Last night had been too intense, too intimate. He'd taken her more than once, taken her until she mewled like a kitten in his arms. But how much could he offer her—or anyone? And he did wonder which of these two cut his phone cords.

He sighed. "C'mon, Nikki, quit squirming."

Nikki ignored him. She was still furious. Seated in front of him on King's saddle, she turned around, staring past him at Christy. Grimacing, he wished the snowplows had come. That way, he could have driven his truck to the sheriff's office. At least the mountain trails were now navigable.

She called out, "Are you *sure* you're all right back

there, hon? It's *awfully* cold. Can you feel all your fingers and toes? If you can't wiggle them, Christy, let your daddy and me know. That means you have frostbite.''

Jon winced. ''Christy's fine. It's not as cold as yesterday, which we spent outdoors.'' Turning, he checked on Christy, anyway. The leads he'd buckled on each side of King's halter were secure; they ran along the horse's flanks and hooked to Jenny's sled, so the horse could pull it through the snow.

Christy waved assurance by wiggling her fingers. ''I'm not frostbit, and I like King pulling me! It'd be even more fun if we went faster! Can we? I'll give you some big fat kisses!''

Jon's tone was gruff. ''No.'' He bit back another sigh, feeling lucky he'd discovered the child's pet snake in her coat pocket on the way out the door. Christy apparently needed to be frequently interrogated and searched.

Nikki squirmed uncomfortably again. Great. She was making sure he understood that the contact between her back and his chest was distasteful. ''Sit still,'' he said through clenched teeth.

''This saddle isn't big enough for two, Jon.''

He tried and failed to tamp down the traitorous huskiness of his voice. ''No kidding.''

''And I can't help but worry about your daughter.''

''If you were *that* worried, you would have ridden the other horse, so Christy could ride with me.''

''I'm a cabdriver,'' Nikki said over her shoulder. ''Not a pioneer. I mean, who do I look like, Sleet? Betsy What's-her-face, who made the flag?''

''Ross. Betsy Ross.'' His voice remained surprisingly calm. ''Now calm down.''

"I am calm." Keeping one hand on the pommel, she used the other to grab the bill of her baseball cap, pulling it more firmly down. "I'm just afraid your daughter could catch a cold. She could get sick. She—"

"Yeah, that's me—" Jon's breath clouded the air "—the lousiest father on earth. You've made your point. Now why don't you sit still? You two'll live for another half hour."

"You mean until you can have me incarcerated for the destruction of your property?"

His jaw setting, he raised his eyes to where patches of cerulean sky glimmered through the thick, snow-laden foliage. An annoyingly long strand of Nikki's hair blew out from beneath her cap and teased his cheek, feeling like silk. "I didn't say you destroyed my telephones."

"You implied it."

Grimly, Jon prodded King's underbelly again with his boot heel. The last thing he wanted to do was argue. Or go into town. He hadn't seen Steve Warwick since last March when Steve had come up the hill to invite him to a potluck, saying Jon needed to start involving himself with the community again. Roaring mad, Jon had told Steve to mind his own damn business.

"You're my best buddy," Steve shouted. "I used to respect you. Everybody did. But you've turned into one mean SOB. What would Mary think of the way you're living now?"

Nobody talked to Jon Sleet that way. Especially not that night, since he'd knocked back a few cold ones. He'd lunged at Steve like a battering ram. It had been a helluva fight, too, with him and Steve rolling on the ground, grappling like roughhousing kids until they were both bruised and bloody. It was hardly the first time; they'd been finding excuses to clobber each other since first grade. But last March, when they'd finally gotten up and brushed off their knees, they weren't still friends.

Jon eased King through a narrow passage, ducking a pine branch that was heavy with snow. A jay swooped, and emotion suddenly pulled inside him. He'd forgotten the quiet beauty of the mountains. He'd forgotten how peaceful it had been to ride here with Mary, and how much fun he and Steve had when they were kids and came here to play cowboys and Indians.

Hell, he'd forgotten a lot of things. He glanced at Nikki. Such as lust. Today he felt more alive than he had in years. Still angry at the cards fate had dealt him, but alive. He was noticing the sun, the singing birds and the crunch of King's hooves on the hard-packed snow. At least until the trail started swimming before his eyes, and he was only remembering how his and Nikki's intimacy had reduced her to moans that shuddered clear through him.

Damn. He almost wished he didn't know how vulnerable she looked when she climaxed. Staring at her flyaway hair now, he wondered what he was going to do. His initial attraction had graduated to a need. And he was too old for her. Thirty-one to her twenty-three, which meant an eight-year difference. Of course, when he'd asked her age last night, she'd teased him about being too old to keep up, and he'd turned the tables, holding her wrists above her head on the pillows and taunting her with slow thrusts inside her, until she sobbed, "Oh, Sleet, I take it back."

But was there more to all this than met the eye? Could she be really from Stern, Wylie and Morrow? Why else would his phone be sabotaged? Her car wouldn't start, either, so he had to wonder if it had been disabled.

Suddenly, she said, "I did not cut those cords."

"I know, but I didn't, either, Nikki." His arms tightened at her sides, and he told himself it was because he needed to get a better grip on the reins.

"Are you sure?"

He squinted at the back of her head. "Why would I cut my own phone wires?"

Her voice was low. "To keep me around as a baby-sitter until we got off the hill and you could return your daughter to her mother."

He bit back a groan. "Eventually, you'll understand what a mistake you're making."

"Jon," she said tightly, "by this afternoon the snowplow would have come. They said so on the local news." Her voice rose. "And if you'd been less anxious to get rid of Christy and me, we could have driven. We didn't have to ride through this dang wilderness on horseback like pioneers—"

"Hey," Christy shouted. "Did you say *pioneers,* Nikki? If we're pioneers, can Jon be a cute Apache who's capturing us?"

"No he can't be a cute Apache," Nikki stated. Lowering her voice, she whispered, "How could you think I cut your phone wires after...after...?" *After we made love.* "Not that what happened last night matters—"

She was fishing for information about how he felt about her. "Now's not a good time to rehash last night."

She wrenched around so fast in the saddle that King trotted sideways. "I'm not rehashing! I don't care about it! We don't even know each other, Sleet."

He didn't know what he felt yet, so his voice turned cool. "Maybe we should keep it that way."

"Maybe we should." After a long silence, she added, "I just don't understand why you're so pissed."

"Because my phone lines were cut."

Her voice spiked up. "But I didn't do it!"

"Please quit fighting!" A choked sob suddenly sounded behind them. "I did it, okay? And Nikki, you're not supposed to say 'pissed' because it's a cussword."

Nikki sighed. "Sorry."

"Whoa." Jon drew up the reins, halting King. Turning, he glared behind him at Christy. "*You* cut the phone cords?"

She nodded.

Hadn't he suspected that? This was the most devious child he'd ever met. "Why?"

She stared back mutely. Only her small face was visible, the rest of her was bundled up in the red snowsuit and hat.

Uttering a soft, barely audible string of oaths, Jon gave up, turned around, clucked his tongue, and said, "Giddy up, King." As soon as he dropped these two at Steve's office, his life would get back to normal. Nothing had felt better than making love with Nikki, but he didn't have the energy to chase love anymore. His love life was over. Forever. By tonight he'd be numb and warm.

Sure, he'd be lonely. But he'd be safe from what

Nikki Ryder did to him last night. Safe from her kisses. And safe from her love.

"DEAR HEAVEN, are my eyes deceiving me?" An elderly woman with blue-rinsed hair, watery eyes to match, and a Carolina accent as thick as mud peered at Nikki through round wire-rim glasses. She smiled. "I'm Mrs. Honey. Folks sometimes call me Mrs. Honey Pie. I own the store. Did I just see Jon Sleet drop you off?"

Dumped her on her rear end in the snow was more like it. Nikki nodded. "In a manner of speaking."

"Oh," the woman said simply.

Hardly wanting to talk about Jon, Nikki made a show of studying items on the counter, checking the prices on jam jars and reading the labels on cracker spreads. *How humiliating,* she thought. When they arrived in town and found a sign on the sheriff's door indicating he was out for lunch, Jon had dumped her and Christy like so much refuse in front of the general store.

"Go inside and wait," he'd said.

She didn't even let her father and brothers take that dictatorial tone. "What do you think I'm going to do?" she'd snapped. "Walk back to True Pines? Move back in with Buck? Hitchhike to my father's in Kentucky?"

"I wouldn't put it past you," Jon said. When it came to fighting, he was apparently the type who always had to have the last word. But then, so did Nikki. He'd hitched King to a post, then headed toward a diner to find the sheriff, while she'd sullenly trudged inside the general store.

As if she *could* go anywhere else. Had Jon completely forgotten that her cab was being held hostage at his house? *Oooh.* Nikki really didn't appreciate his blaming the phone-cord incident on her, even if she was glad his daughter had confessed. Poor Christy was so obviously trying to get her dad's attention. *Geez...so am I.*

It was humiliating to admit, but Nikki was never going to forget how he'd awakened her body last night. She couldn't even look at him today without remembering his face at the peak of arousal—how he thrust back his hair while his jaw went slack and his barely opened eyes possessed her. Against her will, she'd started dreaming that they had a chance together. She wanted him, and she'd grown so fond of his little girl....

And then he'd accused her of clipping his phone cords. She'd lain awake all night in angry shock. How could he think she'd do that? And why? So that she could stay here and seduce him or something? Or was he really ready to grab any excuse, no matter how flimsy, to push her out of his life?

She fought against a wave of depression. Trying to take her mind off him, she stuffed her gloves in her pockets, then took off her bomber jacket and hung it on a coat tree. She glanced around. As they'd passed the iron chairs on the porch of the general store, Christy had excitedly announced this was the store her dad wrote about in his books. "Mrs. Honey's" was stenciled in arching red script on the front window, and inside, the place smelled of the fresh, perking coffee that was free to customers. Feeling calmer, Nikki breathed in scents from the herbs and loose teas in jars while Christy passed a rack of books on home remedies and aromatherapy, then busied herself with kids' books.

Nikki realized Mrs. Honey was staring at her. "Honestly," Mrs. Honey said, as if she couldn't believe it. "That was Jon Sleet from Mistletoe Mountain?"

How many Jon Sleets could there be in Holiday Hamlet? Nikki nodded. "Yes."

"And you are?"

"Nikki. Nikki Ryder." Since the older woman extended her hand, Nikki thrust hers out and shook.

"And you are a...a *friend* of Jon's?"

At best, Nikki felt like a baby-sitter who'd been kept on retainer until Jon could shuttle Christy back to her mother's. At worst, she felt like a dumped girlfriend. "I guess you could say we're friends." Recalling last night's intimacies, a flush stole up her cheeks that wasn't lost on Mrs. Honey.

The older woman pressed her hand to her heart. "I'm so glad Jon's found a new gal and a little romance. Lord knows, he deserves it. We hardly see him in town anymore, you know. Why, ever since his wife and little girl died, well—"

"What?" The hum of the store suddenly seemed louder, and the sunlight reflecting off the snow and streaming through the windows was achingly bright. Surely, Nikki hadn't heard right. "His wife and little girl did *what?*"

The woman looked stricken. "Oh, you didn't know?"

"Well—" Nikki tried her best to recover. "Jon and I only recently met. I mean...he does have a daughter, a *living* daughter." She glanced around, but Christy had conveniently vanished.

Mrs. Honey shook her head. "Well, no. No, he doesn't. Mary was Jon's high-school sweetheart. They both grew up right here, you know. And they only had the one child, sweet little Jenny."

"Please…" Nikki felt as if the floor was dropping out from under her. If Christy really wasn't Jon's daughter, who was she? Nikki's heart hammered. "Please…tell me what happened."

Mrs. Honey leaned her elbows on the counter. "Now, I'm not one for gossip, mind you," she warned. "But I can tell you that Jon lived for Mary. And as far as he was concerned, his little girl, Jenny, hung the moon and stars."

"Really?" Nikki managed. *Oh, geez. He's not divorced.*

Mrs. Honey began talking about the ice storm that had hit the East Coast two Christmases ago. "I kid you not, the weight of that ice was so heavy that power lines fell. A man up in Holiday Hollow got electrocuted and Doe Run—that's the big two-lane up yonder—wasn't even passable."

Suspecting what was coming, Nikki felt vaguely ill.

"Well, I don't like to recount people's tragedies any more than I like to gossip, but I can say that Mary and Jenny were coming back from Mary's mother's over in True Pines. Jon told them to stay put, but they couldn't be without him on Christmas.…"

Nikki's heart thudded dully in her throat, pumping blood that felt strangely thick. Jenny? His daughter was named Jenny? Lord, he'd written about a girl named Jenny. Nikki touched the bill of her baseball cap to steady herself.

Mrs. Honey sighed. "Their car went out of control. 'Course, Sheriff Warwick delivered the news during the annual Christmas Eve party we used to have up at the old inn, and needless to say, Santa didn't show up that night with his reindeer-driven sleigh. That's when everybody realized it was probably Jon who'd been dressing up as Santa all those years. Guess he's still got the reindeers, since Oscar over at Benson's delivers feed for them.''

Mrs. Honey's blue eyes grew distant. ''That sleigh was something to behold,'' she continued wistfully. ''Gold with red velvet seats. Why, you should have heard the little ones ooh and aah as Santa stepped out in his long red velvet robe with the white fur lapels.'' Mrs. Honey suddenly chuckled. ''It was enough to make a little old lady like me believe in Christmas again. 'Course, things are right different now. Back when Jon's children's books hit the *New York Times* list, we had a tourist boom around here. The old inn was full. Folks from the tristate brought their kids here during the holidays, so they could see the town where little Jenny's adventures took place.''

''So, Jenny was Jon's daughter, not a fictional character?'' Nikki managed.

Mrs. Honey smiled kindly. ''Well, she was both. And Jon's pride and joy. Oh, how he loved children! It was a sight when he came down the mountain on that sleigh, then propped the little ones on his knees to hear their Christmas wishes. Then off he'd go again—as if back to the North Pole to fill those toy orders by morning.'' Mrs. Honey laughed. ''Well, maybe it wasn't Jon Sleet at all. Maybe it really was Santa Claus. I've heard tell that no child in this town has ever not gotten what they wanted for Christmas.''

Nikki's heart did a flip-flop. Jon Sleet was a constant revelation. Every time she learned something new about him, she became even more intrigued. What had he been like two years ago, before tragedy touched his life?

"Well," Mrs. Honey continued, "this year, I considered putting my artificial tree in the shop again, but I suddenly thought of how much Jenny loved my decorations. Shirley O'Hare over at the beauty parlor said the same thing. The Sleets were such a vital part of this community that…well, I think we all went into mourning with Jon." She smiled gently, glancing around for Christy. "That adorable little one who came in with you looks a little like Jon's Jenny might have been, with her blond hair and green eyes."

Christy really isn't his daughter. Nikki glanced around in panic as the truth continued sinking in. The cozy shop, with its barrels of goods and sturdy iron furniture suddenly seemed surreal. "No one here celebrates Christmas anymore?" Nikki forced herself to say, feeling incapable of any more small talk.

"'Course we do, but it's never been the same. Oscar Benson dresses up in a Santa suit, but the kids keep waiting for that gorgeous gold reindeer-driven sleigh."

Nikki barely heard. Her mind had reeled back to square one. "They died?" she repeated in a soft whisper. How had she convinced herself Jon was divorced? She thought of the untouched bedrooms with his wife and daughter's things, the funny postcards. *Guess this explains why Mary Sleet didn't take her belongings.* "Did you really say his wife and daughter *died?*"

Mrs. Honey sighed. "Such a tragedy for us all."

Nikki felt she'd spent the last ten minutes in a trance, lulled by the woman's soft Southern accent.

Now she mulled over the details of her meeting with Christy outside the airport. The girl had barked out Jon's address, seemingly knowing where she was going. And she'd seemed familiar with his house, but probably only because she'd read about Jenny's adventures. What was going on here? Her eyes darted around, but Christy was still nowhere to be found. "Did you see the little girl who came in with me?"

Mrs. Honey frowned. "Why, I declare. Your little one *was* right next to the book rack..."

Your little one. Nikki let that slide, having no idea how to explain her relationship to Christy. Nikki raised her voice. "Christy?"

She was hiding. Well, if she wasn't Jon's daughter, that certainly explained Jon's lack of parental behavior. Nikki's heart skipped a beat, and she tried not to think of how she'd pushed Jon and Christy to spend time together. Had Jon really never laid eyes on Christy before she and Nikki were snowbound? *She's not my daughter.* How many times had he tried to tell her? And why was the child pretending she was related to Jon? This was all so strange....

"If she reappears," Nikki said loudly, her eyes scanning the room, "could you tell her to wait right here for me?"

Oblivious to Nikki's confusion, Mrs. Honey smiled. "Oh, I love children, and won't mind watching her in the least."

Feeling completely wretched, Nikki headed for the door—and Jon. She didn't even pause to get her coat.

DEEP SIGH. Everything was going wrong!

Because Christy was such a bad girl, Jon was going to hate her guts! How was she supposed to know what had happened to Jenny? The awful news made Christy's heart hurt and her tummy ache. This was ten times worse than disobeying Jon earlier. If Christy could go back in time, she'd put Noodles back in his aquarium, the way Jon thought she had.

Reaching into her pocket, she petted Noodles guiltily, and with her other hand, she gripped the stick of a grape lollipop Mrs. Honey had given her. She wanted to cry, but she had to hang on to her wits and fix this mess.

"Thank you so much, Mrs. Honey," she managed, fighting back tears and talking around the lollipop. "I knew you'd give me some candy, because Jon wrote about you in his books."

Mrs. Honey's eyes twinkled. "You're welcome, little one. Now let's see. Would you like to play hide-and-seek again while we wait for your mama?"

"Nope. My, uh, mama will be back soon."

But Nikki wasn't her mother! Cringing, Christy stared at the door, considering running away again. She hadn't meant to hurt anybody, least of all Jon. How could she have pretended to be Jenny when Jenny was dead? No girl on earth had ever done anything *that* bad before.

No wonder Jon was so sad. Nobody even celebrated Christmas here anymore! Even Santa got disgusted and quit coming. Christy knew Jon had never dressed up as Santa because Jon would feel too stupid wearing a funny red suit. No, the Santa Claus Mrs. Honey described was the real one. Christy had been hiding under the counter, so she'd heard every word.

"I'm so glad you and your mama are visiting Jon," Mrs. Honey said now. "Now, tell me all about your trip. How long are you staying? And how has Jon been entertaining you?''

"How has Jon been..." It was then that Christy got a great idea. Using a footstool, she hopped onto the counter. "Well, Jon's been keeping us busy!" she enthused, her spirits lifting. "You remember how much he used to like decorating for Christmas? Well, he put us right to work. He cut a tree and baked us cookies...."

"He baked?"

Christy nodded. "He burnt the cookies, but his cocoa's pretty good." She sighed knowingly. "Jon hates that everybody in town feels sorry for him. He says that's why he doesn't even come here anymore. He feels like a big mean Grinch."

Mrs. Honey looked uncertain. "A Grinch?"

Christy nodded vigorously. "Sure, because he steals everybody's Christmas, even though he doesn't want to."

"Hmm." Mrs. Honey's face brightened. "While we wait for your mama, I'll keep you busy, too. Why don't we get out my artificial tree? Jenny used to love it, and I think you will, too, little one. It's back in my storeroom."

Christy tried to look surprised by Mrs. Honey's suggestion. "You've decided to put up your Christmas tree, Mrs. Honey?"

"Well, if Jon's decorating this year, I don't see why not. It'll spruce up the place, no pun intended."

Christy giggled. "I get it. A spruce is a tree."

"You're one smart little girl," Mrs. Honey declared.

Smarter than Mrs. Honey knows, thought Christy.

Just then, the phone on the counter rang and Mrs.

Honey picked it up. "Honey's General... Not only did I *see* Jon, but I've got his new girlfriend's daughter with me in the store, and we're about to get the holiday decorations from the storeroom." Smiling, Mrs. Honey held up an index finger to indicate she'd be through gossiping in a minute.

"Take your time," Christy urged graciously, knowing exactly what was coming.

"Well," Mrs. Honey said into the phone receiver in a low, conspiratorial tone, "I heard Jon decorated the house this year...probably we didn't see the lights because of the power outages. Anyway, since he's in town and doesn't mind, I don't see why we shouldn't throw the party at the inn this year.... I know, Pam, but it *has* been two years. Besides, it'll draw in customers and we need them. As they say, there are still a couple of shopping days 'til Christmas."

While Mrs. Honey listened, Christy caught herself eyeing an open jar of lollipops and thinking about pocketing a cherry one. But that would be stealing. Crossing her arms tightly over her chest, she held her breath, hoping the wicked urge would pass. At this rate, she'd never quit being naughty before Christmas.

"Now that you mention it," Mrs. Honey was saying, "I think yours is a splendid idea. Why don't you have Liz Allen call Lester? He's got the keys to the municipal building where we used to keep the lights for the trees on North Main..."

"Deep sigh," Christy whispered as the business owners talked. She wasn't sure how this would help Jon, but getting the town spruced up was a step in the right direction. Besides, if Holiday Hamlet was in full Christmas regalia, maybe the real Santa would come. Christy hoped so, since only he could grant the wish

closest to her heart—to see her mom and dad reunited.

STEVE WAS NOWHERE to be found. Already, Jon had
tried Prancer's Diner, the Ponderosa Club, and San-
dra's Specialty Sandwich Shop, which pretty much
covered the eateries in Holiday Hamlet. He'd even
spent time in a phone store, picking up replacement
phones, as well as two cell phones, so they wouldn't
be stuck on the mountain without communication
again. He was crossing North Main, feeling relieved
he hadn't run into too many old acquaintances, and
still kicking himself for being such a bastard last night
to Nikki, when he saw her barreling toward him—
baseball cap in hand, her Frye boots churning up
snow, her earlier anger replaced with what looked like
panic.

Something was wrong.

Any anger he'd felt drained from him. Images of
the ice storm filled his mind, and he remembered the
split second before Steve Warwick told him his wife
and child were gone.

And then Jon started running toward Nikki. She
hadn't bothered with a coat, was wearing only jeans
and a sweater, and her hair was blowing wildly
around her face. As Jon got closer, he was aware
something hurt...what was it? And then he realized
it was his chest. It had constricted with such foreboding that there was no denying what Nikki meant to
him. He could love her. Maybe he already did. She'd
come into his life so unexpectedly, pulling him out
of himself and touching his heart.

She ran right into him, pulling up short in his arms
in the middle of North Main, and as her hands splayed

on his chest for balance, her boot slipped on the ice. Simultaneously, he put down the bag with the phones and caught her, wrapping his arms around her waist. His voice was hoarse from worry. ''What happened, Nikki? Is Christy all right?''

She only gazed up at him. Despite his worry, he registered the lovely things the cold did to her complexion, how her pink cheeks made her brown eyes look larger and more solemn. Her panting breath on the cold air looked smokey, and it warmed his lips, drawing his attention to her chapped red mouth; if he traversed inches, he'd be soothing those chafed lips with his own. He squinted, deciding maybe he was mistaken. Maybe nothing was wrong. ''Nikki?''

She still didn't answer, only shivered.

''Why did you— Oh, never mind. Here.'' Quickly, his gloved hand slid between them, flicking open the buttons of his oilskin coat. He spread the flannel-lined sides, drew her close, and then folded his arms around her, closing her inside.

''I—I need to talk to you.'' She shivered, her face hooded by the coat he held around her, her chin chafing against his heavy cable-knit wool sweater.

He needed to talk to her, too. He wanted her, but she had to understand he couldn't offer much emotionally. Maybe he could love her, but he wasn't sure how much. After Mary and Jenny, he couldn't make commitments that left him vulnerable to such destructive pain. He couldn't bear ever having other children. But if Nikki could accept him on those terms, then maybe.... He realized he had vague ideas about offering her a place to stay while she got on her feet from leaving Buck, just until she made up with her father.

"We need to get you back inside," he murmured. But then he merely stood there, holding her tighter in the middle of the snowy road, oblivious of prying eyes. "If nothing's wrong, what sent you running outside like this?" he coaxed. "I was coming for you, as soon as I found Steve."

She still didn't say anything.

"You're usually so talkative, Nikki. This isn't like you." His eyes searched hers and suddenly it was too much—those large, dark teardrop eyes, her pale skin, the shivers of her body against his that reminded him of the shivers of passion he'd elicited from her last night. He licked his lips, feeling the cold air tingle where he'd dampened them. Unbidden heat pooled low in his groin, even though he knew now that he wanted more than sex from her, just not so much emotion he'd hurt again. He rubbed a thumb down her cheek. "C'mon, I know we were fighting. But you can talk to me."

She said something soft, but a gust of wind caught the words, and as Jon ducked lower to hear, another rush of wind blew strands of her hair across his dampened lips. He let them stay there, not bothering to brush them away.

She looked as if she wanted to take back something she'd done or said. "Why didn't you tell me why Christy couldn't be your daughter?"

So that was it. He leaned back a fraction. "Eve Honey always was the biggest gossip in town. Did she give you my whole life story?"

Nikki nodded, looking guilty as hell, and once again, he noted what the cold was doing to her— making her eyes so stark, dark against her windflushed cheeks.

"Don't you cry," he suddenly protested as those gorgeous eyes filled with tears. Blinking, she tried to hold back, but tears fell like the snowflakes that had begun to drift between them.

"Mrs. Honey told me everything." Lifting a hand between them, she covered her mouth in horror. "And if—if you're not Christy's father...then who is she? Where did she come from? Who are her parents? What—"

He took her hand, removed it from her lips and silenced her with a quick brush of his mouth. His soft, seductive murmur curled around her like the wind. "Don't worry, Nikki. Steve Warwick's the sheriff, and he's an old friend of mine. He'll do everything he can." Despite the rift between them, Steve was a professional. He'd do his job and find Christy's parents.

"Oh, Jon..." Worried tears and tears of anger splashed down Nikki's cheeks again. "Somewhere that little girl's parents are fearing the worst, and it's all my fault. I—I first saw her at the airport. But what if she didn't come from inside? She was already on the curb when I picked her up, and I didn't see any other cars waiting. No one seemed to be looking..."

"It's okay." Lightly dampening his lips by licking them again, Jon then grazed his mouth ever so gently, back and forth, over hers. "That's why we're here now. So you can tell the sheriff everything you know."

She stared up, her eyes imploring, her voice catching. "But you could have convinced me."

"I tried," he reminded gently. "I said she wasn't mine."

"But..." Nikki's eyes said he could have forced

her to believe. And he could have. There was plenty of evidence in the house to prove it wasn't probable.

"We were stuck in a blizzard." He tilted his head, a slight shrug lifting his shoulders. "What was the use of worrying you when there was nothing you could do?"

"Oh, Sleet, you're making me feel even worse. I'm a horrible person." Her teeth chattered again, and he pulled her closer, feeling touched that she'd run outside to make amends to him without remembering her coat.

"I didn't want to talk about my wife and daughter," he added softly. "I didn't know you."

A soft sob came from the back of her throat.

Not knowing what to do, Jon kissed her again. "C'mon, you shouldn't have run out in the cold like this," he whispered, though he was strangely glad she did.

She nodded toward Mrs. Honey's. "My coat's there. Christy is, too. But what if her name's not even Christy? And why has she been lying to us like this?" He started to stop her, but knew she needed to get the guilt out of her system. "And the pain I must have caused you. Telling you you were a bad—" She paused again, barely able to say it. "A bad parent. Can you ever forgive me?"

He glanced toward the shops, knowing he should urge her out of the road, even though there were no cars on North Main. He brushed her hair back from her face. "There's nothing to forgive. You know, Christy even looks a little like Jenny," he added. "And the night you two came—" He suddenly chuckled softly at the recollection, surprised he could. "I thought I'd seen a ghost."

She swallowed hard. "I just wish I'd known."

He shrugged. "Talking about Mary and Jenny was too hard. When the accident happened, I…I was in too much pain. By the time I was ready to see people again, it seemed too late." His eyes drifted over her face. "Until right now. Until I got to know you, Nikki."

Her guilt was so overwhelming, she barely seemed to have heard. "I was so sure I was helping you and your daughter mend fences. I'm so sorry I came into your life in this awful way."

He pressed a finger to her lips. "Don't say that."

She stared into his eyes. "What?"

"Just don't be sorry."

"If you don't want me to be sorry, I won't be, Jon."

Suddenly his hands were in her hair. Threading his fingers through the windblown strands, he stared back into her eyes. "*I'm* not sorry, Nikki. You'll never know how much I needed you last night. I…" Bringing a gloved hand between them, he found her naked one. As he warmed it, folding it against his chest, over his heart, it occurred to him that one storm had taken away everything he loved, and that another storm had brought him Nikki. Maybe he could even love completely again, if she was willing to wait, to take it slow. His voice turned gruff. "I'd never been with a woman other than my wife. And some days I felt like I was dying in that house. The holidays have been so hard. And then you and Christy showed up."

She sounded a little less miserable. "We did that, all right."

"You did. And I'll tell you something else. Last night scared the hell out of me, but I want you again.

All night after you stormed out, I lay there wanting. I wanted to kiss these lips.'' He brushed his mouth over hers again. ''Touch these breasts.'' He drew her closer so she'd feel the hard muscles of his chest against her. ''Last night, I wanted you so badly that I got scared and pushed you away. You were right about that. And you were right to confront me.''

''And today, Sleet?''

A smile lifted the corners of his mouth. ''Today, all I know is that I want to kiss you in the middle of North Main.'' His mouth covered hers completely then, his tongue entering just deeply enough to stroke and lingering just long enough to make his voice creak with need. ''Before we get carried away, Saint Nikki, we'd better get you back inside, where it's warm.''

''Saint Nikki.'' She smiled at the new nickname, and the faint rasp of her voice sent another shudder through him. ''Believe me, Sleet. You're already warming me up.''

Pressing his lips to hers, he whispered, ''C'mon.''

The way she squinted at him made her nose wrinkle, making her look incredibly cute. ''Where to?''

''Over there.'' Stepping back, he whisked off his coat and draped it around her. His arm followed, curling around her back. Guiding her attention, he nodded toward Mrs. Honey's store where Steve Warwick was standing on the porch, hand in hand with Christy. ''Looks like they're waiting. Maybe Steve can help us get to the bottom of this.''

Chapter Eight

"Maybe I'm the spirit of Christmas," Christy announced craftily from her perch on a metal folding chair in the middle of the sheriff's office. Wiggling her hands beneath her thighs, she swung her legs, sweeping her pointed toes back and forth. After eyeing Steve, who was still on the phone, she smiled coyly at where Jon and Nikki were leaning side by side against a metal desk with their arms crossed. "Maybe I'm the spirit of Christmas and Santa sent me to fix you two up, so you can get married and have some babies."

Flushing, Nikki narrowed her eyes. "You are *not* the spirit of Christmas, Christy."

Christy, who must have witnessed their kiss in the street, tossed her curls. "But maybe you'll get married, huh?"

"Sorry," Nikki murmured, sounding embarrassed.

A pull of emotion Jon couldn't name made him inch closer to her. Where *was* their relationship headed? Would he ever feel ready to get married again? Under his breath, he whispered, "Questioning her is useless. Believe me, I've tried before now."

From the feel of Nikki's body tensed against him,

he could tell the words didn't help much. She was shaking all over with suppressed frustration, blaming herself and worrying over the search parties that might be looking for Christy. It had damn near broken his heart to watch Nikki squeeze her eyes shut in concentration and rub her temples, desperately trying to recall every detail of her meeting with Christy while Steve scribbled down the information. Afterward, she'd wrung her hands, her voice full of angry self-reproach. "I *knew* something was wrong when she got in my cab. I *knew* something was suspicious."

Now, as Jon traced comforting circles on the back of Nikki's sweater, the rough wool unexpectedly made him think of how soft her bare skin was. "Don't worry, we'll figure this out."

She exhaled an anxious sigh. "I hope so. I just wish she'd talk."

From across the room, Steve motioned that he'd be off the phone soon, then he ran a hand through his dark blond hair and wedged the receiver between his shoulder and jaw. Turning away, he nodded. "Yeah, let us know if anyone remembers a child meeting her description.... Uh-huh, the True Pines P.D. is checking missing persons, and I've faxed a picture I took of her for distribution...."

There was a long pause, then Steve continued, "It's a tough break. No, no one blames you. The blizzard came on fast, and y'all had too many planes grounded, some of which weren't even scheduled to land. No small town airport's equipped to handle that kind of heavy traffic. Just do your best to track down the attendants, even if they're home for the holidays... Yeah, well, the woman's taxi isn't operable now, but she's good with cars and already checked the basic stuff. I sent a snowplow to clear the mountain, and a mechanic with a tow truck. Once the taxi's at the garage, I'll go over it for clues...."

When Steve hung up, Nikki's eyes searched his. "Her clothes were all lightweight."

Steve glanced at Jon. "Notice anything else?"

Jon shrugged, wishing he could say otherwise. "No."

They paused, at an impasse. During the silence, Jon's eyes met those of his old friend. They were the same soft brown Jon remembered. Steve looked good. He'd always worked out, and now he was pacing around his office with the stealthy grace of a panther. Muscles bulged beneath his pressed tan uniform shirt and matching slacks—something that had always drawn the eyes of too many women, which was probably why Steve had never bothered to marry. But he had kind eyes. They could turn steely, making even hardened thugs squirm. And yet right now, it was hard to reconcile those kind eyes with the badge, or to imagine Steve drawing and shooting the gun strapped to his hip. Of course Jon had seen his buddy pick peas off beer cans at a hundred yards enough times to know his aim could be lethal.

But that was years ago. Today they'd exchanged wary nods upon greeting, and the subtle distancing hurt. Steve was playing the consummate professional; a curtain had come down, shuttering the real Steve. Protecting him, Jon thought.

The momentary heaviness he felt as he recalled their last fight reminded him of the ice storm again. The ice had looked so incredibly heavy, pulling down everything it touched. Jon would never forget it. Now, as his gaze pulled back to the eyes of a friend he'd lost, Jon felt the weight of all that ice again. For a second, he felt as if the storm had never ended at all. And his soul felt heavy, bowing under the weight. He reached for Nikki then, rubbing his hand across her back, cupping his palm around her shoulder and squeezing. Finally, he said, "I just don't know, Steve. I went through her carry-on with a fine-tooth comb."

Steve nodded, advancing on Christy. "Only a few summer clothes," he repeated, towering over her and glowering down, looking menacing. Not that the physical threat would work. They'd already cajoled, coerced and pleaded. "Kid," he growled. "This isn't a game."

Only the slight quiver of Christy's lower lip indicated she was the least bit perturbed by what had turned into a long interrogation. "Don't bully me, Mr. Warwick," she warned fiercely.

He leaned, flexed a hand around her upper arm and glared into her eyes. "I said start talking."

"Steve…" Nikki murmured. "Don't." Turning to Christy, she said, "Please, hon. You have to help us out here."

Even as telltale guilt flickered in her gaze, Christy rolled her eyes heavenward. "This is just a good-cop, bad-cop routine," she said. "I learned it on TV, and it's not gonna work."

Stepping back, Steve looked weary. "It's not a routine," he muttered, dragging a hand distractedly through his hair again. "We're trying to get at the truth."

"Her clothes are all so nice…" Nikki said, thinking aloud and shaking her head. "Well made. Good labels."

Steve glared at Christy again, forcing her narrowed

green eyes to lock with his. Finally, she blinked. "Quit staring at me!"

Steve only came closer, piercing her with his eyes.

After another few moments, Christy's chin started quivering. "Are you gonna put bright lights on me now?" she challenged. "Maybe put me on the racketeer?"

Jon winced. "I think you mean the *rack,* Christy."

For an instant, she looked confused. Then she solemnly said, "Racketeers are bad."

Jon sighed. "Yes, racketeers are bad. But they're— Oh, never mind."

Looking into Steve's unsettling eyes again, Christy shifted uncomfortably on the metal chair and stopped swinging her feet.

"If you don't start giving me something to go on," Steve warned, "I really might get out the thumbscrews, kid."

Her eyes widened. "Uh, maybe I was supposed to go to Florida. See, it's real hot down there, so I needed summer clothes."

Jon felt a flash of temper. The kid was obviously lying, but Nikki was so desperate for a lead that she raced forward, passing Steve and kneeling in front of Christy. Nothing more than the concern in Nikki's eyes made his heart pull. The phone rang again and Steve picked it up.

"Florida?" Nikki queried.

Christy nodded. "My parents have a big boat and I have four new bikinis. There's palm trees, and you can pick oranges off the trees for orange juice...."

While Christy did her best to make the false lead sound convincing, Jon's attention shifted to Steve. The phone receiver was wedged between his chin and shoulder again, and he was nodding and listening. Periodically, his concerned eyes lifted to Jon's. Was this bad news about Christy? Had something happened to her parents in the storm? Had they been separated while traveling?

"He's right here," Steve said, looking discomfited. "I guess I could ask him."

Jon realized he was holding his breath and exhaled. Were they talking about him? "Hmm?"

Steve covered the receiver with his hand. "Some folks are talking about throwing our annual Christmas Eve bash up at the old inn." He paused, looking faintly embarrassed. "Uh, they want to know how you feel about it."

For a second, Jon's mind was in the past. Two years ago, he'd been headed to that party when the doorbell rang and Steve told him.... His eyes caught Steve's and he managed a shrug. "Why's anybody care what I think?" Nobody had asked his opinion in the past two years.

Steve fixed his eyes on Jon for long minutes. Finally, he said, "We haven't held that party for two years, Jon."

"Oh." Jon didn't know what to say. Glancing through the window, he saw some guys unloading Christmas lights from the back of a truck, and his frown deepened. Looking down from his house, he hadn't noticed any lights this year, and usually decorations went up after Thanksgiving. Now the street was dark.

Steve was still watching him, his hand over the receiver. "You never did understand what an impact you had on this town," he chided softly. "You were our hometown boy made good. When the books you wrote for Jenny sold so well, it brought in a helluva lot of business...."

No wonder Steve had accused him of being a selfish bastard. Had people around here really stopped having the annual Christmas party because of what happened to Mary and Jenny? "No," Jon managed quickly. "Of course I don't mind about the party." He wished he'd known how much everyone was affected, but Steve had tried to tell him.

Eyeing him, Steve hung up. "You know, a lot of people around here cared deeply for Mary and Jenny."

But Jon had shut them out. Fortunately, another ring of the phone stopped him from having to respond. "Warwick," Steve said into the receiver.

Nikki's voice suddenly spiked. "You're lying, Christy! You are *not* from Florida!"

Christy's eyes filled with tears. "Am, too."

"And what's this?" Lifting the flap on Christy's coat pocket, Nikki stared inside. "Jon told you not to bring that snake! And...and these!" Nikki reached into the other pocket, bringing out a handful of cherry lollipops. "Did Mrs. Honey give you these?"

Christy's voice shook. "She would have wanted me to have them."

Nikki sounded furious. "That's not what I asked."

"I stole them!" Christy suddenly cried out. "I tried not to, but I couldn't stop myself! And I don't care if I'm bad and Santa won't bring me presents. I just want one thing. I won't get it, either, not unless the real Santa comes. You can punish me all you want, too, because I'm bad and I deserve it!" Clapping her hands over her eyes, Christy burst into tears.

Nikki worriedly sighed and crossed her arms at her

waist. Jon snagged her sweater and pulled her to his side again. "I didn't mean to push," she murmured over Christy's sobs.

"We have to," he assured, not feeling half as compassionate. "She's just a kid. And we've got to find out who she is, Nikki."

When Steve hung up the phone, Jon sighed. "Like I said, she told me no one was looking for her and I believe her. For some reason, people might not know she's missing yet."

Nikki glanced up, her eyes hopeful. "You think so?"

Jon nodded, warmed by the relief in her gaze.

Steve glanced at Nikki. "That was the garage on the phone. The kid put peanut butter in your gas tank. It'll take a few hours to flush it out. After that, I'll go over the interior. I figure we can get you back on the road by tonight, and headed toward wherever you're supposed to spend Christmas."

When Nikki's eyes darted to Jon's, it was clear she hadn't thought she'd be leaving tonight. "But I feel so responsible. I...I don't think I can leave until we know where she belongs."

Jon realized again how much he wanted her to stay. Already, he'd begun listening for Nikki in the house, and looking forward to sharing the meals she made. He wanted to explore what was happening between them and, from the sudden softening of her expression, he knew he'd communicated that with his eyes.

Oblivious, Steve nodded curtly. "Good. Stick around town if you want. But you can head on back to Jon's. I'll call welfare to pick up the kid."

Nikki's hand flew to her throat. "Welfare?"

Steve shrugged. "If they can't come tonight,

there's a halfway house for runaways in town that'll take her." He glanced between Jon and Nikki. "That is, unless you want to take responsibility?"

Nikki's gaze shot to Jon's. "Can we?"

The caring in her eyes moved him. "Sure. It's the least we can do."

"Thanks, Jon," she said.

He squeezed her waist reassuringly.

While they pulled on the heavy layers of their clothes, it was decided that Jon would ride King back to the house. Nikki and Christy preceded him outside, heading for the deputy's car that would take them, now that the roads were clear. Jon had just reached the door when he felt Steve's hand on his arm, staying him. He glanced over. "What?"

"I never had the nerve to ask, but since we're having the party this year, would you mind letting me use the sleigh and Santa outfit?" Steve glanced away. "The kids...you know, they've really missed—" Cutting himself off, he said, "Well, Oscar's been dressing up, but that sleigh of yours was such a big production..."

For the second time, Jon was stunned. He'd just assumed that someone else had taken up the mantle, that things in town had gone on the same without him. "It's all yours."

Steve nodded, but didn't move away. "Look, it's really good to see you, Jon."

Feeling slightly awkward, Jon nodded. "You, too."

Their eyes met. "Uh...the little girl," Steve ventured. "She reminds me of Jenny a little."

Jon managed a nod. "Me, too." Somehow, something more seemed to be required. Determined not to make another mistake, Jon made the first move, lifting his hand and clapping Steve hard on the shoulder. Steve reached up and did the same. Briefly, they drew close, their chests brushing. Stepping back, Steve said, "Don't be a stranger."

Jon shook his head. "Call me. Or I'll call you. I'll make sure you get the sleigh. We wouldn't want the kids to go without the best possible Christmas."

Steve didn't respond, merely opened the door, but as the cold wintery air gusted inside, his glimmer of a smile said he thought Jon had just started traveling the long road back home.

NIKKI PAUSED in the stairway, turning off the lights. She turned back toward where weak downstairs lights still shined, and looked at Jon, who was on the step behind her. She said, "Ready to help tuck Christy in?"

"No." Catching her fingers, Jon pulled her back down a step. "I want to know what's made you so quiet tonight."

Turning and leaning against the wall, Nikki tilted her head, surveying him. She looked adorable in a baggy wool sweater that was skimming the thighs of tight jeans. Her hair was down, swirling around her cheeks, and her baseball cap was turned around with the bill in back. "C'mon," he prodded huskily, "what gives, Saint Nick?"

She chuckled softly.

He smiled back. "That's a nickname, no pun intended." Leaning closer, he covered her lips with his in a firm but fleeting kiss. "C'mon, what's on that devious mind?"

"Other than you?"

"Yeah, other than me."

She sighed. "Geez...I—" She glanced up the stairs, toward the room she'd been sharing with Christy. "Well, Sleet, I know it's stupid, but I've been dreading going in there. I feel so bad about the way I made her cry in Steve's office today."

"You apologized."

"I know, but—"

"And she accepted your apology." Snuggling his hands under the hem of her sweater, he settled them on the T-shirt beneath and molded the inward curve of her waist. Propelled by the heat that flooded his groin every time he touched her, he pressed against her, locking hips that fit perfectly. Good and snug, like favorite jeans.

For a second, awareness moved between them, their breaths quickening. The events of the day were forgotten, and they were new lovers who wanted nothing more than darkness and a room with a lock. Sliding his hands slowly down, he curled them over her hips and then grazed her thighs until he found her dangling hands. "You feel so good," he said raggedly, twining his fingers through hers. "And about Christy. Don't forget she's lying. We have to get the truth out of her."

Nikki glanced away, exhaling her short rush of breath against a cheek dark with evening whiskers. "I know. I guess it wasn't so much that I made her cry."

"Then what was it?"

"The way I felt. I was so mad. I know she's just a confused kid who doesn't understand all the implications of this, but…I felt I was losing control with her."

He nuzzled her face, careful not to burn her soft cheeks with his stubbled jaw. "But you *didn't*, Nikki. And sometimes with kids, you want to. I was a parent…" When sadness twisted inside him, it didn't hurt as much as it had a week ago, before Nikki came. Maybe nothing could have healed him more than her loving.

She disengaged one of her hands and brought it to his chest. "Sorry, I didn't mean to make you think about…"

He shrugged, angling his head further downward, sweeping his lips across hers again. "I was just going to say that kids can try your patience." A low throaty chuckle escaped him, then his lips curled ruefully. "The first few years, they keep you awake and dirty their diapers when you're miles from a changing station. Toddlers are worse. And when they start talking, they repeat every word you say."

She smiled against his chin, her voice raspy. "You make parenthood sound like a blast, Sleet."

He sighed, emotion pulling him. "It was." He folded a hand over where her fingers were curled on his chest. "Anyway, Nikki, I believed her when she said no one was looking for her."

"Hard to imagine. I can't figure out why her parents wouldn't look."

He shrugged. They'd mulled over the possibilities countless times since leaving Steve's office. "I don't know, but I really think you can rest easier about that. Eventually, though, someone will want to know where she is." Gazing down, he frowned when he saw the pensive pout of Nikki's lips. "C'mon, I hate seeing you be so hard on herself. You're good with her, you know."

Her eyes lifted, searching his. "You think?"

"Not every woman would step into the role of mother the way you have for the past few days. She respects you for it." His voice lowered huskily. "So do I."

An uncertainty he didn't completely understand crossed her features. "Thanks, Sleet. When I got mad at her, I guess I felt like I'd make a lousy parent."

"No, you'd be good." She had so much ahead of her. He was eight years older than she was, and in that eight years he'd started and lost both a family and a career. But she still had all those things to explore. Which meant he couldn't be the man for her. She needed a husband who could give her babies. Who could help with P.T.A., Little League, Brownies, Girl Scouts. Jon couldn't try again when the wounds were still open, not when he knew how fast love could vanish. Staring down and brushing a lock of hair from Nikki's cheek, he couldn't have felt sorrier their lives were at such different places.

"C'mon." As he stepped away, releasing her from the wall, his whole front felt bereft. Trying to ignore the stirrings that had him thinking of his bedroom, not Christy's, he said, "Ready to tuck her in now?"

"I think I can handle it."

In the bedroom, Christy was already under the covers, and she stared at them warily through red-rimmed eyes. The scene in Steve's office had gone a long way toward making her realize how her actions affected others, and the references to child-welfare offices and halfway houses had shaken her up.

Seeing her look so remorseful touched Jon. Not

that he'd make this easy for her. She needed to understand how much worry she was causing. It was
called growing up. And it didn't stop when you were
seven or seventeen, Jon suddenly thought ruefully.
God knew, he was still learning.

He watched how fiercely Christy hugged Nikki's
neck. "Are you mad at me, Nikki?"

Nikki's voice caught. "No, hon. I just want you to
start talking to us."

As Nikki stepped back, Jon leaned and nestled the
covers more snugly under Christy's chin. Glancing
toward the aquarium, he made sure Noodles was
tucked in, then he rested a finger on the bridge of
Christy's pert ski-jump nose, as he often did, and ran
it down to the tip. She wiggled up to hug him, her
slender, gangly arms feeling so tight around his neck
she almost cut off his breath. "Christy," he said
softly, hugging her back. "You know you need to
help us out. Could you sleep on that for me?"

She scooted back, tears shimmering in her eyes.
She nodded solemnly. Her voice was tremulous. "Before I came here, I read your books, Jon. And I—"
She hiccuped, then her voice rose as she raced on. "I
wanted to meet your daughter because I thought
maybe you modeled Jenny on her. I didn't know
Jenny was your real little girl! Jenny was like my best
friend, because I don't have any brothers or sisters!"

So, Christy was an only child, and she'd known he
was an author. "And? Did you come here because
you read my books, Christy?"

She merely kept hugging him. Once more, he
thought of how Steve said the changes in his life had
affected people in town. How many children had enjoyed the stories he'd written? Thousands, anyway. It

was a sobering thought. And a tremendous responsibility, he now realized.

Christy snuggled her face against his, her breath soft and sweet as her voice cracked with unshed tears. "Do you maybe want another little girl someday, Jon?"

Was Christy thinking about herself? Was she a runaway? Had she come here after reading his books, thinking he'd make a good father? It was a crazy idea, but kids' minds worked in mysterious ways. *No, sweetheart. I never want another child.* Aloud he said vaguely, "Maybe someday."

Christy lay back on the pillows, looking like a pint-size Camille, with her face drained of color and her eyes bright pink. She sighed as if Jon's answer wasn't good enough.

"Look, Christy," he said gently, seating himself next to her on the mattress. "If you don't want to talk to me and Nikki, is there anyone else we could get? Anybody you'd feel comfortable with?" If he kept pushing, maybe she'd divulge a relative's phone number.

After long moments, she nodded. "Yeah."

His heart missed a beat. "Who?"

"Santa." Tears welled in her eyes again. "But there isn't really a Santa, is there, Jon?"

Looking at her stricken little face, he felt an overwhelming urge to lift her into his arms again. Her mouth pursed tightly as she tried to hold back a sob. He didn't get it. If she was so upset about the worry she was putting them through, why wouldn't she talk? Gently, he kissed the tip of her nose.

"That's where you're wrong, Christy," he found himself saying against his better judgement. "Of course there's a Santa.'' And right now, no little girl could have looked as if she needed one more.

She sniffed. "If he hears my wish, then maybe I could go home and my house would be the way it used to be."

So, something had changed in her household. A death in the family, maybe? Divorce? Jon felt Nikki come behind him, her hands settling anxiously on his shoulders. He said, "The way it used to be?"

Christy nodded. "Uh-huh. Could Santa grant that wish?"

Hard question. Jon couldn't promise that things would work out for her. "I believe...Santa will do his best."

A tear fell, as if she'd expected that pat adult answer, too. "Sometimes," she said with a wisdom far beyond her years, "Santa's best just isn't good enough."

Which meant, Jon thought as he kissed her again and turned out the light, Christy wasn't going to drop any more hints about who she was or where she'd come from.

Chapter Nine

"Knock knock."

Startled, Nikki glanced up from her perch on the edge of Jon's desk. He looked windblown and cold, having just come in from the barn. Belatedly, he rapped his knuckles against the open door. "Mind if I come in?"

"Sure, Sleet." Her mouth quirked. "It is your study." She glanced toward the books he'd written, which she'd collected and stacked on the corner of the desk, since she and Christy had finished the last one. The covers had fanciful scripted gold lettering and glittering bindings that shined in the low lamplight. They were books any child would cherish.

Jon didn't make it past the threshold, but leaned lazily against the door frame, his eyes taking in the dark wood paneling and packed bookshelves. "Haven't been in here for a while, not since the night you came."

The sudden change in his voice made her realize he might dread being here. Once, he'd spent so many productive hours in this room. Would he ever write again? Her tone was gentle. "Well, come on. A bunch of books won't bite."

He glanced toward those on the desk. "Gearing up for some heavy-duty reading, huh?"

She smiled back easily. "*All I Want For Christmas*," she said, reading a title, then leafing through a large-print book. "It does appear to be difficult material, but I figured I might stretch my mental muscles by burning the midnight oil. Or at least get a glimpse inside the mind of the author." She arched an eyebrow. "Hmm. Wonder what kind of guy he is."

"A Quasimodo type," Jon suggested darkly.

She sent him a sage nod. "No doubt."

"But sexy, don't you think?"

Jon Sleet was that and so much more. "I'll take the fifth."

A playful smile curled the corners of his mouth. "So, you're trying to analyze me by reading my books?"

Nikki shrugged. "When a woman wants to understand a man, she has to start somewhere."

"Are you sure you want to know what makes me tick?"

"Hands down, you're the most fascinating man I've ever met," she said honestly. So many things he'd done had helped her get over Buck. Initially taciturn, Jon had been so kind. He'd warmed to Christy just because she needed a parental figure, and he'd wound up sheltering them during the storm in spite of the pain it caused him. He hadn't even really tried to prove Christy wasn't his, just so Nikki wouldn't worry. When he made no response, she said, "Scared because I'm gathering all this information about you?"

"Not really. But if you keep getting your impressions from children's books, you might decide I've got the sensibilities of a five-year-old.''

"But the body of a man," she offered. And then she said, "A five-year-old, huh? Well, keep growing and eventually maybe you'll come into your own, Sleet."

"Hate to disappoint you, Ryder, but *All I Want For Christmas* won't be that illuminating."

"Well dang," she murmured, even though she wasn't the least disappointed as she watched his broad, weathered hand slide down the scarred brown leather of his jacket, popping open the buttons. Beneath, tucked into his jeans, a long-sleeved white shirt hugged his chest, and she couldn't help but notice that his nipples were still stiff from the cold, nestled in dark untamed chest hairs that made the shirt fabric pucker. Her eyes dropped down below his belt, cruising over jeans that were worn to white and that left a subtle outline where he was pressuring a frayed button-up fly.

Quick, unexpected heat unfurled in Nikki's limbs. Abruptly glancing up, she pressed a hand to her chest, over where her heart had suddenly started to beat too wildly. Like this room, which smelled of well-oiled wooden furniture and leather bookbindings, Jon was unabashedly masculine. Lifting her baseball cap by the brim, she set it on the desk, then tossed her head. Using her fingers, she loosened the strands, knowing full well he liked to see her hair around her face.

He smiled his appreciation. "Looks nice, Ryder."

"Thanks, Sleet."

He pushed away from the door frame, and as he approached, his eyes turned shades darker, gleaming with sudden intent that sent her hand to her heart again. Immediately, she was thinking of his firm mouth, of how hot it felt when he'd closed it over hers in the cold, snowy street today. She knew she shouldn't feel this way, not so soon after Buck. Maybe she should never feel this for a man such as Jon, who'd promised her nothing. But after last night, there was no turning back. One night with Jon could never be enough.

Nothing more than his slow, green-eyed caress of her body was making her yearn for his touch now. She'd taken the liberty of going braless, since she'd worn a bulky sweater, but now her silk long-underwear top was worrying her nipples, the thin fabric chafing worse than the sweater's coarse wool ever could have. By the time Jon halted in front of her, her breasts were unaccountably at attention, and while her sweater hid the hardened peaks from his eyes, her sharp inhalation alerted him to what she was feeling. It also brought the warm, leathery, masculine scent of him deep inside her lungs, charging her body with excitement.

He smiled. "Ho, ho, ho."

Her voice caught unexpectedly. "Next thing I know, you'll be climbing down chimneys. I see your mood's improved."

"So's yours."

She nodded. Talking to him earlier on the stairs had made her feel better. Jon could be so soothing. And he was right. They'd find Christy's parents, with or without the little girl's help. "Hmm. So, is Scrooge finally getting into the Christmas spirit?"

"Afraid so." A flirtatious grin tugged at his otherwise uncompromising mouth. "And now Santa wants to hear all your secret wishes."

"Does he?" Reaching, she finger-combed the hair at his temples where it was tangled from his trip to the barn. She toyed with the few silver strands. "Was it cold out there?"

"Freezing. Windy, too." His lips stretched into another unsettling smile. "*Brrr.* Come on, warm me up, Saint Nikki."

"After all that time at the North Pole, I don't get cold."

"No, but maybe all your little elves do."

"Is that what you are? A little elf?" Leaning back a fraction, Nikki studied him, trying her best to keep a straight face. Jon was a man of letters, and she was beginning to understand how he used flirtation as foreplay.

"C'mon, let's hear your Christmas wishes."

She sighed sadly. "I'm afraid they might give you a heart attack." She fluffed his few gray strands. "Given how old you are."

"The gray's premature."

When she brushed it from his forehead, wavy hanks fell between her fingers. She tucked some strands behind his ear, then traced her nail all the way around the rim, making him shiver. She laughed, sending him a glance of bold, pure challenge. "Well, old man, they do say some things improve with age." She teasingly patted his thigh. "Still, I'd hate to break Santa's infirm legs."

"Come closer or you'll break my heart."

She wanted to sit down because his proximity was making her legs feel like rubber. "Be careful what you ask for, Sleet."

The predatory gleam of challenge shimmered in his eyes as he slid his palms around her waist and under her sweater, heating her skin through her silk top. "C'mon." He angled his head closer, nuzzling her ear. "What's Saint Nikki want for the holidays?"

"Here..." Her breath suddenly caught as she changed the subject, and he shut his eyes, leaning his head back with pleasure as her hands began kneading his strong shoulders. "You feel so stiff."

He released another throaty chuckle and half opened his eyes, peering at her from under heavy lids. "I'm definitely that."

"I didn't mean—"

Lifting a hand, Jon trailed one finger slowly, gently down her cheek. "Ah..." The coarse undercurrent in his voice barely masked desire. "Didn't you?"

Maybe. Because the man was unashamedly aroused, and when he bent his knees, and drew her closer with his hands, she felt the swollen heat of him at her thighs. Her hands trailed over his shoulders and down the front of his chest. Beneath her fingertips, his nipples tightened, and the bones of his ribs seemed to ripple; his tummy clenched. She said softly, "I think I just figured out what I want for Christmas."

Even though she knew his kiss was coming, its greed took her by surprise. Right before his mouth moved on hers, he murmured, "Let's see if Santa can't accommodate you." He was still licking her lips when he drew away, and his voice was octaves deeper. "Trouble is, there're still a few more shopping days till Christmas."

"But everybody gets to unwrap one gift before then."

He caught her sweater by the hem and pulled it over her head in one smooth motion. When he saw her, he released a moan, then licked against the dryness of his lips. Obviously, he'd expected to find another shirt or a bra, not her breasts, fully visible through the transparent top.

"Merry Christmas, Jon," she whispered.

His gaze said he meant to take all night with the rest of the wrappers. And she hoped he did. She wanted to be lying with him when the sun rose. *And to be with him for a lifetime, Nikki? Isn't that what you really want? What you're too afraid to admit?* Ignoring the troubling thoughts, she tried to tell herself that if no deeper relationship came of this, she could handle it. She'd never be sorry for this intimacy.

"Wait." Jon sounded strained.

"Where—" She didn't even get to ask. He'd already turned on his heel, strode across the room and vanished. Her lips parted in protest as he headed down the hallway, the heavy tread of his boots audible on the hardwood floor. Frustration had her silently cursing him. At least until he reappeared—and her heart did flip-flops. Swiftly, Jon locked the study door and crossed the room, and when his strong arms circled her waist again, she felt her throat close from need and emotion. He tossed some foil packets on the desk.

"So that's where you went."

He didn't even bother to answer, just kissed her again with a hungry force that made her open for his mouth. She opened her legs, too, parting and arching, while he teased her lower lip with his mouth, tearing gently with his teeth. The warmth of his breath and kiss flooded her with fever, and when he plunged his tongue between her lips again, a rush of need such as she'd never felt answered, making her throb. Leaning back with their hips still locked, he palmed her breasts, gazing down as if he'd never craved a woman more. She felt the love in his eyes as he caressed the roundness of her breasts and the dusky cinnamon tips shimmering through her shirt. Lowering his mouth, he teased the taut tips with his tongue, dampening the shirt.

A low moan was torn from her when she felt the flex of his erection through their clothes, and an answering guttural sound came from deep within his throat. After that, they were both gone. As he dragged his damp mouth across hers, she surrendered to a kiss that was hot and dark, while both their hands tangled, stripping off each other's jeans. Just as she pushed his down on his thighs, hers came loose, and the hot head of his swollen flesh brushed her intimately, making her sob. "Oh, Jon…"

"Nikki, hold—hold me, Nikki." The broken command was as unsteady as the hands on her breasts that suddenly shook. Feeling her readiness was too much for him. Abruptly breaking the kiss, he got a condom and urged her around the desk.

"Where—"

Sitting back in a chair, he molded his hands over her hips, urging her to straddle him when he was ready. Only when he was poised to enter her did the strong hands stay her, and his soft pant was an aphrodisiac that took her last remaining sense. "What *do* you want for Christmas, Nikki?"

She couldn't help the hitch of her voice, the jerky inhalation of breath. She was so far past joking or repartee. "You, Sleet."

Though his arms bore her whole weight, they no longer shook as he lowered her, eliciting whimpers as he let her take him inside just an inch, stretching her enough that she could feel his heat through the condom's thin barrier. Leaning near his ear, she gasped, "This. Oh, Sleet, I want this."

"Me, Nikki?" One of his large splayed hands dropped, curving downward over her backside, and right before his mouth closed over hers, he whispered, "You want me?"

"Hurry, Sleet," she pleaded.

"Yes," he whispered simply, lowering her completely. "Yes."

"COME BACK under the covers with me, Nikki."

"In a minute." She was sitting with her back against the headboard, hugging her knees. The past few hours had made her feel so full, so loved. She barely remembered how they'd gotten from Jon's study to the room where he slept. Now, through the window, she noticed the skyful of scattered stars, and she stared at the pearl yellow surface of the moon long enough to see a sliver of its dark side; it wasn't really full, after all.

Glancing down, she whispered, "You look good in the moonlight, Sleet."

Smiling, he edged closer, pulling the sheet to his waist as he rose on an elbow. Curling his head against her side, he traced a finger over her sheet-covered knees, then lightly pressed his lips to the sloping side of her breast. "Want to tell me what you're thinking?"

Not really. Conscious of the dampness still between her thighs and of her flushed skin, she was afraid the afterglow of lovemaking could make her admit too much. She barely knew him, and yet she wanted to stay here with him. "Geez..." She sighed. "I guess I'm thinking it's beginning to feel a lot like Christmas."

"Thought you might be worrying about Christy."

"That, too." Looking into Jon's half-closed eyes, she wondered if she was wrong to feel so much for him so soon, to want to hold him tight and not let go.

His voice was as lazy as the hand stroking her hip. "Should I be offended?"

"Offended?"

"Since being in bed with me didn't make you forget our troubles?"

Our troubles. She liked the sound of that. She smiled. "I forgot for a while."

"Not long enough. Next time I'll work harder."

"I doubt you could."

"We'll see." He laughed. Pulling her into his arms, he turned so that they spooned together, both looking out the window with his chin resting on her shoulder. He snuggled his forearm across her belly, and his voice dropped even lower. "It *is* beginning to feel like Christmas," he agreed.

"You're less of a Scrooge."

"We aim to please."

Sighing, Nikki felt wistfulness twist inside her. This moment was so perfect—stargazing with Jon and feeling so warm in the cold night. She knew all such moments were fleeting, but sure wished this one would last.

"Nice moon," he whispered simply.

Looming in the window, it looked so close she could almost touch it. She chuckled softly. "For years, I stayed awake on Christmas Eve, staring at the moon, hoping I could catch Santa."

"Was this recently?"

She laughed. "No. When I was a kid. Doesn't every kid do that? Just once, I wanted to see him fly across the moon in that sleigh."

Jon smoothed back her hair, then rested his face in a hollow of her neck he'd laid bare. He sighed. "Me, too. Once when I was a kid, I even snuck downstairs and sat in the fireplace, hoping to catch him when he came down the chimney."

"You didn't."

He nodded. "That's where my folks found me on Christmas morning, all covered with soot." He chuckled. "The presents were under the tree, so I guess my parents worked awfully quietly that year."

"Or else the real Santa came."

"Maybe. You know, they do say you can see him here on Christmas Eve. That at midnight, in Holiday Hamlet, if you look hard enough, you'll see him fly across the moon while the trees in the mountains wink with lights because they've been decorated by the angels."

"You wrote that in a book, Jon."

The low hum of his voice curled through her. "Yeah, I guess I did." After a long moment, his lips pressed against her shoulder. "Thanks, Nikki."

"For what?"

He didn't answer immediately, merely glided a hand over the sheet, from her knee all the way to her waist. Snaking around, his hand came to rest on her belly again, slightly pressuring it, so she fit more snugly into the cradle of his lap. "Thanks for being here with me." His fingers found and twined through hers. "Really, Nikki, I couldn't have wished for more this Christmas."

Still feeling the warm pressure of his hand against her belly, she thought of the very special gift she carried there, her baby. These past days, the pregnancy had begun to feel real. At odd moments, she'd catch herself wondering if it was a boy or girl, or thinking about things she'd need to buy—clothes, carrying bags. It would be tough financially, but Nikki could make it. She was *not* going to start wishing Jon would become a permanent part of her and the baby's life. No matter what they'd just shared. No matter...

"See Santa yet?" Jon drew her from her thoughts.

She stared at the moon. "Not yet." But she did feel a sudden flood of well-being. Rubbing his forearm, she toyed with the rough hair, feeling her pulse quicken. A lump formed in her throat. "Jon?"

"Shhh. Before you say anything, I have something to say."

She swallowed hard, waiting. And then he turned her toward him, finding her eyes in the darkness. "Nikki," he said gently, "I know it's crazy, but I want you to stay here with me." His eyes searching hers, he took her hand and brought it to his lips.

She realized her heart was hammering dangerously hard as her free arm circled his neck. "It *is* crazy, but I've thought about it, too. I feel like—"

"Like you'll go nuts if you don't get to know me better?"

"Eloquent, Sleet. That sums it up."

"I feel the same way."

He drew back, caressing her. She felt the warmth of his hand gliding between her breasts to her belly, pressing the spot over her child. Ever since she'd come here, she'd wanted to tell him, to share the gift with someone. No one else on earth even knew. And now, given what they were talking about, she couldn't wait any longer. "Jon...I'm—I'm pregnant."

His hand stilled. She was sure it stopped moving right over the baby. "Jon?"

"Dammit, Nikki."

Her eyes stung as she watched how quickly he moved from the bed. As if in a dream, she watched his broad, bare shoulders turn in the moonlight until he was facing her. Gazing down, he didn't show a trace of modesty for his partial arousal, and even though she'd seen that part of him before, even though he was rejecting her now, her blood thickened with desire. Passion, wariness and anger seemed at war in his face, and yet his voice was strangely calm. "You're pregnant?"

She sat up, snapping the sheet to her breasts, her heart stuttering. "Are you hard of hearing? That's what I just said."

Tantalizing moonlight glanced off his chest as he stepped forward. An hour ago he'd done things to her body she'd now crave for a lifetime. And she'd shamelessly begged for more. He'd asked her to live with him, too. And now she felt so exposed that she wanted to crawl under a rock. "I said I'm pregnant," she challenged. "You got a problem with that, Sleet?"

His voice was a growl. "Damn right I do."

No way was she going to cry. She should have known he was just like Buck. Tossing her head, she gathered her forces, determined not to show him how much his rejection was hurting her. When Buck pushed her away, she'd just been angry. But now...now... *Oh, God, I'm in love with him.*

Her voice was tight. "Why should *you* have a problem?'' Glaring at him, she suddenly wished for less moonlight. Would the darkness cover emotions her eyes couldn't hide?

"Nikki…" Jon cast his eyes about as if he couldn't find the right words. "This isn't…fair."

"Fair?" She threw back the covers. Moving on the momentum of her anger, she whirled toward him and swiped her clothes from the floor. "I don't owe you anything."

He circled the bed and caught her wrist. She stepped back, leaning against the window frame. "Sleet," she warned. "Get your hands off me."

He didn't. His voice was unsteady. "You don't sleep with a man, then tell him something like that."

"It didn't come up before now."

He stared at her for long moments, looking well beyond anger. "I wanted you in my life, Nikki."

Wanted. Her heart hammered and a lump lodged in her throat, strangling her words. "Oh? What exactly had you *wanted* me for? Another live-in maid?"

"A *what?* Maybe that's how you felt with Buck, but don't bring your past into this bedroom, Nikki. It's just you and me here. And I wanted you for this." He stepped close, his heated skin grazing hers, and the abrupt contact was so unsettling that she almost dropped her clothes. Her fist clenched around them as she fought a wave of desire she could never deny. Blushing, she tried to calm the pulse in her throat, but her breath was gone and her lungs burned for air. Just moments ago, she'd reveled in what this man did to her. "This," she said now, ignoring the energy between them, "is not enough for me."

His voice was rough with arousal now, thicker with anger. "I know that, Nikki."

She glared right into his eyes. "You're just like Buck."

"I said don't bring the past into the bedroom we're sharing."

"Why not? You have."

"Don't you understand?" he exploded. "I *had* a child. Losing her didn't just break my heart, Nikki. It *destroyed* me. I can't live through that again."

"Are you saying *my* baby's going to die?"

"God, no!" he gasped.

"And I'm not getting rid of my baby, Sleet."

His jaw went slack, his eyes widened. "What? Oh, no, is that what Buck wanted you to do?"

"What do you care? You don't want a family. You're not ready for love. All you wanted from me is sex."

His hand tightened on her. "Dammit, Nikki, that's not true."

Her heart beat harder when she saw the raging fire her comment had brought into his eyes. Silently, she damned him for making her love him. But she couldn't have stopped herself, any more than she could stop the hurt that was driving her to provoke him. "Geez...guess I was perfect, Sleet, wasn't I?" She wrenched from his grasp. "Because I'm a stranger. Just some transient lady stuck in a snow-storm."

He surprised her by shutting his eyes, taking a deep breath, then running a finger gently down her cheek. "Nikki, please..."

She jerked away. "What?"

His hand dropped to her collarbone, and there was something almost broken in his voice now, something that would have elicited sympathy if she wasn't hurt-

ing so much. "Don't you see, I can't give you what
you need? You need a man who wants to give you
more babies and be a father to this one." The way
he dropped his hand again and molded it over her
belly brought tears to her eyes. Her chin quivered.

He was right. And she knew it. So, why didn't the
knowledge stop her flood of wanting him? And why
couldn't Jon be that man? Right now, she wanted to
beg him to be that man. She had to get away from
him—from his naked body and the aroused warmth
it brought, and from the sensual fingers that had
touched her in such unlikely places…fingers that now
rested so easily on her belly as if he really cared about
the baby.

His voice was low. "I'm not Buck, Nikki. So, don't
make out like I've treated you badly here."

She could read between those lines. It was over
between them. "If you want to live the rest of your
life alone, that's fine with me," she managed. "Go
for it, Sleet."

With that, she shoved his chest so hard he actually
staggered back. Clutching her clothes to her chest, she
ran for the door. When she was through it, she turned
around and slammed it hard, putting her whole weight
behind it. She was halfway down the hallway when
she heard it jerk open behind her. She could feel Jon's
eyes between her naked shoulder blades.

But Nikki Ryder had plenty of pride. And she
wasn't about to look back.

Chapter Ten

No wonder she'd been so concerned about whether she'd be a good parent, last night when they'd talked on the stairs. Jon pulled on a robe, not bothering to tie it, and then he seated himself by the window and stared into the dark night. How could Nikki be pregnant? For the first time in days, he needed a drink. A stiff one.

He'd watched her eyes fill with tears she hadn't wanted him to see, watched the angry twitch of her naked backside as she'd run away, and it had torn him up not to follow her. He could kill Buck, too. Didn't the man know Nikki would never consider an abortion? Jon's heart ached for the pain she must have felt when Buck rejected her, but he was mad, too. While they were lying in bed, he'd been thinking about getting married again... But this? A child with her? And so soon?

"Marry Nikki?" He'd better get a grip on his imagination because, after a two-year dry spell, it seemed to be running wild. He wanted her, but he could never be a father again.

No, no way was he going to continue sleeping with her and risk that much emotion. A wry smile twisted his lips. Maybe he'd never made love to Nikki at all. What if the Ghost of Christmas Future had conjured her to haunt him with the vision of everything he was missing in life? Maybe Nikki and Christy were phantoms, Christmas angels sent from heaven to bring him out of the self-imposed hell where he'd been living.

Or more likely, Nikki's lovemaking had dislodged some major writer's block. If he kept up this fanciful thinking, he *might* start writing again. Anyway, Nikki was no phantom. And she was pregnant. Which meant it was over between them.

Would things have played out differently if he'd been able to take the sex for what it was, without wanting to make promises? *Who knows?* Too bad he was the kind of man who made commitments. Before this, he'd only been with his wife, and now he wished Nikki could share his life for a while, and his bed. Since she was so different from Mary, being with her had felt like a fresh start, and he'd felt whole again.

Mary…well, Mary had been his girl as far back as he could remember. After they were married, she was his biggest fan, pushing him and supporting his writing. Hundreds of nights, she'd nestled in his arms, sipping wine and talking books. She'd appealed to the poet in his soul.

But there was nothing practical about wanting Nikki Ryder. She was a constant challenge—angry and too young for him, with a sharp tongue and too much pride. They hadn't grown up in the same town or shared social ties, the way he and Mary had. And yet she'd touched him, and, somehow, he needed her.

He did not need a baby.

He'd never have slept with her if he'd known. So, why hadn't she told him? Did she think he could make love to her without caring? Without starting to dream about starting a life together? Had she forgotten that he'd already been a daddy, and that the heartbreak of loss had nearly killed him?

So many moments were printed indelibly on his mind. Jenny, at seven pounds, resting on his broad hand. How he, Mary and Steve had laughed at her christening because Jenny hadn't cried, but merely licked the holy water from her lips. How beautiful she'd looked, cuddled under the covers when he read to her every night.

Nobody would ever know how dark it had gotten after the ice storm, how weak he'd felt because he wanted to follow Mary and Jenny. He'd loved them the only way he knew, with every fiber of his being, and when they were gone, the damn truth was that Jon had wanted to die, too.

Nikki made him want to live again.

Which was why the thought of giving her up filled him with gnawing emptiness. Trailing his eyes over the moon's surface, Jon studied the dark craters and the barely perceptible sliver crescent of the dark side. How could he battle his own dark side now? How could he forget the ghosts of Christmas past? How could he hold another baby to his heart—and accept the joy, pain, and responsibility of fatherhood again—when nothing more than Christy's youthful presence here had choked up the pain of the past?

No answer came. And so he simply sat like that, staring at the moon. After a while, his imagination sparked to life again—and Jon could swear the man in the moon was looking back with eyes full of judgment.

NIKKI TURNED from the moon and glanced down to where yellow-gold licks of the fire's flame cast shadows on the open book in her lap. Reading Jon's stories was the worst thing she could do, of course. But because she'd feared Christy would awaken and wonder why she was storming around stark naked at 3:00 a.m., she'd ducked into the study to pull on her jeans. She wound up taking the stack of books she'd left on the desk. Now she was curled in the armchair in front of the fire, dressed in a sleep-shirt and wrapped in a blanket. It would have been cozy if Nikki could have quit crying.

Abruptly she gripped a poker with more than the necessary force and stoked the fire until it snapped and sputtered in the warm silence. Replacing the poker, she leaned back again, her tear-blurred eyes straying to the bed. Her gaze softened as she looked at Christy. The little girl was asleep on her back. Soft, blond ringlets curled on the pillow, her face was relaxed, and the corners of her lips lifted as if she were having pleasant dreams. She looked like an angel.

Staring down at the book in her lap again, Nikki read another page. The story was about a little girl's attempts to make inattentive parents love her, and each sentence attested to Jon's magical imagination. How many kids had cherished these wonderful books? How many people had felt more alive because of the life Jon created through words?

Sighing, she stared into the fire again. It would be so easy to make excuses for him. But she carried the gift of life, too, and she couldn't forgive his rejection. She drew in another bracing breath. Too bad her willpower was pathetically lacking when it came to Jon Sleet.

"Nikki?"

Swiping quickly at her eyes so Christy wouldn't see the tears, Nikki glanced toward the bed. "Shush, hon," she whispered gently. "It's late and you need your sleep."

"Can't." Christy wiggled from beneath the covers, slid down the side of the mattress and padded across the hardwood floor. She'd insisted on wearing one of Jon's T-shirts to bed, and it was so long it nearly hit the floor. "I can't sleep by myself, Nikki."

Nikki smiled. "Well, I guess I'd better come to bed then."

"That's okay," Christy croaked, squirming beside Nikki in the armchair. Scooting to make room, Nikki put her arm around the little girl's shoulders. As she smoothed her fine, soft hair, Nikki wondered who had read Jon's books to Christy. Had it been a loving parent? Or had the precocious girl read them to herself?

I can't wait to read to my little girl, she thought. *If I have a girl.* She'd be just as happy with a boy, but she'd love to give a girl all the things she'd craved from a mother—and missed—during her childhood. Things, she thought now, that Christy already seemed to know, such as how to mix and match her clothes and apply makeup. Things that led Nikki to believe Christy must have a loving mom out there somewhere.

She realized Christy was still gazing up at her.

"I know that other book," she murmured, pointing at the stack. "Can you read it to me?"

"Sure." Nikki leaned, trading books. Opening the new one, she glanced down at the large-print page, at words that had first come to life in her lover's imagination. Where had he been when he'd written them? In the turret, where he'd been the night she'd come here? Or maybe shut up in his study, where he'd made such remarkable love to her? Her heart suddenly wrenched, and she knew if Christy wasn't with her, she'd weep.

Shaking away the thoughts, she cleared her throat. "'Once upon a time in the sleepy little town of Holiday Hamlet,'" she began, watching Christy's eyes drift shut with the words. "'There was a little girl named Jenny who didn't even know her most secret dreams were about to come true at Christmas...'"

As she read, Nikki wished that Christy's dreams would come true. And then thinking of Jon, Nikki suddenly wished that for herself.

JON WAS BEHIND HER in the kitchen doorway, and Nikki was so aware of him that she could feel his eyes and smell his scent. He said, "I'm sorry about last night."

She managed to glance his way, nodding coolly. Otherwise, she didn't look up from the magazine she was pretending to read. Staring hard at the words, she was still seeing how Jon looked in the doorway. He was wearing a heavy, ribbed, bone-white sweater that made his upper body look mouthwateringly powerful and that hugged the hips of his black jeans. Taking a bite of cereal, Nikki wished Christy hadn't already finished her breakfast and taken off for parts of the house unknown. *Pretty grim, Ryder, when you want to use Christy as a buffer between you and Jon.*

"C'mon, Nikki. I don't want to fight. I care about you."

Not enough, Sleet. She was half tempted to say she

liked him better when he roamed the house until the wee hours and then slept all day. At least she didn't have to see him then. But such comments might be construed as juvenile. Angrily tossing her head and keeping her eyes riveted on the magazine, she shrugged. "Well, geez, let's not fight anymore."

"We're fighting now."

She felt him come up behind her. All last night, she'd schooled herself not to react with anger—or to give in to physical temptation. If Jon Sleet wanted to reject her, fine. But why was he trying to pretend they were friends this morning? She'd expected him to avoid her, the way he had when she'd first arrived. Fresh anger suddenly coursed through her. Or did he really expect her to make him feel *good* about rejecting her? *Oh, poor, poor Jon,* she thought. *You've been through so much.* Not that she wasn't deeply sympathetic, but… She finally said, "At the very least, you could have congratulated me on having a baby, Sleet."

He stretched his arm under hers and molded his hand to her belly, splaying his long fingers on her sweater. She felt unwanted desire pool beneath his palm; the warm, liquid sensation spread to the rest of her. Still, wounded pride made her chin shoot up even as his slow, gentle drawl tugged at her heart.

"Congratulations, Ryder. You know, I've always loved kids, and this is going to fulfill you in ways you haven't even imagined. I—I wish I could share more of this with you, but I can't."

"Because of your past, right?" She couldn't help but say. "Oh, please spare me, Sleet. Because this isn't your past. The kind of past you have is calculated to last forever. And—" She glared down at his hands. "I really think you've lost any right you had to touch me like this."

Jon sighed. "Do you really mind so much?"

Her eyes stung with tears, and she blinked rapidly. "Yes. As a matter of fact, I do." Feeling frustrated at her own lack of resolve, she clinked the spoon into her bowl, took a bite of cereal and chomped it loudly enough that he'd get the point. When he didn't, she shot him a long, sideways glance. "I'm trying to eat breakfast here. Do you mind?"

"Of course not, Nikki."

She glared at him, wishing his voice wasn't so steady and unaffected. Hers was shaking and her heart suddenly turned over when he squatted next to her chair. Her face felt tight with the need to cry. "If you don't want to get to know me better because I'm pregnant," she said, "then why can't you just leave me alone?" She wished she hadn't said it, especially when he trailed another stupid finger down her cheek. She told herself she hated it when he did that.

"I've tried to be honest. What do you want from me?"

He was right, of course. He hadn't done anything wrong. She forced herself to take another bite of cereal. "To be left alone in peace to eat my Wheat Chex."

Now he uttered a frustrated half grunt.

She sent him what she hoped was an unconcerned glance. She wished she hadn't. There was something entirely too close to helplessness in his devastating eyes. Not that she'd break down and cry. No way was she falling for a man who didn't want her in his life.

"Please, Nikki," he ventured. "Can't we be friends?"

"We've never been friends, Sleet."

"Nikki…"

She whirled on him. "You just want me to absolve you of guilt because it'll be easier for you if I make nice and smile pleasantly even though our relationship is over. But what happened meant something to me."

"It meant—it *means*—something to me, too."

"Could have fooled me."

Gripping the back of her chair for balance, he released another frustrated sigh. "You could leave, you know. I'm hardly holding you at gunpoint." He glanced around. "Hmm. No bars on the windows. No ropes, handcuffs, duct tape. Which means you must have some interest in continuing to communicate with me."

"Oh, I get it. Now that I don't want to have sex with you, you're throwing me out!" As fury washed over her again, she thought that was only going to make this worse. Why was she doing it? Was it because his response would assure her he was telling the truth, that their lovemaking had touched him?

His slow drawl remained tender, only further teasing her anger. "I'd never throw you out, Nikki."

Somehow, she managed to turn and crunch another bite of cereal. "Well, I brought Christy here," she said between chews, "which makes her my responsibility. And I'm not leaving until I know she's reunited with her parents. Now, if you'll please let me finish my breakfast, she and I have things to do today."

Still hunkered down beside her chair, he was squinting up at her, his eyes looking smoky with emotion. "Look…" Lifting a hand, he cupped the back of her neck. The touch made her skin tingle, and made her wish she was wearing her baseball cap—as if the boyish hat could really protect her from the female needs Jon stirred inside her. She eyed where it was resting on the table.

He continued, "You don't know how sorry I am that I reacted badly last night."

"Thank you for saying so." She turned her attention back to the magazine.

"I'm not just *saying*—" He blew out a quick breath, giving up. "Uh...where are you and Christy going?"

Nikki didn't lift her eyes. Vaguely, she noted that the article in front of her was about how to improve one's communications skills. Be direct, it said. She turned to Jon. "I told Mrs. Honey we'd help decorate the inn. Tomorrow night's the annual Christmas Eve party." Despite her desire to act as if their affair had ended amiably, she wound up leveling a cold stare at him, and her voice was a challenge—a very direct challenge. "Would you like to come?"

He shook his head.

She nodded. "I didn't think so."

His eyes glazed, looking distant, and his words were laced with suppressed anger. "And why's that, Nikki?"

She shrugged. "Because you'd rather stay up here by yourself," she returned tightly. "I could read between the lines when we were in town yesterday. You don't keep in touch with Steve, even though he's your best friend. And according to Mrs. Honey, you used to be an active member of the community."

"Times change."

She slapped the spoon into the bowl, snatched the

napkin from her lap and dabbed at her lips. "They sure do. There's been a big change since last night."

His sudden grip on her arm took her by surprise. "If I didn't know better," he muttered, "I'd say you're provoking me."

"Yes." She turned to him. "You know, I think I am, Sleet."

He looked thoroughly exasperated. "Why?"

"Because I think you're a selfish son of a bitch, Jon Sleet!" Embarrassed heat flooded her face at the sudden admission. She'd practiced all night what she'd say this morning, how cool she'd be. As if their lovemaking hadn't meant a thing to her.

Now his eyes were almost begging her. Maybe he was recalling Jenny, how he'd felt when he held her the first time, the moment he understood that he'd really become a dad. His voice implored, "I'm trying to be honest about what I can give you and the baby, Nikki."

Unable to stand the judgment in his eyes, Nikki abruptly stood. Unfortunately, he did so at the same time, and they wound up chest to chest. She tried to edge around the table, but he laid a staying hand on her waist.

"Dang it all, Sleet!" she suddenly exclaimed, "if you don't want to come into town with me and Christy, don't! I wanted to be cool about this morning, but I can't. I can't help the way I feel! I think I'm in love with you!"

"You're in—" He sucked in a deep breath. "Don't you understand?" he growled, abruptly dragging her against him and bringing his lips close. "A part of me doesn't *want* you to help the way you feel, Nikki."

Her eyes widened. "You don't?"

"No, dammit," he cursed. And then his lips crushed down on hers, making her body flash with heat. This mouth was so familiar now. She knew his lips—how they stretched into grins, thinned with displeasure, and twisted into wry, wise smiles. She loved the hard, hungry way they were moving on hers, how the thrust of his tongue weakened her knees and made her cling to his shoulders. Only when his hands began slipping, dragging down her spine, did she manage to pull back, telling herself that any further contact with him would hurt too much in the long run.

"You were right last night," she managed breathlessly. "I deserve better. I deserve a man who wants a family."

His lips were wet, and the way his starved eyes were still roving hungrily over her mouth made her want to kiss him again and again, until he caved in and loved both her and the baby.

"I didn't mean to hurt you, Nikki. But I can't be with you."

The sudden rapid beat of her heart sent too much blood rushing through her at once. She grabbed her baseball cap from the table and jerked it down on her head. "Oh, I don't know," she bit out, even though her rapid respiration made speech difficult. "A second ago you were doing a pretty good job of being with me, now weren't you, Sleet?"

His half moan of frustration was more telling than a thousand words. "I'm trying to do the right thing by you, Nikki. But when you're so close, I can't stop wanting to touch you."

She smiled. "I believe you're the first man to ever complain about that."

"That's not a complaint. Quit deliberately misunderstanding me."

"Shut up while you're ahead, Sleet." Adjusting her baseball cap, she grabbed the cereal bowl and dropped it into the sink with a loud clink. Turning, she glared at him. He was still standing behind the chair she'd vacated, his strong hands gripping the chair back. She said, "What you don't seem to be getting through your thick skull is that I don't want you." *Lies, lies, lies.*

But they woke him up. He circled around the chair, coming toward her. "Then why are you so mad?"

Good question, Sleet. I don't know. Why are you? Hasn't it occurred to you yet that I'm not the only one who's accidentally developed feelings here? "You want honesty," she said, edging back around the dining table and toward the door, "I'll give you honesty."

He nodded.

Glancing at him again, some of the anger left her and was replaced by heartbreak and disappointment she'd rather ignore. Sighing, she leaned against the door frame and shook her head. "Sleet, last night, I sat up reading your books...."

His eyes narrowed, as if this was the last thing he expected her to say. "And?"

"And don't you understand?" she muttered, not caring how much she exposed herself. "You're amazing. Inventive and funny. You make worlds come alive for people, and you make readers feel things."

He leaned against the counter, crossing his arms. "What's this got to do with you and me?"

"Everything! You should have heard Mrs. Honey talk about your love of kids."

He was squinting at her. "So?"

She sighed. "For a rich, smart guy, you're beyond dense." Tilting her head, she surveyed him a moment, her eyes drifting lovingly over that fabulous body—the tight jeans and bulky sweater. Swiping at her hat and grabbing it by the brim, she brought it in front of her and studied the electric-blue bill. Then she looked at him again. "I've learned my lesson," she continued, her voice calmer than it had been all morning. "I was so anxious to leave home that I pretended Buck could give me what I needed, even when there was plenty of writing on the wall to say he couldn't."

"I know that, Nikki."

"Sleet—" Her voice suddenly gentled. "I've never made the same mistake twice." Her hands moved to her belly. "I'm having a baby. And you're right. My child needs a father."

He looked strangely stunned. "And you've decided I'm out of the running."

"Afraid so."

There was real pain in his voice. "But you just said you were in love with me. I don't understand—"

She pushed herself off the door frame with her shoulder, wishing she wasn't still tasting his kiss...wishing she wasn't wondering if it wasn't the last time their lips would ever touch. "I don't want you, Jon," she said, putting her cap back on again. "I want the man who used to dress up as Santa and drive the reindeer into town on Christmas Eve. I want the man who loved his wife and child. Sleet—" She suddenly begged him with her eyes, feeling her chest constrict with emotion. "I want the man you used to be."

"You're really going to buy me a leotard so I can be an elf?"

Nikki ruffled Christy's hair, then hung some gowns and leotards in the dressing room. "If I do," she said, once they were inside with the door shut, "will you tell me where your mommy and daddy are?"

Christy's lower lip puffed out. "Nope."

"But you saw how upset Sheriff Warwick was when he came into the inn today, didn't you? Hon, he's trying so hard to find your parents. We're afraid they're looking for you." When Christy's lips clamped more firmly shut, Nikki sighed. There had been no new leads, although two flight attendants thought they remembered Christy. Unfortunately, the rush of Christmas travelers had required their full attention and they recalled nothing else.

Christy's lower lip suddenly quivered. "Don't get me a new leotard, then."

Nikki frowned. The child was so charming and adorable, at least until you tried to wrench information from her. Despite Steve Warwick's concern, Christy had nearly charmed the pants off the man while they'd decorated the inn's Christmas tree.

"C'mon—" Nikki slipped a green leotard off a hanger as Christy wiggled out of her sweater.

"I thought it's a costume party, though, Nikki," she said.

"It is."

"But you're not dressing up?"

"Nope. Here..." She offered an arm for balance as Christy stepped into the legs of the leotard. "The sleeves are too short on you," Nikki murmured, helping the girl pull it off and try another.

"Won't you look funny if you don't have a costume?"

"You'll look cute enough for the both of us, Christy." While the child beamed at the compliment, Nikki thought about the town's party.

When Jon's books hit, tourists began visiting Holiday Hamlet, and locals had started wearing costumes to the inn's annual party. In fact, the inn still kept costumes in a back room. There were elf masks, one of which Christy would be wearing, and a collection of reindeer antlers secured by headbands. Nikki had even found puffy white snowman suits, not to mention Santa suits in various sizes. She'd heard that one local man even used to come dressed as a decorated Christmas tree, while his wife came as the gift. Someone else had made a suit shaped like a stocking. Apparently, both the local and visiting children loved the costume party. The old fellow who managed the inn had told Nikki it was better than going to Disneyland. Clearly, he hoped business would start booming again.

And maybe it would. The inn was magical, and scents from the professional kitchen promised a buffet of succulent hors d'oeuvres.

"That leotard fits better, Christy," she said.

"I don't know." The way Christy turned this way and that, surveying herself in the mirror, made Nikki suddenly sure that Christy's mom liked to shop. The little girl was far more comfortable in a fancy boutique than Nikki. Nikki reached for a third leotard. "Ready to try the last one?"

Christy frowned at herself in the mirror. "Not yet," she said, sounding very grown-up. "I'm still thinking.

I don't want my costume to be like everybody else's. Maybe I should be a red elf, 'stead of a green one.''

Nikki started to say that elves were supposed to be green. "If you want. I think all the leotards come in red, too.''

Christy was still staring at herself. "Which dress are you wearing?''

She wasn't sure. But she did want Jon to see her, just once, in a gown. She glanced uneasily toward the party dresses she'd chosen. *As if a dress could change the way he feels about you, when the issues are so complex.* "What about this one, Christy?''

"Wow.''

Nikki slipped the red velvet dress from the hanger, holding it against her. It was backless, with a low, scalloped neckline. Already, she could tell that the red brought out the reddish highlights of her hair. Still holding the dress against her, she lifted the lid of a shoebox, and stared down at the sinful, spike-heeled red shoes inside.

"Dangerous,'' she muttered.

The dress was hell to get on, too. Tight as Spandex over her butt. At least it was good and snug up top. Otherwise she wouldn't have the nerve to wear it. Reaching behind her, she managed to zip it up.

Christy suddenly giggled. "It'll look pretty funny with a baseball cap.''

Nikki smirked. "For your information, kid, I wasn't going to wear my baseball cap.''

Christy clapped her hand to her forehead dramatically. "Thank you!''

Nikki's eyes had fixed on her own reflection. "You really think the dress looks all right?''

Christy nodded, her eyes wide. "Uh-huh. Real good."

Turning back to the mirror, Nikki had to fight the urge to gape at herself. Especially when she slipped on the shoes that added a full three inches to her height. She might be the only partygoer without a costume, but she was going to make sure Jon Sleet got a good look at what he was missing.

And then they'd find Christy's parents.

And then she would say goodbye to Jon. Painful emotion suddenly twisted inside her, but she ignored it. After a moment, she felt a tug at her dress and glanced down. "Hmm?"

Christy still looked thunderstruck. "I'm still the same human being," Nikki said dryly. "I wasn't born in jeans and a baseball cap, you know."

Christy scrutinized her. "Can I do your makeup?"

Of course not. The words were almost on Nikki's lips, when she realized Christy probably knew more about lipsticks and eyeliner than she ever would. She'd come with a carton of the stuff. "What do you have in mind?"

"Kohl pencil and Mousse Café lipstick. There's still some Chanel Number Five left."

Nikki was sure the perfume cost a fortune. No one bought that kind of stuff for a child. Her eyes narrowed. "Did you take that perfume from your mother, Christy?"

Christy crossed her arms. "Do you want my help or not?"

"Yes." Right now, she felt she could use all the help she could get. Turning back to the mirror, Nikki's eyes trailed from her bare shoulders down the length of the red velvet sheath. It made her look busty, but otherwise slender. She might not have made any headway with Christy today, but the dress would give Jon Sleet a start.

Unwanted pain suddenly made her heart pull again. Why did she have to meet Jon now? Why couldn't it have happened sometime in the future, when he was ready to move on with his life? Of course she wished his life had followed the path he'd initially chosen, that he still had Mary and Jenny.

But he didn't. And now she wanted him. Because he was too good a man to go to waste, she was going to put this dress on her credit card, even though she'd now missed a week of work and couldn't really afford it. And then maybe she'd try, just once, to put some sense into Jon.

Unless, of course, she toppled off these dangerous-looking spike heels first and killed herself.

Chapter Eleven

Jon glanced up, his breath catching. "Nikki, you look so...elegant."

Pausing at the top of the stairs, she tossed her head with a light gesture that sent hair cascading around her shoulders, and as she floated downstairs on legs that suddenly seemed impossibly long, Jon realized that the shoes bringing new shape to her calves also added to her height. When she reached the first floor, her eyes were nearly level with his. Kohl pencil rimmed them, turning darkened irises to lush black, and mascara lengthened the lashes. She settled a slender, manicured hand on the newel post, and Jon swallowed hard. "Makes me wish I was going with you."

"You still could."

But he couldn't. He might never be ready to take up his old life. Or a new one. Sadness touched his eyes, but his smile was genuine. "I've never seen a woman look so good."

When she smiled, the dark evening seemed to light up. "Thanks, Jon."

Not Sleet, he noted as her soft, twanging drawl stroked him, but Jon. It was hard to believe this was the same woman who usually wouldn't part with her baseball cap. Feeling compelled to step closer, even though he knew he shouldn't, he settled his palms on her waist, cupping where the cinched, red-velvet dress nipped in. He sighed.

"What?"

He shrugged. "I can't take the cold shoulder anymore. Don't be mad at me." He needed to feel her melting against him. Leaning toward where the strapless bodice had left her shoulders bare, he brushed a kiss there. "But your shoulders aren't really cold at all," he managed huskily as her cool, naked skin warmed to his lips. Inhaling a deep breath of her, he whispered, "God, you smell good, Nikki." *I want you so much.* His chest tightened as a slow, drugging heat flushed through him. And then he murmured, "Sorry…"

"I know—" Her seductive eyes remained steady, but in such a practiced way that her real feelings were bare. She was in love with him. More than the words she'd spoken, her eyes told him. "You just can't stop yourself from kissing me, right?"

"Can you stop kissing me back?" he murmured.

Her eyes said no. "Under the circumstances, sure."

They wanted each other so much, but he knew she was right. It wasn't fair of him to keep touching her when he never meant to give more. *Don't be so sure of yourself, Jon. She's been burned once. Even if you knew you wanted to try, maybe she wouldn't have you.…*

At the thought, panic he refused to name curled inside him, and against his better judgment, he was powerless to resist sweeping his lips across her bare shoulders once more—kissing one, then the other—until Nikki visibly trembled and he saw the tips of her breasts constrict against the velvet. *So soft,* he wanted to whisper in her ear as his lips touched her skin a final time. *And so hard.*

Her voice was unsteady. "Jon…"

Stepping away a pace, he let his eyes trace the curves of her legs. "You really are beautiful tonight, Nikki."

Her words were tremulous. "I'm glad you like the dress."

His gaze met hers. "You know I like the woman in it." *So much.*

Her eyes said, "But that doesn't matter, does it?" His returned, "I wish I was ready to move on. Because if I was, you'd be the woman." At least Jon hoped that's what his eyes said.

Their gaze was linked a second too long—long enough that another, deeper silent conversation took place that neither of them wanted to have. Then even the silence beneath the silence was gone, and all that remained was the look of two people who'd pleasured each other in the dark. Cries were remembered. Whimpers. The slow touch of a hand, and a particularly deep kiss.

Jon could see how hard her throat worked when she broke the gaze and swallowed. With a sharp intake of breath, she glanced back toward the stairs. "Christy?" she suddenly called out. "C'mon, hon, you'd better hurry! The buffet starts soon, and we're late."

Small feet pounded above. "I'm ready!" Christy's cry was so shrill that Jon winced. "But I've got to kiss Noodles goodbye."

Jon called, "Take your time." Then he lowered his voice. "While you and Christy are out, I thought I'd look over the gifts we'd planned to give Jenny before the accident. They're still unwrapped. There's paper here…some tape and bows.''

The softening of Nikki's eyes made them look like liquid chocolate—and made his heart squeeze. ''You mean, to put under the tree for Christy?'' she asked.

It shouldn't have been hard to breathe, but it was. Was this a sign he was letting go? That maybe he could bring Nikki into his life? He nodded. ''No use letting good things go to waste.'' He paused, the words echoing, making him think of the love he and Nikki had shared. *Why are you letting it go to waste, Jon?* ''If her parents aren't found by tomorrow,'' he continued, ''I figured we'd better do something, so she'll have Christmas.'' Giving another child Jenny's gifts was such a small thing, and yet he'd expected it to hurt. It didn't. It felt good.

''Are you sure, Jon?''

He shot her a quick smile. ''Jenny would have wanted it. Besides, it's Christmas. Isn't it supposed to be the season of giving?''

Nikki nodded. ''I got Christy a few things in town, too. They're in the trunk of the cab.''

Of course Nikki had done that. He'd never met anyone so thoughtful. Another smile curled his lips. ''Good thinking, Saint Nikki. Not everything here will work, since Christy's a couple of years older. Still, there's a vanity set she'll go nuts for. Some stuffed animals and board games. More than enough to make her know Santa didn't forget her.''

Nikki's hand on his forearm warmed him right through to the bone. So did his suspicion that she'd worn this dress for him. ''She'll love it, Jon. I—I can help you wrap the things later.''

"Deal. When you get back, I'll help Christy fix snacks for Mr. and Mrs. Claus. Which would you rather have—sugar cookies or the chocolate-chip angels?"

She chuckled, though longing and sadness were still in her eyes when she looked at him. "What do you think?"

He hadn't a clue. "No idea."

"Try both."

He smiled. "Both it is."

Even though he could barely tear his eyes from Nikki, Jon glanced at the stairs as footsteps pounded nearer and the cutest elf he'd ever seen bounded toward him. He said, "Now who's that?"

"It's me!" Christy squealed.

As if he didn't know. Making a show of bending over and squinting at her, he did his best to sound perplexed. "Christy?"

"Of course it's me! He can't even tell, Nikki!" Suddenly, she gasped. "What if Santa doesn't recognize me? What if he doesn't know who gets the presents I ask for?"

Jon grinned, taking in the green leotards, tights and eye mask. "Santa'll see right through your costume. Now go ahead, kid. Nikki'll meet you by the door."

Christy took off like a bullet just as Nikki said, "No, I'm coming right now, Christy."

"Are you that afraid I might try to kiss you goodbye?"

Nikki managed to shoot him a droll glance. "Don't worry, Sleet, I think I can withstand your kisses by now."

"Is that right?" Even without touching her, he could see her weaken. Her gaze dipped to avoid his, and her hands trembled slightly until she clasped them in front of her. *Well, Jon, she's right for not pursuing a relationship that you've told her is headed nowhere. Why don't you have a heart—and just let her go?*

"C'mon," he found himself saying as his gaze dropped over the dress again. "Let's get one of Mary's dress coats. Your bomber jacket won't do the outfit justice. But then nothing could ever do that outfit justice." He flashed her a grin. "Except you, of course."

She frowned back—either at the flirtation or because she hadn't thought about a coat—he wasn't sure which. Then she brushed past him, leaving perfumed air in her wake, and opened a closet. He watched her slip the bomber jacket off a hanger.

"My jacket will be fine."

He didn't blame her for not wanting Mary's. Just thinking about Nikki with another man bothered Jon; Buck had already rented far more space in Jon's head than he'd ever admit.

"You're right," he conceded, taking the jacket from her. "This'll do just fine." He held it out with such care that it could have been a mink stole. Sighing, he watched her slender bare arms disappear inside, then he gently pulled the jacket around her shoulders.

"Thank you," she said again.

This time her voice was almost stiff, fostering a distance. Which was just as well. He had no right to want her so much. "It might snow again," he said, reaching into his jeans pockets for his keys as she turned toward him. "I'd rather you take my Jeep. The four-wheel drive might come in handy. While you're gone, I'll unload the things you got Christy from the trunk of the cab.''

She considered, then plucked the keys from his palm. ''Sounds good.'' When she glanced up, her eyes lingered on his a moment too long, then she turned away and headed for the foyer.

''Nikki, wait...''

She turned back, her eyes now looking reddish-brown in the light, like her hair. ''What?''

As if she didn't know how badly he wanted that kiss goodbye. *Unless you can give more, you've got no right.* He shook his head. ''Nothing.''

Barely masked disappointment was in her eyes. ''Sure?''

He nodded. ''Just do me a favor and drive carefully. The roads are slick. I'll take the cell phone to the barn when I go, so if you get stuck, call me from the one I left in the Jeep.''

Emotion turned her eyes glossier, and he guessed she realized he'd been thinking of Mary and Jenny's accident. ''Don't worry,'' she said gently. ''I'll be careful. I'm a professional driver, remember?''

He smiled again, shaking his head. ''In that dress, you look like a supermodel, so it's pretty easy to forget just about everything.'' He chuckled. ''I figure every man at that party's going to feel like he's got amnesia.''

Despite the regret in her eyes, she laughed softly. ''Christy and I'll be careful.''

He wished he was closer, so he could lean and catch her slender fingers in his. ''Promise?''

''I promise.''

And then she turned and was gone.

Sighing, he watched from a window as she pulled

out of the driveway, and then he shrugged into his
oilskin coat and headed to the barn. The air was crisp;
the temperature had dropped when the sun went
down. Beneath his ropers, the hard snow crunched,
and in the distance, he could still hear the diminishing
sound of the Jeep's motor. When it faded completely,
something twisted inside him—a swift pull of panic—
as if Nikki was never coming back.

And she wasn't, he realized, not if he didn't change
his mind and go after her before it was too late…

Inside the barn, King and Mister Ed neighed. Pausing briefly, Jon rubbed between their ears before moving on to feed the reindeer. When the chores were
done, he strode to a locked double-doored tack room.

Flipping the light switch, he glanced around. In the
corner was a sturdy, locked metal armoire where the
Santa suit was kept, wrapped in plastic. Tugging back
a heavy tarp, Jon tossed it aside, then looked at the
sleigh. It was deceptively heavy-looking, of gilded,
carved wood. Yesterday, while Nikki and Christy
were in town decorating the inn, he'd come out and
polished it. Now, after he'd harnessed the reindeer
team, he could call Steve and tell him the sleigh was
ready. Steve could drive up, leave his truck here, and
then come back after he'd visited the inn. But instead
of getting on with the work, Jon leaned against an
uncovered window and stared into the night.

Or maybe you should go instead of Steve. Right
now, his world seemed full of so many *maybes*.…

After a moment, something cold brushed his shoulder, drawing him from his thoughts. He tried to shake
off the chill, to tell himself it was nothing more than
a cold gust of wind, but as it blew past, it seemed to
leave fanciful images in his mind. There was nothing

beyond the window but the black winter's night, but he suddenly remembered countless things he'd told his little girl. Maybe they were even true. Maybe if you looked closely enough, the circular roads in town were really paved with diamonds, and maybe lights winked in the mountains on Christmas Eve because angels had decorated the trees for the holidays.

Maybe…

Why was it so hard for adults to keep believing in magic? he suddenly wondered as he felt that softly whistling gust whisper past him again. Blinking, he felt half-convinced that it was the cold finger of the Ghost of Christmas Past. Or was that Christmas Future? Because Jon suddenly pictured Nikki months from now, big with the baby and grinning, glowing with health. She was going to be an amazon of a pregnant woman, he knew, strengthened by the power of her undeniable femininity. He could just see her— her hands on her hips, her sharp tongue lashing everyone in sight when her contractions started. No doubt she'd deliver in that baseball cap. *And I want to be there.* Jon's heart swelled with the truth of it.

He had no idea what Nikki thought. She had feelings for him, but could she truly envision more? Or was she simply hurt by his doubts? Was she really in love with him?

When a third swirl of wind teased his neck, Jon could swear it ruffled his hair as sweetly as fingers before settling on his cheek, like a goodbye kiss. And then, just as abruptly, it was gone. For a moment, he couldn't move. Whimsically, he was sure it was Christmas Past, giving him a push toward Christmas Future. In any case, Nikki's lovemaking had restored his imagination. And he knew now that he was being a fool for letting fear stop him from loving her.

Reaching into his coat pocket, he pulled out the cell phone and punched the buttons, remembering the number even though he hadn't called it for a long time. It was answered on the first ring.

"Steve?"

He sounded relieved. "I just tried to call you, Jon, but there was no answer."

"I'm out in the barn, on the cell phone."

Steve started right in. "Well, I can't make it tonight. I've got a lead on Christy's parents...."

Jon listened while Steve filled him in, feeling relief wash over him. "You really think you've found them?"

"I'm pretty sure, but don't tell her. It's just a lead, and I still don't have her parents' names. I don't want Christy bolting again before someone can pick her up. Trouble is, before I can run down these leads, I've got to find someone else to play Santa tonight. The kids are expecting the sleigh and reindeer. The whole works."

"I'll go."

Steve drew a surprised breath. "Come again?"

"Happy to do it for you, Steve. It's why I called." And maybe by doing so, Jon could show Nikki that he'd changed his mind. Maybe he wasn't the man he used to be—yet. But he was ready to move on. He couldn't lose the woman who'd just waltzed down his staircase in red velvet.

As if reading his mind, Steve said, "Welcome back to the human race, buddy. And if you ask me, she's the best thing that could have happened to you."

She was, Jon agreed silently, disconnecting the call.

If Sleet insisted on missing a spectacle such as this, it was his problem, Nikki bravely told herself as she glanced around the festive party. The costumes she'd found earlier in the inn's storeroom had come to life, and now life-size ornamental Christmas balls walked past, followed by waddling puffy snowmen who sported rubber carrot noses, top hats and twig arms. Cardboard boxes, covered with decorative paper and bows, were worn over bodysuits, transforming adults into gifts, and two firemen even came as a reindeer. Their four, brown-clad legs danced beneath the costume while the leader tried to uphold a giant head comically weighed down with antlers. Elves mingled, making Christy hard to find, but after a moment, Nikki spotted her. She was beside Santa's throne, where she'd been waiting most of the evening.

"It's getting so late," Nikki said, nervously chomping a celery stick liberally coated with blue cheese. "Why do you think Steve hasn't shown up, Mrs. Honey? He should have been here hours ago."

"His deputy just came in—" Mrs. Honey nodded toward a large figure dressed as a Christmas tree. "Said Steve might have a lead on Christy's parents."

As relieved as she was by the news, Nikki was unprepared for the sadness. She'd been so intent on hoping Christy's parents would be found that she hadn't completely realized how attached she'd gotten to the little girl.

Same with Jon. Dammit, it was so hard to care, knowing you needed to pull back and withhold the feelings to protect yourself. Not that Nikki could stop loving Jon now; she was lost the first time they'd made love. Sliding her hand over her belly, she felt a rush of gratitude. At least she wasn't walking away from the last cataclysmic week of her life without something.

But she wanted Jon.

Just as she was getting ready to excuse herself so she could talk to the deputy, Mrs. Honey said, "I'm sure Steve will make it."

"He has to." All day, Christy had been so excited. She said she had a special Christmas wish that only the real Santa could grant. Nikki glanced at Santa's throne. It was at the far end of the room, opposite the fire, and it was very regal, high-backed and painted gold with a red velvet seat. The steps leading to it were covered with white, gold-glittered felt, and a camera had been set up, so children could have their pictures taken.

Mrs. Honey clasped her hands anxiously in front of her. "If Steve doesn't show soon, the little ones will be so terribly disappointed."

Nikki nodded. For most of the evening, the children had been running to and from the wide windows facing the mountains, watching for Santa. Some were in costume, some not, but all had cheeks that were flushed with excitement. Now the kids were beginning to scoot closer to their parents, or climb sleepily into their laps. As glad as she was that Steve had a lead about Christy's case, Nikki hoped it wouldn't stop him from meeting his obligation here.

Glancing toward the deputy, who looked deep in conversation with someone, she caught the eyes of an older man. He had a paunch and thick gray hair, and something in his bearing reminded Nikki of her dad. She swallowed around the lump in her throat. Her father and brothers might be overly protective, but they loved her. And it was Christmas Eve. It was definitely long past time for her to call home.

"Santa!" a child shouted.

And then Nikki heard sleigh bells. The child in her took hold, and along with everyone, she moved toward the wide windows through which she could see a gold sleigh gliding over the snow. Smiling as she caught up to Christy, Nikki felt as if her own childhood wish to see Santa had just come true. Outside, the reindeer pranced to a halt beyond the wide windows, and Christy gasped as Santa stepped regally from the sleigh and tied off the reins.

"I'm pretty sure it's the real Santa, Nikki," she said, anxiously pulling at her green leotard.

"Sure looks like him," Nikki returned, taking in the white locks, thick beard and velvet suit. Santa's roly-poly belly became visible beneath his fur-trimmed robe as he raised an arm, ringing a bell. Coming toward the doors, he boomed a loud, "Ho, ho, ho."

Nikki grinned. She'd known Steve Warwick would come through. Jon Sleet might have chosen to stay home on Christmas Eve, but Steve simply wasn't the type to let a bunch of little kids down.

NIKKI HADN'T recognized him.

Not that he had time to so much as shoot her a wink. "Ho, ho, ho," Jon called, still feeling the effects of the sleigh ride—a rush of pure cold air and adrenaline. That's how it felt to be with Nikki, he thought now. Free, like he was flying.

Leaning, he ruffled a child's hair, shook another's small hand, then he headed for the throne, letting his robes swirl around him for effect. He'd expected

Nikki to at least recognize his voice, but she was busy, helping parents marshal the kids into a line and breaking up a petty squabble about who got to go first.

Soon enough, a proud-looking couple took the small treasure chest from a wise man and pushed him gently from behind. Jon winked encouragement, suddenly remembering how shy kids could be. This one looked to be in first grade, younger than Christy. He stared ahead, wide-eyed, as his stubby legs strained to take the steps to the throne.

"I'm headed straight back to the North Pole from here, son," Jon said confidentially as he pulled the wise man onto his knee. "So, what do you want for Christmas?"

The little boy cupped a hand around his mouth, wiggling up to Jon's ear. "Could you please make Leslie in my day care like me?" Before Jon could answer, or even suppress a chuckle, the boy lost his shyness and rushed on. "If you can't, it's okay."

"It is?"

"Yeah, Santa, 'cause I'd rather get me a bike. I mean, if I gotta pick between her and a bike. It's a mountain bike with really good training wheels. And…" His shyness diminishing, the wise man continued for long moments.

Nodding sagely, Jon listened carefully to all the items. And more, as countless children took their turns, squirming onto his knee. Most of them sounded sweet-voiced and hopeful, their every wish followed by a question mark. And they wanted so much. Battleships and brand-name trucks. Ice skates and batons. Puppies and kittens. They wished for things that adults would never guess unless they donned Santa suits. For more friends. And higher IQs, so they could do better in school. One little boy wanted to see an angel, so it would be easier to believe in God, the way his Sunday-school teacher kept telling him to. How could Jon have forgotten the heartbreaking tenderness he'd felt for years while he'd sat here, listening as the wishes washed over him in these tentative soft-spoken voices that trembled with hope?

Christy pulled back until the very end. Jon's chest tightened as she, the very last child, nervously straightened her elf outfit and approached him. Patting his knee, he helped her climb up, then he mustered a voice he hoped was unlike his own. "What would you like for Christmas?"

She gazed up, her eyes narrowing suspiciously. "Your eyes are supposed to be blue, not green."

"Trick of the light, m'dear," he assured her.

She relaxed. "Are you the real Santa? I have to ask, because if you aren't, you can't get me what I want."

"I'm the real Santa."

Shimmying upward, she whispered, "I don't want toys. I just want my mommy and daddy to get back together. They're divorced. I came here because I thought maybe Jonathan Sleet could be my new daddy, but really, I want my dad back. Okay?" Reaching up, Christy suddenly rested her fingers on his beard and gazed at him through her green mask with imploring eyes. "Please, Santa?"

Before he could answer, she turned away and slid from his lap, as if she couldn't bear to hear the answer. Lord, Jon thought, watching her go, maybe if Steve had found her folks, Jon could talk to them... *As if I could really fix someone's broken marriage.*

Was that why Christy had run away? That she'd loved his books enough to think he'd be a good father moved him.

Christy had nearly reached the edge of the platform when she turned around again. The tears shimmering in her crystal green eyes brought Jon to his knees. She called out, "Can you do it, Santa?"

Looking at her, he had no choice but to lie. "Yes."

Her quick, brave smile was worth it. Whirling around, she skipped down the steps as if a burden had been lifted from her tiny shoulders. Jon started to rise, but then he realized Mrs. Honey was behind Nikki, pushing her toward the platform. Now, what was that old gossip up to?

Nikki was laughing and protesting, but soon enough other adults—mostly men, judging by the catcalls and whistles—were stomping their feet and demanding that Nikki sit on Santa's lap.

Jon couldn't help but smile, feeling a rush of proprietary pride. Nikki Ryder was so damn sexy in that dress that he wanted to rip off his robe and drag her into the nearest unoccupied room at the inn.

He watched the unintentionally provocative sway of her hips as she came close. Just as she reached him, before she noticed his eyes, Jon stood and whirled away, grabbing her hand. He tugged her down the platform, then across the ballroom.

She laughed breathlessly. "Taking me for a ride, Santa?"

Hadn't she guessed who he was? "Some other time."

"Then where are you—"

Urging her through the door, he pulled her into the cold night air, under the dark velvet sky and the full

pearl moon. "I want to hear your wishes in private."
But of course there wasn't any privacy here. Everyone
had rushed to the windows and countless noses were
pressed to the glass.

Not that Jon cared. Stepping closer, still avoiding
her gaze, he murmured, "What do you want for
Christmas, Nikki?"

Sighing, she flung her head back. Lovely dark eyes
that were as bright as the night sky searched the stars.
Even though her shoulders were bare, the cold didn't
seem to bother her, though it brought a healthy pink
into her skin. His eyes trailed down her slender neck.

"Oh, Steve…" she murmured, staring at the stars.

So, she hadn't guessed. Disguising his voice, he
murmured, "Yes?"

As her eyes searched the heavens, she bit her lower
lip. "I want…" She sighed once more. "I want your
buddy, Jon Sleet, to fall hopelessly in love with me.
That's what I want." He watched her blush with the
confession, and then watched as her glossy eyes
turned toward him and widened in shock.

"Nikki," he said smoothly, coming closer and letting his lips hover above hers, "I think your dream's
come true."

"Really?" she said huskily.

"Really," he returned. His eyes settled for a second on the lower lip she'd bitten, and his mouth followed, his eyes shutting as her lips, so cool with the
air, warmed his mouth. As the velvet of her tongue
touched his, he reveled in how thoroughly she yielded
to a kiss meant to claim and promise.

And then Jon stepped back, smiling. With a final
wave to the crowd, he hopped into the sleigh, leaving
Nikki just like that—stunned and well-kissed by
Santa, standing in the snow.

Chapter Twelve

The reindeer flew over the packed snow, guided by Jon's hold on the reins and by the full moon illuminating the path across the mountains. Flurries were spiraling, glistening in the night air, and a freezing wind seemed to race past as the team approached home, but Jon still felt warm inside—from the voices of the children that kept replaying in his mind and from the pleasure in the eyes of neighbors who'd missed him, and most of all, from Nikki's kiss, which had started a fire roaring in his belly.

"Whoa!" He tugged the reins as the team pranced through the barn's open doors. "Whoa there, Dancer. Prancer, do me a favor, hold up."

Quickly unharnessing the animals, Jon sped through the routine of getting them back into their stalls, then he headed inside the house, changing into a suit he hoped would do Nikki's dress justice. If he made it back to the party in time to meet her, he thought when he saw that the snow was falling in earnest again. With his luck, he'd pass Nikki on the road.

Stopping in the hallway, he frowned. Where had he left the keys to the cab? He'd used them when he unloaded the gifts Nikki had gotten Christy. Oh…the dish on the table in the foyer, next to the cell phone. Snatching both the keys and phone, he pulled a shearling coat over his suit and went outside.

"I hope they're still there…" As he slid into the cab, he glanced through the windshield. The night didn't look promising. The snow was heavy and wet now; with these low temperatures, it would ice the roads. Leaning over to readjust the seat, he dropped the keys.

"Damn." As he ran his hand along the floor, searching for them, his fingers hit something hard…a book. Pulling it from under the seat, he tossed it beside him.

"Here you are." Bringing up the keys, he slid them into the ignition. The car was old, but now that the peanut butter was out of the tank, it turned over like a dream. Snapping on the headlights and wipers, Jon pulled out, wondering if he'd wind up leaving the cab and driving back in the Jeep with Nikki and Christy. This was definitely turning into a four-wheel-drive kind of night. Fortunately, not many rowdy types were out looking for a fight on Christmas Eve. No telling who might object to a grown man driving a hot-pink car.

Jon had reached the bottom of the mountain when he glanced at the seat beside him—and did a double take. He'd never seen the book before, but it bore his name. Edging to the road's shoulder and braking, he flipped on the dome light, then lifted the book. It was a trade-size white paperback galley proof of his last children's story *Christmas is Forever*. If the book had been published last year, the final cover would have depicted a father reading to a little girl in front of a roaring fire.

But where had it come from? After the accident, he'd bought back the rights to this book in a substantial settlement, never wanting to see it in print. How could the proofs have gotten into Nikki's car? Not even he had a copy of them. Flipping open the cover, he felt his chest constrict when he saw that this version included the dedication: "To Mary and Jenny, my two best girls." Turning another sheet, he whispered, "So that's it." Because written across a blank page with a flowing fountain pen were the words: "To Christmas with love, Mom."

He'd recognize the writing anywhere. It was Joy Holt's, his editor at Stern, Wylie and Morrow. He should have known she'd hold on to a copy; she'd always been so supportive. Shaking his head, he realized he'd nearly met Christy some years back, but when he arrived at the Holts' apartment in New York for dinner, their little girl had just gone to bed.

But the Holts had been so crazy in love. They were the kind of couple who fed each other from their dinner plates and used every excuse to brush against each other or share a kiss. Why would they divorce? Something horrible must have happened.

At least this explained the connection between himself and Christy. Lord, the Holts would be frantic. Jon's frown deepened. "Unless Christy fooled one parent into thinking she was with the other," he muttered. It was definitely her style to play both sides against the middle.

Putting the car into drive and steering with one hand, he took the cell phone from his pocket and tried Steve. As the phone rang, Jon's heart suddenly squeezed painfully tight. By solving the mystery of who Christy's parents were, he'd just lost another little girl. And if Steve's leads had panned out, the divorced couple was probably on their way here.

"God, I'll miss her," he said softly over the hum of the car's engine and the rhythmic pass of the wipers.

But then, with any luck, he was about to gain another child, the one he wanted—and was ready to share—with Nikki.

JON LOOKED like a million bucks, Nikki thought, watching him from across a makeshift dance floor where costumed couples were now swaying to "White Christmas." He'd changed into a soft, cream-colored, V-neck sweater, and the dark brown jacket of his suit perfectly hugged his broad shoulders and wide chest. His slacks, heaven help her, hung in such a way that Nikki started remembering the intimate contours of the man beneath. Her heart thudded against her ribs. Why exactly had he come back? What was he going to say to her? He was coming her way.

Or at least he was trying. People kept stopping him and patting his back. Even from here, Nikki could see their lips moving as they wished him a Merry Christmas, or told him how much they'd missed seeing him.

"Finally," he said.

Grasping her fingers, he led her away from the crowd at the food tables. When they reached a secluded archway, she turned—darn gracefully, she thought, given the shoes—and leaned her back against the wall. She pointed up with a red nail, still trying to get used to the manicure. "Should have watched where you were going, Sleet."

His eyes followed hers. "Ah. Mistletoe." Leaning closer, he slid his palms around her neck, and when he'd brought his lips a breath away, he whispered, "But I *was* watching. The mistletoe was intentional."

She shut her eyes briefly, letting him guide her head back, then she felt the soft brushings of his mouth on hers and the tender stroking of his fingers through her hair.

When he drew away, she half opened her eyes, her voice sounding drugged with the kiss. "You came back."

He chuckled softly. "Thought I'd better. I heard some rumors you were being naughty."

She raised an eyebrow. "Me? Naughty?"

"Yeah, Ryder," he teased softly, nipping her lips once more. "I heard you were going at it hot and heavy with Santa Claus before I got here to mark my territory."

She managed a smile. "And Christy promised not to tell you, since she was afraid you might get jealous." Nikki sobered. "It was a good thing you did tonight," she said, her voice raspy. But had he meant to imply he loved her? She replayed the words in her mind, wondering if she'd misconstrued them. *I want Jon Sleet to fall in love with me.... I think your dream's come true.*

Looking into his eyes now, she barely heard the music. Her heartbeat sounded in her ears as he rubbed a thumb back and forth across her cheek. "What took you so long to come back?" she managed. Had he come to tell her he wanted more with her? That he still wanted her to stay? She tried to ignore the yearning hope inside her.

"Well, I had to put away the sleigh..." His breath stirred against her lips again, making her feel strangely weak. "And Steve found Christy's parents. I talked to him while I was driving over. I also found one of my unpublished books in your cab, and it was signed by Christy's mom. I guess when the deputies searched the car, they didn't realize the book connected Christy to me."

Nikki was a little lost. "A book?"

Jon nodded. "It was under your seat."

She squinted. "What were you doing under my seat?"

"Dropped the keys."

"Oh...and so who *are* Christy's parents?"

Jon glanced toward Christy, who was with the remaining children in a half circle in front of the fire. They were listening to Mrs. Honey read *The Night Before Christmas*. "Joy Holt's her mother."

"Joy Holt?"

"My editor at Stern, Wylie and Morrow." He shook his head. "Definitely not the type of woman to lose her child. I figure Christy conned both parents into thinking she's with the other. Steve says her father's on his way, but they haven't tracked down Joy yet."

"They're separated?"

"Divorced. But...they were the most loving couple I've ever met." Pausing, Jon touched Nikki's face again, this time tracing his thumb over the arch of her eyebrow. Staring into his eyes, Nikki noticed a sheen in his eyes that looked more like emotion than a trick of the firelight. She could swear he was thinking that the Holts had shared the kind of love he wanted with her.

She thought her voice was obviously unsteady. "Wonder what happened to the marriage?"

"I can't imagine." Jon shrugged, glancing at Christy again. "But Steve doesn't want us telling her that her folks are on their way. He's afraid she might bolt again."

"Must have been a nasty divorce if she ran away."

Jon looked perplexed. "They're such good people."

"Sorry to interrupt—" A woman dressed as an angel suddenly stopped beside them and patted Jon's arm. "Annie Hamilton," she said, lifting a gold mask. "I doubt you remember me…"

"Jenny's kindergarten teacher. Of course I remember you. How could I forget?" Jon's voice carried a hint of surprise as if he couldn't believe how easily the words came. "So good to see you again, Annie," he was saying. And Nikki knew he meant it.

"Annie Hamilton," he continued. "She was a great kindergarten teacher. Kids love her. Maybe she'll be working when…"

He paused. And no man had ever looked at her this way—as if she were at the center of his universe. His head was tilted slightly as if he was studying her from a new angle, and his moss green eyes were hot and fixed right on hers. Lips she'd kissed only moments ago were parted as if he had every intention of lowering his mouth to hers again. Nikki felt conscious of the pulse beating in her neck. "When…"

He was looking so deeply into her eyes that she didn't notice his hands seeking her waist, but only felt their warmth when he touched her. His voice low, he said, "When the baby comes."

She tried to tell herself she hadn't heard right. "A kindergarten teacher for a newborn?"

"Well...I guess it wouldn't be for a few years."

Don't mess with me, Sleet. Her eyes stung and she knew he'd already seen their sudden brightness. "Sleet," she said softly, "you'd better be careful what you say right now."

A tender smile curled his lips. "Why?"

Her voice caught. "Because I'm listening with my heart."

He merely shook his head, and his voice was hoarse with emotion. "I'm through with being careful, Nikki. I've been careful for years." Leaning back, he ran a hand raggedly through his hair, and she watched as the few silver strands caught the light. "I blamed myself, you know," he continued, his eyes finding hers again. "Not that there was anything I could have done." Lifting a hand, he trailed a finger across her forehead, brushing back her hair. "But if you mean careful about you..." He shook his head again. "I'll never hurt you, Nikki. I promise you that."

She believed him, but wished he'd said more. "How—how do you feel about my having...the baby?"

His eyes widened in faint surprise, as if she hadn't understood a thing he'd said. Circling her waist with his hands again, he rubbed his thumbs up and down on her belly. "I think I'll be missing Christy soon. And that I'm ready to have another kid around the house."

"I—" Her heart was hammering. "I'm not sure what you're saying…"

Both his hands found hers and their fingers twined. "I'm asking you to stay, Nikki. If it's marriage you want, that's fine by me. I'm ready. I know it's right. It's…fast. I know that, too. If you'd just like to stay in town and set the rules, I'll do whatever you want." His smile was almost tentative. "I'll take you on a million dates. Just don't go back to Kentucky."

She realized that one of her hands had disentangled itself from his somehow, and now it was resting on the narrow lapel of his suit. "What changed your mind?"

"Realizing I love you. I can't lose you."

"Just like a man," she managed, tears of joy making her eyes sparkle. "Forgetting all about a woman's career."

His eyes widened. "But you own your own cab, right? Doesn't that mean you can set up here?"

"Yeah, Sleet." She laughed softly. "Did you really think I'd let a pink taxicab come between us? Haven't you figured out that I don't wear killer heels for just any man?"

For such a guy-type guy, he looked downright misty. "You wore those for me?"

She glanced around. "Well, you do have some rivals."

"You mean other than Santa?"

"Well…I did call my dad. He and my brothers were so glad to hear from me that they hopped in the van and are headed here to make sure I'm all right."

"They're coming from Kentucky?"

"Ought to be here by morning." Suddenly, her

shoulders were shaking with laughter. "I gave them your address."

He looked wary. "So, how are these Kentucky boys going to feel about finding you pregnant and engaged?"

Engaged. She still couldn't believe it, not really. "If they don't kill you, I think things'll work out."

"Comforting." He pulled her closer, pressing his mouth to hers for a blissful moment. "Any man who knows you're worth fighting over is a friend of mine. And I'm glad you called home. I know it's been on your mind."

"It was good to talk to my dad."

"And, Nikki…"

Her eyes leaped to his. "Yeah, Sleet?"

"I know it's soon. But promise me you'll stay."

"I could marry you tomorrow, Jon Sleet."

His voice caught. "But will you?"

"Yeah, Sleet," she said breathlessly before his mouth found hers again. "I will."

"NIGHT, NIKKI," Christy whispered.

"Night, hon," Nikki said. From the doorway, she stared into the cozy, firelit room while Jon seated himself on the edge of the mattress and tucked the covers around Christy's shoulders. Nikki couldn't take her eyes off him. Flames from the fire he'd built sparkled in his hair, making the silver strands glint, and the cream sweater pulling across his upper body outlined the muscles of his chest. Her eyes trekked down to where the well-made suit jacket draped across his dress slacks, brushing strong thighs she longed to feel naked against her skin again. His voice wasn't meant to be seductive, but it was. It wasn't meant to tease her, but it did. And listening to him now, she knew it always would.

He said, "Ready for a bedtime story?"

Christy shot him a drowsy-eyed look of disbelief. Her voice was scratchy with the need for sleep. "I thought you're too sad to tell stories anymore, Jon."

"You made me remember the magic, kid."

As Christy yawned, her eyes drifted shut, then she opened them again. She blinked. "I did?"

He nodded. "You and Nikki."

She made a sleepy, snuffling sound. Clearly thinking Nikki wouldn't hear, she whispered, "That's why I ran away and came here, Jon. Because I love your stories. Tell me a new one."

Yes, do. Smiling wistfully, Nikki realized this would probably be her and Jon's last night with Christy. Leaning, she slipped off her shoes, then leaning against the door molding, she massaged her aching feet through her stockings. She'd have to tell Jon it was a good thing he proposed tonight. She definitely wouldn't have been able to bear these three-inch heels another night. Although, if he wanted her to put them back on in the bedroom....

"Once upon a time," he was saying, "there was a man who lost everything he loved in an ice storm. The storm came on fast, and along with the ice that weighed down the power lines and made the roads treacherous, there were winds that banged the window shutters and howled around the house. The man stayed inside, trying to keep himself safe, and only when the storm was over, did he realize he'd lost everything he loved. When he realized that, he got so mad that he turned to ice inside...."

Christy gasped. "Inside? You mean, in his heart?"

Jon nodded gravely. "After that, he lived all alone, high on a hill. People came to see him, but he was so cold that he sent them all away. And because he'd become colder by the day, everything he touched started turning to ice, too."

Christy's eyes were completely entranced. "Like his house and everything?"

"Everything. The cups and saucers froze, and if he tried to turn on the faucet for a drink of water, the water froze into icicles before it hit the sink. He'd had a working man's hands, but now his fingers turned into foot-long icicles. And there'd been a beautiful garden, but now the sunflowers, pansies and tulips were so brittle that they snapped right in two." Jon snapped his fingers to illustrate. "The blades of grass in the man's yard were so sharp that your feet would bleed if you stepped on them."

Christy's voice trembled. "Your feet got cut up?"

Jon nodded again. "Cut to ribbons. But the man was so mean that no one visited him, anyway. Which was good, because if anybody touched him, they'd freeze, too. In a split second, they'd be turned into an ice statue."

"Did the man get lonely?"

"Sure. He didn't have a friend left in the world. Until one day, a little girl called out to him from the road. She didn't believe what she'd heard about him, and she wanted to find out the truth for herself. When he looked outside, she was edging closer, walking on the grass, on shoes she'd made especially for the purpose. They were built like snowshoes, but of metal, so she glided right over the tips of the frozen blades."

"And she didn't freeze?"

"No. She was a brave little girl."

Nikki watched Christy fight to keep her eyes open as Jon detailed the little girl's slow approach. He said she brought gifts of love—bread that stayed piping hot, and pictures of faraway places she wanted to visit someday. She brought a bucket of fire, so the man could start melting his dinner. And a knife, so he could carve messages into the ice, since his writing paper was frozen. And then one day—it was Christmas day, in fact—the little girl kissed him.

Christy gasped. "And *then* she got turned into ice?"

Jon shook his head. "No. Not even then. You see, she was the only person to ever even try to love him. And she was fine. It was just a light peck on his frozen cheek, but that one kiss made everything finish melting. Most of all, his heart. And you know what the little girl's name was?"

Christy sighed deeply. "Jenny?"

"No. It was Christy." Jon suddenly dropped a finger down her ski-jump nose. "That little girl was you, sweetheart."

Christy laughed softly, blushing with pleasure. "It's a good story, Jon," she said. "But if you ever write it up in a book, you can call me Christmas."

"Christmas?"

"That's my name. I just told people to start calling me Christy because I didn't believe in Christmas anymore."

Setting down her shoes, Nikki crept quietly forward and rested her hands on Jon's shoulders. As she gently kneaded the muscles, she gazed down at Christy. "But you believe in Christmas now?"

"Oh, Nikki, I do. I just wish Jon hadn't missed

Santa." Christy's eyes shined, catching flickers from the firelight, and a secretive smile curled her lips.

Nikki chuckled. "I'm sorry he wasn't there, too. But you'd better get some sleep, hon. Because I suspect Santa's on his way."

The words weren't necessary. Christy's eyes had drifted shut, and a moment later, she was asleep.

SHE'D SURE FOOLED them. "Merry Christmas, Noodles." Christy giggled mischievously, gingerly lifting Noodles from the aquarium and liberally peppering him with kisses. Looping him over her shoulder, she skipped barefoot to the window and stared up at the moon. "He was the real Santa, Noodles. You should have seen him. At first I thought it was Jon because his eyes looked so green, but then I got my wish and saw Daddy on the road, so it had to be the real Santa."

Christy just hoped she hadn't already missed seeing Santa fly across the moon. Her eyes burned from the lack of sleep, and her bones felt so achy that she could have been seventy instead of seven. But her excitement was so intense that she was fighting not to hop up and down. She would, but then Jon and Nikki might hear her....

Christy still couldn't believe she'd seen her daddy. He was driving toward the inn in a car so ugly that it had to be a rental. Her dad wouldn't be caught dead without a sports car, which meant he was probably steaming mad. Not that Christy cared. Because if Santa had found her dad already, he'd found her mom, too. Christy guessed they'd get back together tonight, since Christmas was tomorrow morning.

Santa sure worked fast.

Christy even figured that Jon and Nikki would get married. In fact, maybe Jon and Nikki and her mom and dad would have a double wedding. Lifting Noodles higher, Christy snuggled him against her cheek. "Double deep sigh," she whispered.

Breathing in as deeply as she could, she held her breath for a second, then blew out a long, relieved breath. She'd known running away to meet Santa was the right thing to do. By morning, her mom and dad would be in love again. And soon, Santa would be riding across the moon. Christy planned to wave. She hoped Santa knew it meant thank-you.

CARRYING NIKKI'S shoes in one hand, Jon twined the fingers of his other through hers. *My future wife's,* he thought as they made their way down the dark hall. He could barely believe the gifts that had come into his life this Christmas.

Nikki's voice was throaty. "Jon, we'd better go downstairs now and wrap Christy's gifts."

"Afraid if we go in the bedroom we'll never come out?" He laughed softly. "I already wrapped them, Nikki. Everything's under the tree. That's another reason I was late getting to the inn."

"I thought we were playing Mr. and Mrs. Claus tonight."

He urged her from the hallway into the dark bedroom. "Oh, we still are." Crossing to the window, he nodded down to where a glass of milk was chilled on the windowsill. On the bedside table was a dessert plate piled high with cookies. "Both kinds," he whispered, coming behind her and wrapping his arms around her waist. He rested his chin on her shoulder and stared out the window with her at the moon. "In case our nocturnal exertions made Mrs. Claus hungry.''

She tried to sound shocked. ''Exertions? How romantic.''

''You want romantic, Ryder? C'mere.''

Just as he drew her even closer, she turned in his arms. ''You really want to marry me?''

He understood her need to hear him say it again. It was so new, so exciting. ''Yes,'' he said simply.

''Why?''

''Because I love you so much, Saint Nikki.'' He smiled. ''Because only warmth like yours can melt an iceman's heart.''

''Mine and the little girl's down the hall.''

''Hers too.''

With a smile, Nikki turned to face the window again. Silently, staring into the night, they shared a cookie, one of the chocolate angels. The longer Jon looked at the sleepy town below, the more the glistening snow started to look like diamonds, and for just a second, he could swear trees in the periphery of his vision had winked with lights, as if they'd really been decorated by angels. His lips settled on his own angel's hair, and his hand slid over her belly. ''I don't only want this baby, you know,'' he suddenly assured her, his voice husky. ''I want other children with you, Nikki.''

He could hear her swallow hard. ''You're sure?''

Lowering his head, he nuzzled the side of her neck. ''You bet.'' He leaned away long enough to gently pull down the zipper of her dress. Slowly, the red velvet parted, revealing delicate skin bathed in moonlight. He kissed between her shoulderblades.

''Twelve midnight,'' she suddenly whispered in a

voice that deepened with desire. She nodded toward the bedside clock.

Midnight. There were still so many things to do. Jon should call Steve again, to get the details about Christy's father's arrival. For all Jon knew, the man would be on the doorstep within the hour. Maybe Jon could even talk to him about the divorce, for Christy's sake. Without even knowing the reasons for the separation, Jon wished the Holts would refind the love that he and Nikki now shared.

He sighed, bringing another deep breath of Nikki's perfume into his lungs. There might be things to do, but right now, all he could think about was the moonlight on her bare back. Bending, he began kissing each ridge of her spine.

She suddenly tensed. "Hey, Sleet. Look."

He glanced up. "What?" And then he saw it. Over Nikki's shoulder, in the black night sky, in front of the round moon... He inhaled sharply. It came and went in a flash. So fast he knew his eyes had been deceiving him. But for a moment of time, he could swear he'd seen a man in a golden sleigh driving a reindeer team across the moon.

Nikki gave out a short gasp. "Sleet," she said in a voice made throaty by his kisses, "I thought I saw—"

"Santa?" As he turned her in his arms once more, Jon's hands caressed her back. "Could have been," he whispered. "Rumor has it that Holiday Hamlet's a magical place."

Her voice was a little shaky. "It was just a trick of the light, Sleet."

"Right, Ryder. Or our imagination."

"Right," she echoed. "Our imagination." Suddenly smiling, she stretched on her toes, seeking a sweet kiss. He gave her more than she asked for. Pressing his tongue deeply, wetly inside her mouth, he tasted the chocolate they'd shared as he languidly stroked her. As she arched against him, he realized he was aching, trembling with need for her. Tilting his head back, Jon smiled into her eyes. And then, just as his mouth descended to capture her lips once more, he heard a far-off but unmistakable voice shout, "Merry Christmas to all. And to all, a good night."

Next month, don't miss #757
SANTA SLEPT OVER
only from Jule McBride
and American Romance!

When Joy Holt arrives in Holiday Hamlet on Christmas Eve, to take her runaway daughter Christy, home, she winds up at a costume party at the local inn. Before the night's over, she winds up in the wrong bed, too. And with a man she's been trying to forget—her ex-husband!

Christmas Is For Kids

This Christmas, some of your favorite
Harlequin American Romance authors bring
you brand-new stories that will warm your heart!
In December 1998, don't miss:

#753 SMOOCHIN' SANTA
by Jule McBride

#754 BABY'S FIRST CHRISTMAS
by Cathy Gillen Thacker

#755 COWBOY SANTA
by Judy Christenberry

#756 GIFT-WRAPPED DAD
by Muriel Jensen

Available at your favorite retail outlet.

HARLEQUIN®
Makes any time special ™

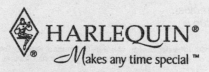

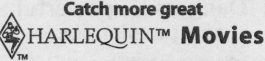 

Fill your holiday with...
excitement, magic and love!

Mistletoe Kisses

December is the time for Christmas carols, surprises
wrapped in colored paper and kisses under the mistletoe.
Mistletoe Kisses is a festive collection of stories about three
humbug bachelors and the feisty heroines who entice them
to ring in the holiday season with love and kisses.

AN OFFICER AND A GENTLEMAN
by Rachel Lee

THE MAGIC OF CHRISTMAS
by Andrea Edwards

THE PENDRAGON VIRUS
by Cait London

Available December 1998
wherever Harlequin and Silhouette books are sold.

HARLEQUIN®
Makes any time special ™

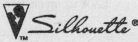

Silhouette®

HARLEQUIN®
AMERICAN ◆ ROMANCE®

COMING NEXT MONTH

#757 SANTA SLEPT OVER by Jule McBride
The Little Matchmaker
Christmas morning...on the trail of their missing mischievous
matchmaking daughter...in a swirling snowstorm...how did Joy and
Ryan Holt wake up in an inn bedroom—together, smiling and wearing
only a Santa hat?

#758 DADDY'S LITTLE DARLINGS by Tina Leonard
Gowns of White
When Alexander Banning learned his estranged—darn stubborn—
wife was pregnant, he set out to win back her love—and his male heir of
his Texas family ranch. But Daphne didn't make either easy for the
determined daddy. Not only did she deliver triplets, but they came
wrapped in ruffles, white lace and satin!

#759 THE COWBOY IS A DADDY by Mindy Neff
When Wyoming cowboy Brice DeWitt placed an ad for a housekeeper-
cook at his Flying D Ranch, he expected a sturdy, mature woman—not
a petite, pregnant applicant who was about to deliver on his doorstep!

#760 RICH, SINGLE & SEXY by Mary Anne Wilson
The Ultimate...
With a seductive smile and knockout kisses, Connor McKay truly was
"The Ultimate Catch." But this sexy billionaire aimed to keep his
bachelor status. Then he met Maggie Palmer....

Look us up on-line at: http://www.romance.net